ALL'S WELL THAT ENDS

All's Well
That Ends

AN AMANDA PEPPER MYSTERY

Gillian Roberts

BALLANTINE BOOKS · NEW YORK

Copyright © 2007 by Judith Greber

All rights reserved.

Published in the United States by Ballantine Books, an imprint of The Random House Publishing Group, a division of Random House, Inc., New York.

BALLANTINE and colophon are registered trademarks of Random House, Inc.

ISBN 978-0-345-48021-7

Library of Congress Cataloging-in-Publication Data

Roberts, Gillian
    All's well that ends : an Amanda Pepper mystery / Gillian Roberts.
        p.   cm.
    ISBN-13: 978-0-345-48021-7 (hc)
    ISBN-13: 978-0-345-48022-4 (mm)
    ISBN-13: 978-0-345-49718-5 (el)
    1. Pepper, Amanda (Fictitious character)—Fiction.   2. Philadelphia (Pa.)—Fiction.   I. Title.

PS3557.R356A78 2007
813'.54—dc22   2006051088

Printed in the United States of America on acid-free paper

www.ballantinebooks.com

9   8   7   6   5   4   3   2   1

First Edition

For Abby and Matt
—all's well that begins, too!

Acknowledgments

Many thanks to Sarah Burbidge and Paula Jaffe for helping Casa de Angeles Orphanage in Guatemala and in so doing, giving Amanda two new super-smart students, Margaret Burbidge and Eddie Schneider.

Gratitude beyond words to a trio who tried their best (and their best is as good as it gets) to pull out the weeds and cut through the brambles in this book: Jo Keroes, Betty Schafer, and Louise Ure. Thank you for all the TLC. And though I felt obliged to change titles midstream, thank you, Betty, for the original and clever: "Beth Be Not Proud." Next time?

For two decades, I've been privileged to have the late Marilyn Wallace as my dear friend and first reader. This would be a better book and a better world had she been able to stay longer.

ALL'S WELL THAT ENDS

One

"She was the best of mothers, she was the worst of mothers. She had wisdom, she had foolishness. . . ."

Dennis's words made me want to snatch the silver martini pitcher from his hand and smash him with it, even though that would make my behavior as inappropriate as his was. We were paying our last respects, except for Dennis, who was paying his final disrespects.

Inappropriate didn't begin to describe posthumously clobbering the Dickens out of your own mother. I don't care how literary Dennis thought he was—not that familiarity with the opening lines of *A Tale of Two Cities* qualifies as anything special.

"It is a far, far worse thing you do than ever you have done before," I muttered to Sasha. Unfortunately, that probably wasn't accurate. To put it as charitably as I could: Dennis Allenby was a jerk.

He'd been a jerk in tenth grade when his mother was married to Sasha's father. Twenty years later, age had not withered nor custom staled his infinite jerkiness. He had a reputation as a specialist in the nearly-illegal scheme, the loophole-finding arrangement, the deal that shamelessly preyed on the gullible.

His mother had been Sasha's favorite stepmother. Despite the divorce, Sasha managed to maintain the relationship through three more of Phoebe's marriages, and two of her own, until Phoebe's untimely death two weeks ago. Sad, or ironic, that having pledged five separate times to be with a man till death did them part, Phoebe wound up alone, dead by her own hand, with only Dennis as a sorry by-product.

I blocked out his drone, forced his voice to dissolve into the bright December morning, to be no more than the crunch of twigs underfoot, the occasional birdcall, or the murmur of the stream; although in truth, the water was silent. It was so chilly, it was probably icing up. So was I.

My chattering teeth helped drown him out. I looked around and could see that my irritation was shared. Maybe we could rush Dennis, push him into the creek along with the urn's contents.

Sasha, dressed intensely in black, from the oversized broad-brimmed hat that wobbled and shivered with each wintry gust to her high boots, looked flamboyantly in mourning. But her face was set with anger, not grief. She opened her eyes wide, the better to glare at Dennis. "You see?" she hissed. "You see?"

She wanted me to see a murderer, but I saw only a middle-aged jerk.

I once again let my eyes travel around the group. On this bright winter day, about twenty people had gathered by the river to remember and honor Phoebe Ennis. The group included her cousin Peter, who hadn't seen Phoebe in fifteen years but had memories so vivid that he'd made the trip from his home in West Virginia; four women who'd identified themselves in such a rush that I never got them straight; a woman who looked in her eighties and who'd identified herself only as "a former neighbor," though of which time period and/or house she didn't say; and near her, Phoebe's flame-haired business partner, Merilee Wilkins, standing so rigidly she looked planted in the spot. I'd met her a while back when I went to Top Cat and Tails, the shop she and Phoebe owned. I was amused by the idea of a pet boutique, which probably shows what a shallow, uncaring cat-owner I am. But the admittedly funny sight of sale items such as a Halloween costume for a dachshund that made the pup into a hot-dog on a bun did nothing to make me take the place more seriously.

I went for entertainment value, not to buy, and apparently, so did too many others, because the business was about to fold. Merilee's husband was withdrawing his financial support and, not coincidentally, withdrawing from the marriage as well. Somehow, Merilee blamed Phoebe for the weak revenues that she believed had led to her husband's defection, and in her agitated state she'd accused Phoebe of larceny.

Judging by Merilee's grim expression today, the bad blood between the women had stayed bad, which made me feel a twinge of sympathy for the otherwise annoying woman. There couldn't be many things much worse than having a friend die in mid-quarrel. Surely both women hoped, if not expected, that they'd find a way through their anger, that they'd resolve their issues and restore the friendship. Now it was impossible.

Looking less profoundly upset, two men in their forties who had identified themselves in unison as "the Daves—we're just her friends" stood at the back of the small group. Only one of Phoebe's ex-husbands had attended, Max Delahunt, the fourth of "the Alphabet boys." Phoebe's love life had been frenetic, but her marriage partners turned out to be as systematic as if they'd been chosen by a file clerk. She'd wed, in order: Harvey Allenby, Charlie Berg, Bert Carnero, Max Delahunt, and Nelson Ennis. Among the wedding gifts for Phoebe and Nelson had been a set of towels that had the entire alphabet embroidered along the hem. "Pre-emptive monograms," the gift giver called it. Nelson Ennis should have seen the writing on the towel and known he was a short-timer, and indeed, he didn't make it to the getting-divorced stage. He was done in by an out-of-control motorcycle, barely a year into his marriage.

Phoebe probably would have found herself Mr. "F," too, except that she ended the progression by killing herself.

Max's son, Lionel "Lion" Delahunt, a slender, balding man, stood close to his father, looking pensive, representing along with Sasha Phoebe's many temporary stepchildren. He was next to a man I didn't know, but the teenager by that man's side was a Philly Prep student, Mitchell "Jonesy" Farmer.

At lunch, before this ceremony began, Jonesy had told me he was here because it was his weekend with his father, and his father said it was the right thing to do. His father had known Phoebe, Jonesy had said grudgingly, and I assumed that meant the senior Farmer had dated her. I wondered if he'd been optioning for a position as next husband. Alphabetically, at least, he was appropriate.

There were a few other mourners I didn't recognize. At least one, I suspected, was someone who'd been out for a walk, bundled in his sweats and parka, and had spotted something out of the ordinary and opted to join in for the novelty factor.

We stood in a glorious sylvan setting of trees and water, even if the stream wasn't burbling and the trees were bare under the December sky, and we did our best to ignore the human traffic nearby. This part of the park was called Forbidden Drive, which sounds more exciting than it is. Cars are forbidden, but pretty much everything else is allowed, except, I suspect, what we were about to do. In any case, the bucolic silence, if you ignored Dennis, which I was trying my best to do, made Philadelphia's stone and brick feel galaxies away. You don't realize until you're away from it how nonstop noisy a city is, a perpetual motorized grumble, air being pushed aside by crowds of people, gears churning.

But at this point, the idea of a city's enclosed heated spaces trumped the beauty of our setting. I shivered, and my teeth chattered uncontrollably. I stomped from foot to foot and watched my breath frost and puff in the air, envying the joggers on the path behind us for the body heat they'd created. Sasha bent toward me, nearly blinding me with the brim of her hat. "I can't believe he's doing this," she whispered. "It's so openly hostile!" Earlier, she'd said a few heartfelt words about what Phoebe had meant to her, as had almost everyone else who'd gathered here, including the Daves and even Ex-Husband "D."

Not the man in the parka, not Jonesy or his father, not I, not Merilee.

Dennis had taken control of this event, although Sasha had planned and organized it. "I am the only blood relative," he'd snapped. He was in a perpetual fury because his mother had included Sasha in her will. Not that Phoebe had much beyond a modest house, but however much it was, Dennis wanted it all, and his mother had said he could have only half.

He'd been in a sulk ever since he'd flown into Philadelphia. When he bullied his way into running the memorial service despite years of ignoring his mother, Sasha capitulated.

The fact that he'd saved himself and this performance for last was all the more offensive.

"You have got to find out where he was the night she died," Sasha whispered. "Maybe he hired somebody. Maybe somebody else flew using his name and he was here before then. Maybe . . ."

She'd wanted me here for reasons of friendship, but also because after I finished my days teaching, I was training to be a private investigator. I had a long apprenticeship to go before I could get my license, and I meanwhile co-moonlit with my husband, C. K. Mackenzie, who was licensed because he'd been a homicide detective before opting for grad school. I did mostly clerical chores. You don't get points toward your license for teaching high school English.

That didn't matter to Sasha. She refused to accept the idea that Phoebe had committed suicide, no matter what the police said, and no matter that she had nothing beyond a gut conviction to support her theory.

So with her talent for ignoring the obvious, she'd begged me to observe—as if this were all a grade-B movie, and I was the obligatory cop lounging at the back of the funeral home. I didn't even know why they were there in movies, let alone in real life. What did they expect to see? A killer suddenly throwing himself on the coffin and confessing? Villains twirling moustaches and chortling over their evil accomplishments? Meaningful glances among conspirators?

Why would a murderer attend his victim's funeral?

But since Sasha's current craziness was a by-product of her sadness, I honored it and stood here, wishing I knew what I was supposed to notice beyond a clump of shivering red-nosed people.

Instead, I thought about the one attendee I couldn't see, the one in the martini shaker. When I was in junior high, and Phoebe was Sasha's stepmother, the things that initially made Sasha cringe with embarrassment amused me. I could afford to feel that way—Phoebe wasn't part of my household, so her delusions of grandeur, her fantastic stories of her family's past glories, her regal sweep of arm, her lorgnette (a family treasure, she insisted), her irrational aspirations for us: "Why not the stage? Why not become supermodels, movie stars, or roller-derby gals?" seemed colorful and exciting. I made my mother know that her drab pronouncements about how to live: study, do your homework, clean your room, were pitiable "bourgeois middle-class values," a term I'd learned from Phoebe, of course.

The fact that my parents didn't put me up for adoption during that phase is testimony to their saintly goodness.

Phoebe was bigger than life and her dreams were still larger. She dwelt in the waiting room of an alternate universe populated by the glitterati because, she would remind us with a conspiratorial wink, she was of "royal blood."

When we'd barge in after school, as often as not Phoebe

would be working on her never-finished family tree. Her grandmother had told her that *her* grandmother was the descendant of
a king. Or sometimes, instead, of a "world-famous man." The
story had been handled so often, had tumbled through the generations like a long game of whispering down the lane, and as
surely as it did in the game, it had acquired polish and spin with
each retelling. For all any of us knew, the original message was
that she was the descendant of the man who cleaned the king's
boots. Or simply, a very nice man who once caught a glimpse of a
king. Add to it that grandma had been a tad senile, and fuzzy as
to what principality or how far back that royal bloodline began.

Most people would laugh gently at their grandmothers' romantic visions of themselves, and that would be that. Not
Phoebe. She searched in vain for that missing golden link. I remember coming to Sasha's house one afternoon and seeing notebook pages taped together covering the dining-room table. Each
sheet had webs of lines, circles, and question marks. "A genealogical chart," Phoebe had said. "Mine." I couldn't make head nor
tails of it.

Phoebe's pretensions drove Sasha berserk for about a year before the two of them reached détente. After that, they developed
a lasting fondness for each other's quirky, loveable selves, and that
lasted long after Sasha's father decided that this marriage, like all
his others, had been a mistake.

I wondered if he remembered the good parts of his marriages, the attraction and the initial wedded bliss, and if he would
have attended this memorial were he not in Spain, honeymooning
with whatever number wife or fiancée this one was.

"Phoebe was never mean-spirited," Sasha whispered.

True. She was silly. She was pretentious and possibly delusional. She was probably not the world's best wife. She was a cluttered, distracted housekeeper, though an elegant, extravagant
cook and hostess when she put her mind to it, and it now appeared she'd not been much of a businesswoman, either.

But not mean. Not ever.

"If he does not shut up immediately," she said, "I'm going to speak ill of the living. Loudly."

Perhaps he felt the heat rising from his former stepsister. In any case, Dennis wound down, grudgingly admitting that his mother had been fun and had always been there in a pinch. "And," he said, "she made a mean martini, so here's to you, Mom." With a smirk, Dennis lifted the silver martini shaker he'd been clutching.

"Hear, hear," the group said with little enthusiasm. Nobody looked directly at him, nobody gave the almost-obligatory encouraging smile that would normally be expected.

The cocktail shaker had been Phoebe's requested resting place till her remains were emptied into the Wissahickon. All of this had been written out years earlier, along with the request that anyone mourning her should "carouse" on the banks. She'd wanted us to drink champagne from the crystal goblets she'd collected over the years, to toast her here, on Forbidden Drive, the spot where, apparently, she'd enjoyed a few romantic dalliances in her time.

She apparently forgot that Philadelphia has four seasons, and she envisioned us in sheer summer dresses, barefoot and dancing on the grass. She also hadn't considered the park's rules that forbid alcohol, let alone carousing. And while the official rules kept mum about our particular situation, I doubted that dumping charred human remains into the clear creek was permitted. Launching Phoebe into a different existence therefore had a hurried, surreptitious air. Raising bubbling crystal glasses while walkers and runners witnessed it would have been too flagrant. Raising empty glasses felt terribly wrong. Dennis had forged a compromise by using innocuous white Styrofoam cups and hiding the champagne in a duffel bag.

He now extracted a bottle and opened it, and then a second, pouring a small amount in each cup. I hadn't heard of screw-top champagne until then.

"A toast to Phoebe," Sasha said, but she said it too softly for the passing jogger to make note of it in the unlikely event that he had his MP3 player turned off and could hear.

"Safe journey, Phoebe," people said.

The fizzing liquid Dennis was trying to pass off as champagne managed to be both too sweet and too tart, and after one sip, I tipped my cup over and hoped it was good for the dormant grass.

Dennis popped off the top of the martini shaker and leaned over the creek. I watched Sasha frown as she watched him. Ever since the terrible night she'd found Phoebe dead, she'd been blaming herself. I'd heard the refrain, and I could almost see it circle her skull like a roll on a player piano, the same tune over and over. She'd been away in England for too long while anything might have been troubling Phoebe. She'd been a poor correspondent. She hadn't visited enough since she'd been back. She could have, should have, saved Phoebe.

Sasha's self-flagellation was without grounds. She had indeed visited Phoebe as soon as she'd returned to Philadelphia, three months ago, and several times after.

Demonstrating how upset and confused she was, not only did Sasha accept responsibility for Phoebe's suicidal depression, but she simultaneously insisted that Phoebe had not been depressed in the first place.

"She laughed a lot" was part of the loop going around and around in Sasha's head. "She was *sad* about Nelson, but not depressed. I'm not sure that marriage was destined to last much longer even if he'd lived. She said he was a whiner. She said lots of things, but then—*wham*—he was gone. Sad, you see. Not suicidal! And look, she was dating again, she was optimistic, not depressed."

Part of what bonded the two women was the irrational belief that the next man would be better, despite their own histories, which proved that the next ones were seldom as good as the ones before.

Sasha had even used her professional skills to help the hunt for number six by taking photos of Phoebe for an online match-making service. She'd needed new ones because all her portraits were in wedding attire.

She never got to see the photos. Sasha was delivering them the night she found Phoebe dead.

"Is ordering photos the behavior of a clinically depressed woman about to end her life?" Sasha had demanded. "Posing, preening, worrying about the lighting and how it would make her look?"

People are unpredictable. Maybe the need for updated photos and an online dating service would make you realize all you'd lost, and drive you into depression. I didn't know Phoebe well enough to know if she'd been putting up a façade for Sasha's sake, or if she was subject to rapid mood changes.

But my private opinion was that this was all about Sasha, who, being human, couldn't deal with the painful irrationality of the situation.

Eventually, Sasha noticed the disconnect between what she'd observed and the guilt she felt over what had happened, and had found a way to reconcile them. Phoebe had not been depressed and Phoebe had not taken her life. If someone else had ended Phoebe's life, then Sasha could feel pain, but not guilt.

Dennis uncapped Phoebe as, with perfect mistiming, the wind changed course and her airborne ashes caught a thermal and landed on Dennis's expensive dark overcoat. All over it.

Retribution for that eulogy, I was sure.

Dennis scowled and brushed, which smeared but didn't remove the gray blots, and he looked as if he was about to shout at his mother one last time. Instead, he took a deep breath, leaned low and shook out her remaining remains, turned away from the stream, left the silver mixer on the ground, and wiped his leather gloves clean before facing Sasha.

Because of Dennis's flight schedule, there had been a lunch before the memorial service, rather than the more traditional gathering afterward. Now Dennis pushed up his smeared coat sleeve, checked his watch, and came over to Sasha. "Keep me in the loop about the house," he said.

She nodded. He'd talked her into finding a realtor and disposing of Phoebe's "treasures," since he lived in Chicago while Sasha lived nearby and was sharing in the profits. To me that meant they should also share the work, but Dennis was Phoebe's executor, and life was complicated enough without getting into this particular battle.

Sasha put her hand on Dennis's sleeve. Her forehead had a long, vertical wrinkle down its middle. "Before you go," she said, "I've been wanting to ask . . . do you . . . did you wonder . . . when you heard . . ." She took another deep breath and cleared her throat. "I don't believe Phoebe would take her life that way."

"She wouldn't use pills and booze? Why not?"

He'd spoken too loudly, so that people nearby turned to watch. "I mean she wouldn't commit suicide," Sasha said. "It doesn't fit her. She was upbeat, looking forward—"

"Wait a minute! What are you suggesting?" Dennis's face darkened as if his blood had been rerouted and was pounding its way toward the skin.

"I'm not comfortable with the official version. Why would she—"

"Damn it, Sasha!" he said, his voice loud enough to scare the Daves, who'd approached to express condolences. "*You're* not comfortable? This is not about you. For once in your life can you not be histrionic? You're just like her—everything's dramatic and oversized. You want headlines, investigations, your fifteen minutes of fame? Find it somewhere else. She killed herself."

"And it's just like you to want to believe your own mother killed herself. Why would she? She didn't even leave a note." At six feet, Sasha was as tall as Dennis, and with the high-heeled boots and enormous hat, taller still, so she held her ground. The hostility radiating off him would have floored a smaller woman.

"She wasn't one for writing," he snapped. "Or for thinking things through. This was probably an impulse like so many others. That's how she was, an emotional infant!"

Sasha was silent for a moment, very unlike her normal behavior. Then she said quietly, "Don't you even want to know why I think that?"

"I've got a plane to catch." Once again he checked his watch.

Sasha lowered her voice still more. "Are you at all sorry that your mother died?"

"Let me know what's happening about the house." He turned and walked away from us.

Two

I t makes me angry and sad," Sasha said over dinner. She had the silver martini shaker on the seat next to her, and she looked at it, as if Phoebe, alive, might still inhabit it.

"We are all angry and sad," Mackenzie said. He'd joined us for the meal and looked almost as troubled as Sasha did. While we'd been bidding farewell to Phoebe, he'd spent Sunday on the phone with his parents, three cousins, and two uncles, who'd lost their homes to the devastating hurricane that had leveled too much of Louisiana, including his parents' parish and the home he'd grown up in. No lives lost, which was the very good news, but three months after the catastrophe, everyone was still scattered, unsure about what to do—or what they could do—next.

Their pasts had been eradicated; their futures were murky, and each day was progressively more difficult to wade through.

His mother, the usually buoyant Gabby Mackenzie, compared their situation to having Vaseline on your glasses while trying to read the fine print. Jobs lost, contacts lost, supplies lost, friends made into distant refugees or missing altogether, promises unkept, seasons passing. All the supports society had built were gone.

They'd never had much in the way of material goods. In fact, C.K. had said he hadn't realized till he was out in the world that they'd been "something close to poor." And now, they had still less. His father, Boyd, called "Boy," had been a construction worker when young, then a partner in a country hardware store. The fact that he couldn't rebuild on his former site or supply the tools for others to rebuild was driving him up the wall. If, of course, there had been a still-standing wall to be driven up.

We'd offered the loft to them and to Cary Grant and Katherine Hepburn, their dogs. Either we and our sure-to-be-miserably-unhappy cat would share the space with all of them, or we'd give it to them for as long as they needed, and we'd find friends willing to house us for the duration.

His parents had politely—they were southerners, after all—declined. Exile did not seem a solution to them, and they needed to be closer to where they hoped to rebuild their lives. One of Boy's cousins had a spread of land with lots of room for the dogs up in West Monroe, and though that was too far away from home to be efficient, they could stay as long as they needed to. It was no solution, but the only available one. Mostly, they'd been on long forays close to home, staying wherever they could find shelter, working at rebuilding their store and life, and then retreating north to West Monroe.

We sat glumly in a tiny Ethiopian restaurant, each of us sad and/or angry for our own reasons. We favored third world cuisines—they were generally hearty and inexpensive, although it did feel out of kilter to be dining on the cuisine of a country with a starvation problem. Perhaps it should have put our problems in perspective.

"Is your cousin really named Junior Bear?" Sasha suddenly demanded of Mackenzie. Then she waved the question away. "I thought you were all supposed to be named Bubba. Except you, given that you don't even have actual names, only initials. But really—what kind of a name is Junior Bear?"

Mackenzie smiled for the first time since he'd entered the restaurant. "Northerners have no common sense. Isn't it obvious? Junior Bear would be the child of Senior Bear."

We sat at an hourglass-shaped wicker table, Sasha and I on stools, Mackenzie on a low sofa. To his credit, he had offered to switch, but we figured we'd be as Ethiopian as possible and let the male keep the comfiest spot.

"Those stools of yours," he said. "To be authentic, they should be covered in monkey fur."

I was glad they weren't. But still, "How do you know that?"

He raised an eyebrow. "I read."

He did read, and mostly the sort of things I did not, but wished I did. Aside from the varied texts he had to read for his doctoral program in criminology, his leisure reading was mostly history, biography, and cultural studies, and he was becoming a world-class master of the justifiably obscure factoid.

His observation did not relieve the gloom. We were on hold until we were presented with an enormous plate covered with a gray, rubbery-looking pancake. "Injera," the waiter said, and he then demonstrated how the various stews we'd ordered—chicken, lamb, and vegetable—were to be wrapped into a piece of pancake and popped into the mouth. I liked this part. No utensils, although they had provided forks for the timid.

The waiter also poured us honey wine, but it isn't my favorite, so I ordered sparkling water.

"It makes me sad and angry," Sasha said. Again.

"Junior Bear?" Mackenzie asked. "Or the lack of monkey fur?"

She shook her head.

Mackenzie and I both sighed. "What?" we both asked with no enthusiasm.

"That nobody cares."

"I care," Mackenzie said. "It's breakin' my heart." The devastation in his home state and his distance from and inability to help his family grew less tolerable with each passing week. "Can't imagine why you'd think I didn't," he added.

"You do?" Sasha said. "I can't tell you what that means, you of all people."

"Wait—" I began. "You two are talking about two sep—"

"So you won't let this pass as a suicide, either," she said before I could finish my sentence. "Will you help me?"

Mackenzie frowned. "What are you talking about?"

I'd spared him Sasha's obsessive post-Phoebe discussions. He had enough real and terrible things on his mind. He didn't need figments and rationalizations.

Sasha looked surprised. "Phoebe, of course," she said. "Phoebe's murder. What else?"

"What else? My God, there's an entire . . ." Mackenzie let his thought go unsaid and he looked at me as if he wanted to read what was behind my forehead.

It wasn't always great being with two people you knew well, who didn't know each other well enough to read the signs. Sasha turned and looked at me with the barest hint of a frown. Her unspoken dialogue was fast and furious and irritated that I hadn't bothered to tell my husband her worries and theories about Phoebe's death.

Having made sure that I knew that she knew what was up, she rolled a piece of the rubber pancake around the chicken stew, chewed, leaked only a little bit of the sauce, nodded approval of the taste, then took a deep breath and used her fingers to tick points off rather than eat. "It's obvious that somebody wouldn't take sleeping pills when they're still in their street clothes, nowhere near their bedroom. It feels wrong. Wouldn't you be on the bed and not on the living-room sofa if you were headed for either a good night's sleep or your eternal rest?"

"She was downstairs?" Mackenzie asked.

"Dressed to go out." Sasha spoke with new urgency. Her anger over my failure to involve the great detective in the case was now replaced by this opportunity to make a convert to her cause. "Wearing really nice slacks, a red silk blouse, chocolate velvet blazer, and great shoes. And to think I always worried that she'd break her neck on those spike heels. Life's ironic, isn't it? She was wearing jewelry, too, of course. Not too wild, not too overdone, but . . . perfectly accessorized for company, curled up in the corner of the sofa, her head on the armrest."

Mackenzie shot another glance my way. I think he wanted me to stop her, or to explain why any of this was at all important. But I knew either attempt would be futile.

"The front door was unlocked," Sasha said.

"Why were you there?" Mackenzie asked. "Was this night-time? Did she expect you?"

Sasha shook her head. "It was a spontaneous visit. She hadn't mentioned any plans to go out. I phoned from my car, twice and no answer, but she did that sometimes, opted not to answer the phone. I do that, too. I had photos of her—she'd asked me to take them—but mostly, I was out and in my car anyway, and I had a good story to tell her. I thought we'd have a glass of wine and a lot of laughs. Worst case scenario, she would have gone out, and I'd have left the photos for her anyway."

"Okay, I bite," Mackenzie said, and he finally did, on the injera. "This is good," he said with audible surprise. "Gingery. I could do with a good story and a few laughs. Or is it a for-girls-only thing?"

"You judge. Somebody Phoebe liked, a friend, had acquired a stepson via a recent marriage. Got that so far? An artist. Divorced, available. And since I'm a photographer, divorced, and available, when she heard about him she was sure it was a match made in heaven. Two artists!" Sasha shook her head, her eyes lowered in mock horror. "I met him that night. The night Phoebe . . ."

"And?" Mackenzie prompted when it was obvious her thoughts had drifted away from the story.

"He hadn't sounded all that stupid on the phone, not world-class stupid, but for all I know, he had somebody else speak for him. And I say this despite the fact that I have low standards when it comes to men, so—"

"Actually," I interrupted, "I'd say you have no standards whatsoever."

She nodded. "I was surprised to find out that I did. We met at a restaurant. I was there first, and in he swaggered with the kind of missing-link looks that prove not everybody fully evolved from the apes. Can you remember the experience of praying that an approaching person is not your blind date? I got religion the minute he entered the restaurant. I know you shouldn't judge a book by its cover, so maybe that's why my prayers were not answered. Instead, he raised his eyebrows when he saw me, wiggled them, and gave two thumbs-up. That was meant as a compliment."

She wrapped another morsel of hard-boiled-egg-and-lamb stew and pointed at the gray roll. "This injera has twice the I.Q. he had." She chewed for a moment, then said, "A better personality, too." She bit off another piece. "Better-looking as well.

"This restaurant in Old City, near you guys, was once some kind of retail outlet, and it still has the big storefront kind of window. So he gets the conversation rolling—that's how he put it— by ordering us beers without asking me what I'd like—which wouldn't have been a beer—then by telling me at great length, especially for a man with an extremely limited vocabulary, what a bitch his ex-wife was, and why. And how lucky he was to get rid of her, because ever since he had, he was 'getting plenty'—his romantic description of his love life. More eyebrow wiggling.

" 'I'm a lucky guy,' he said, 'in every way.' And apparently his great good luck had just been proven once again by the parking spot he found. And then he waves and says his car is outside, and indeed it was, driver's side facing me.

"It was orange, with black graffiti all over it. 'My art,' he said. 'Art on wheels. Unique, huh?' So there's my soul mate, the other artist. Outlines of naked women with bosoms so large they were like deformities, and sayings like 'Ready, Freddie' and painted flames coming out from the wheel wells—and yellow crime-scene tape pasted on the side. And on the rear door facing me it said 'Honk if you're horny.' "

She put one finger up to squelch any editorial comments on our part. "That's when I told Nick-the-Artist that I had suddenly developed a terrible gastrointestinal problem and had to leave immediately. He didn't understand 'gastrointestinal' so I translated into his language. He sulked, shrugged, and said, 'Suit yourself.' He didn't even say good-bye and before I made it out the door, he was downing my beer."

She shook her head. "Talk about the bottom of the barrel! He was the sludge that's under the barrel. So I decided to drive to Phoebe's and tell her how her matchmaking with the artist—artist!—had turned out. I mean she's—she was—practically right across the bridge. She was there, on the couch, the TV playing, all dressed up, and it took me what feels way too long to realize she was dead. It does not make sense."

"Any sign of forced entry?" Mackenzie asked.

Sasha shook her head.

"Anything missing?"

The question made it clear that he had not known Phoebe.

"Who could tell? Nothing was turned over, and nothing looked rifled through. Drawers weren't open, but she wasn't into minimalist décor. She believed that less was less."

That was putting it mildly. Divorce was Phoebe's only method of getting rid of excess possessions.

"What are you thinkin', then?" C.K. asked.

"She had a date. She simply hadn't told me about him. Dressed up. Drinks—well, at least she had one."

"But why, Sasha?" I asked. "Why would anybody want to do that to her?"

"I don't know!" she said. "I'm not a detective. You guys are."

"Hardly," I murmured. I am tired of needing to demur, but neither can I speed up the process of becoming an actual investigator.

"You have an idea who she might have been seein'?" Mackenzie's accent had increased since the hurricane, as if carefully preserving that remaining bit of Louisiana, no matter what.

Sasha shook her head. "The photos were for an online dating service."

"One she belonged to or was going to belong to?" C.K. asked.

Sasha sighed, and her shoulders lowered. "I don't know. I think—I think she already belonged somewhere because she mentioned getting inquiries from guys who 'weren't it,' she said. She thought she looked too stuffy in the photo she was using, a half of a wedding photo. I offered to Photoshop out the hat and veil, but she said the whole dressed-up 'granny-thing'—that was her phrase—wasn't the image she wanted to project. Neither was undressed." Sasha looked down at her hands. I was sure it was so that we couldn't see her face, but we could see and understand what the rapid eyeblinks meant.

I patted my friend's shoulder. "You miss her a lot," I said quietly.

Sasha nodded, her head still downcast.

"Maybe the date was with a woman," I said. "Maybe she had plans to paint the town with another woman, or be fixed up for a double date."

"And what?" Sasha asked. "They had drinks before facing the evening out, and then Phoebe said, 'Oh, wait—I need to commit suicide instead, so would you please go wash out your glass and hide it?' How does that work?"

"Then maybe they were simply spending a quiet evening together. We do that sometimes, you and I. Why not Phoebe?"

"Or maybe a man drugged her," Mackenzie said softly.

Sasha shrugged.

"Do you know her women friends? Know how those relationships were going?" he asked her.

Sasha turned and stared at the side wall. A couple at a table frowned at her, thinking she was staring at them. She wasn't, and they finally realized it, shrugged, and returned to their meal. Finally Sasha blinked and returned to this planet. "Friends," she said. "The ones there today. Joanie and Harriet something, Carolyn and . . . a neighbor, though I think in a different time, husband, and neighborhood. I could look them up, but I don't think any of them were hanging-out-together kinds of friends. She was in a book group a year or two back, but I don't know if she saw those people nowadays. And there's her business partner—former partner because the place is going under—that flake, Merilee. They've been friends for years. Since when Phoebe and my dad were married."

Two years ago, when Phoebe and the pampered Merilee had been funded by Merilee's husband, supposedly via his trust fund, I took it as a given, though I never asked, that nobody expected the biz to actually make money. How could it? Does any dog need a manicure set or a pair of sunglasses? Are there doggie gourmets who prefer hand-shaped and home-baked "cookies"? Do kitties feel better if their litterbox is in a turreted castle enclosure or they're eating their food off hand-painted plates? How about feather boas and tiaras for your pets?

"Her husband pulled the plug," Sasha added.

"Phoebe must have been furious."

"More like acutely disappointed. Merilee was the furious one—but with Phoebe, although it was ridiculous. Marc Wilkins was very dramatic about the closing. He came to the store, and not surprisingly there were no customers, and he used that as the trigger for exploding. He chewed out the two women—blaming Phoebe in particular because she hadn't risked a cent of her own. He said they were bleeding him dry and he wasn't going to stand for it anymore. They were out of business as of that moment." Sasha sighed again and shook her head, though nobody had offered her anything. "The real story was that Marc Wilkins was revving up to dump Merilee. He'd found somebody newer, and the floundering pet shop—his lost trust fund cash flow—was the pretense for his splitting. The crazy thing is that instead of being furious with him, which would have been rational, Merilee turned on Phoebe. Acted as if Phoebe's need for this business, or Phoebe's bad business sense or outright thievery, had driven Marc into the arms of whoever it now was. She revved up to the point where she accused Phoebe of having stolen the money or cooked the books—she could never decide which, but stealing in one form or another. And Marc snapped up that theory as well.

"I'm sure the fit of insanity would have passed and they'd be friends again, and in fact, before the big accusation of stealing, Phoebe was trying to show Merilee how to come out on top after the divorce, to make things really hard on Marc. After four divorces, Phoebe was, after all, something of an expert."

"I'm sure those efforts further endeared Phoebe to Mr. Wilkins. And perhaps Merilee as well," Mackenzie said quietly.

"But then—Phoebe died."

"And not by accident, you believe."

"Right." Sasha realized what Mackenzie had implied. "But Merilee? No. There'd be no point."

"How big a point do you need?" He pulled off a part of the remaining injera and surveyed what fillings were left. "Revenge is a pretty time-honored response if you think somebody ruined your life."

"Merilee's too—too silly to do something like that. Too engrossed in playing games. I mean like a little kid plays games. She likes to spend her spare time dressing up her bulldog. When last I saw him, he was in a top hat and a bow-tie collar." She shook her head again.

"Silly people in danger of losing everything can do stupid things. She could decide removing Phoebe would endear her to her husband. And what about him, in fact?"

"I'd love it to be him—the creep—but I don't know if Phoebe'd have dressed up that way for him, welcomed him after the way he treated her."

"Any other enemies?"

"Ex-husbands?" I prompted.

She shook her head. "You saw, one was there today."

"Even his son came," I added.

"That's pretty amicable, don't you think? The recent one's dead, my dad's in Spain, and the other two . . . she never had huge court fights or got enormous settlements or whatever keeps those kinds of feuds going. She's always managed to get by, but she isn't—wasn't—rich. The stuff she was trying to teach Merilee was based on what she hadn't done."

"It's very sad," Mackenzie murmured politely. At some point within the past minute, I'd seen his attention drift again, and while he was properly sympathetic and even asking questions by rote, Sasha's friend and former stepmother, Phoebe, no longer occupied much of his mind.

"Can you help me?" Sasha asked.

Mackenzie snapped back to attention. "Me? How?"

"Find out who killed her. I can pay you. I'm getting half of the sale of the house."

"Sasha," he said softly, "grief does strange things, including making us look for a villain, a source, an explanation. Phoebe must have been lonely. Fifth marriage and she's widowed within months. Her only son's worthless and uninterested. His only virtue's that he lives far away from her. She drank; and either by a sad accident or by design, she mixed booze and sleeping pills and killed herself. Nobody wants to believe that, so we look for outside reasons, when rationally speaking, there do not seem to be any. You yourself just said so."

"I said I couldn't think of any, but they must be there, and you'd find them. That's your job, and I know you're good at it, Mackenzie. Please?"

"I'd feel unethical. I surely wouldn't take your money for this kind of thing, Sasha, and I'd feel I was stringing you along. I hate to disappoint you, but you know, I'm pretty involved now with my family, not to mention school and work, and this . . . Well, I'm sorry, but nothing you've said makes me think it's anything except a sad accident or a deliberate act on her part. There's nothing to investigate."

"Wait." I'd been re-rolling the conversation, looking for how the pieces fit, at least for Sasha, and something had hit me. "Could you describe her shoes?"

"Shoes?" Mackenzie asked.

I nodded. "You said they were great, that her whole outfit was great."

Sasha had done a small double-take, but proceeded with gusto. "Very sexy. Very high," she said. "The kind that made me afraid she was going to break her neck in them. These were red strappy things, maybe alligator—or fake alligator—four-inch or five-inch stilettos, with a strap that buckled around the ankle. That enough?"

"Good Lord." I was sure Mackenzie was about to put his hand on both our foreheads to test for fevers.

"Was she wearing them when you found her?" I continued.

Sasha nodded, rather absently, and then she looked at me and her eyes widened. "Of course!" she said, and turned to Mackenzie, smiling triumphantly. "You see?" she said.

"What?" he asked. "What?"

"No woman curls up with that kind of shoe on," I said. "No woman. In our teens, we'll do most anything to look cool, be in constant pain if a cute guy's around. But Phoebe was way beyond that stage. Do you know how uncomfortable they had to be under her that way? Buckle digging into soft flesh? Ankle straps cutting off circulation when you pull your legs under you? Heel ruining the sofa and whatever body parts it touched? No woman leaves on shoes like that while she sedates herself to death. So Sasha has a point. Somebody else was there when and as she died. Phoebe had no intention of making that position her last one of this life."

His jaw hadn't actually dropped, but his lips were slightly parted, as if too many words to contain were stacked inside them.

"I take your expression to be one of awe at my deduction," I said. "And that we'll look into it."

He crossed his eyes, then he shut them.

I took that as a yes.

Three

Margaret Burbidge looked worried, and that was not an emotion that I'd normally associate with her. The ninth grader had the spirit of a bouncing ball, and when she perceived a problem, she almost immediately rebounded with a potential solution.

Eddie Schneider, also normally a cheerful person, stood beside her, looking serious and nodding agreement with everything she said.

"It doesn't make sense." Margaret's face was barely able to register the worry lines she was forcing between her eyebrows.

I was only half-listening, most of my mind pondering why there couldn't be a pot of coffee in my classroom. In every classroom! Would it hurt anyone if we were all more awake?

I'd stayed up too late the night before talking with Sasha about love, death, and realtors and had gotten up this morning with the sinking sense of having promised not only to look into Phoebe's death but also to help Sasha get Phoebe's house ready to be sold.

All through my groggy morning rituals, I kept hoping I was misremembering my promises, but when I stopped in the office before class, I picked up a message saying, "See you at four at Phoebe's. Dinner provided." And then a set of directions as to how to get there.

I agreed that Phoebe's lifelong need to acquire anything that was flounced, pleated, ruffled, gilded, or labeled "a collectible" needed to be smoothed over so as to avoid terrifying away prospective buyers. Still, I didn't know how I was going to manage my life plus what now seemed like managing Sasha's as well. I consoled myself with the idea that I might be able to combine the two acts of friendship by interviewing Phoebe's neighbors while I was also housecleaning there today. That would have felt like a more efficient use of my time if I had a clue as to what I was going to ask them. What, in fact, I wanted to find out. I stifled a yawn.

"Something is very wrong," Margaret said with dramatic flair.

"The bulletin this morning was wrong," Eddie said, his eyes wide and his expression still solemn. "Our homeroom teacher read it to us, but it was wrong. I mean about the money for Louisiana."

"We asked her to read it again. And then we asked her to check if there was a typo," Margaret said.

I shook my head, still not sure what their point was.

"The holiday gift?" Margaret prompted me.

"Wrong, how?"

Eddie cleared his throat. "Me and Margaret—"

"Margaret and I," I said before I could censor it. Even without enough coffee, some parts of my brain work.

"Yeah. Margaret and I have been keeping a record."

"Like our own charts. Not official," she said.

"But we know we're right," he said. "And what they said we collected is wrong."

"Eddie's really, really good at math," Margaret said, and I wondered if her proprietary air meant that they were a couple. "And I *know* we collected more than the big total in the bulletin this morning. Look!" She waved the notice sheet that goes to all homerooms every day. "It says congratulations to everybody for being so generous, but we know that number? The fifteen hundred dollars? It's wrong."

"Backtrack a little," I said. "You kept the records?" Since the start of December, the school had been collecting donations to be used to buy Christmas gifts for hurricane victims. The collection drive was going to end this week, and this morning's bulletin had published the tally to date, probably as an incentive to those who hadn't yet donated.

Both of them shook their heads. "The office kept the records of the whole thing, but we asked everybody's homerooms what they'd collected."

"Every day," Eddie added.

"And then we added it up," Margaret said. "Every day."

My thoughts wandered back to coffee. Margaret and Eddie meant well, but surely numbers the homeroom collectors remembered were not a solid basis for a challenge.

Besides, I had nothing to do with the collection except to be delighted that the students had thought of it.

Margaret waved the bulletin again. "It says we've collected one thousand five hundred dollars and fifty cents so far."

I nodded. "I know. I receive the bulletin each morning, too. I was impressed with how much you've all donated." I was. After all, aside from my own household, the hurricane wasn't front-page news anymore, and teenaged memories are no longer than their adult counterparts'. Not only had this idea been suggested by the student council, and to my reckoning had been a success, but there was talk of a New Year's resolution to adopt a group of still-closed schools in New Orleans, and to send money for books and supplies for six months.

"Well, it would be nice, except we know it was close to two thousand dollars!" Margaret stood with her bottom lip and one hip pushed out. I thought fleetingly of comic book superwomen.

"One thousand, nine hundred and forty-seven dollars," Eddie said.

"You sure?" I looked at my watch. "A nearly five-hundred-dollar discrepancy?" Their classmates would be here any second, and I had some necessary preparation. "Sorry," I said. "I'm still listening, but I've got to do this." I wrote *A Tale of Two Cities* vocabulary list on the board: *Cessation. Soliloquy. Inexorable. Epoch.* I was so tired that I stared at "epoch" as if it were a word I'd never seen before. A silly-looking word, too.

I finally turned around.

Margaret's expression, which she'd obviously carefully maintained while I wrote on and studied the whiteboard was, if not quite withering, then a combination of having been betrayed and outraged.

Eddie's expression was more discreet, but no less unhappy with my reaction.

"Okay, you're sure," I said. "Sorry. I'm not great at math, and the collections came in somewhat randomly, I think, so I'm always ready to believe I've made a mistake. But did we really collect nearly two thousand dollars? That's huge."

"It's not that huge, Miss Pepper," Eddie said. "If you do the math, it's around four dollars a student in fourteen days. Two dollars a week. Less per capita if you include the teachers who donated. And the cafeteria workers. All those people. Most of us waste a whole lot more than two dollars a week."

Margaret rolled her eyes for emphasis, to make sure I comprehended just how much cash our students wasted. She mutated from a mini-superwoman into an avenging angel. Or Madame Defarge, knitting while the cash-wasters were beheaded.

"I am impressed with your calculations; and I trust them," I said. "It isn't that, but isn't it also possible that the people you asked about the daily takes miscounted or misremembered?"

I wanted coffee. The ninth grade class was bearing down on my room. Plus, why come to me with this set of woes?

How did I keep getting myself entwined in things that had nothing to do with me—like Phoebe's death? Last night, having shoes on while supposedly committing suicide had sounded so significant. Sherlock Holmesian. Make that Cher LaCombs, the new female sleuth. C'est moi.

I realized that two entirely likeable young people were staring at me with expressions that belonged on a Save the Children poster.

"Let me just remind you that lots of the donations, at least in my homeroom, are in small coins, so it's easy enough for the person tallying it up to mix up a nickel and a quarter or . . ."

Wrong response. If anything, their eyes grew wider, their lips more tightly compressed.

I continued on with the vocabulary list. Sad that Dickens could assume his magazine readers already knew the words I was writing on the board, all of which were still in use, and none of which my ninth grade class would be likely to have in their vocabulary. *Sonorous,* I wrote. *Levity. Evanescence. Supplicatory. Gradations.*

"The totals are wrong," Eddie said. "Nearly five hundred dollars wrong." His voice, still in the process of changing, betrayed how uncomfortable he was with all of this. He was accusing somebody in this school of embezzling funds meant for the children of a disaster.

I conspicuously looked at my watch, then at the open doorway. The sounds of the approaching horde were clear. "I think you have a case to make," I said. "But I think you have to take it up with Miss . . . the secretary . . ." I had again forgotten the new secretary's true name, because she'd only been in school for one week so far, and I had labeled her "Miss Odd" as a way to remember her actual name. Unfortunately, I forgot what the link was.

Lately, the occupants of the main office's desk had been arriving and departing too quickly for my wee brain. "Did you ask for a recount?"

Margaret shrugged. "Mrs. Codd says she did."

Codd. "Like the fish, but with an extra 'd' so you know I'm not tonight's dinner," the sweet woman had said. "Opal Codd." I felt a wave of irrational relief at having her name once again.

"She says she recounted it twice. I don't know if she even listens to me, because I'm not in charge of anything. Just a concerned citizen."

"Are you suggesting Mrs. Codd can't count?" That sounded like a word game, but they both remained grim-faced. "Something else?"

"We aren't saying Mrs. Codd's *stealing,*" Eddie said. "Just wrong."

"Eddie's our class treasurer, too," Margaret said. "He'd know."

"You know, class is going to begin in less than a minute, so maybe this discussion—"

"I certainly never let the money I collect out of my sight," Margaret said, pressing her case as long as she could. "It's sealed and in my backpack until I take it in. Everybody else does the same. That's the rule."

Sometimes my room looks like the aftermath of a natural disaster with objects the students "never let out of their sight" flung in wide arcs around their desks. They have lockers, but they find them inconvenient, or they don't have time to get to them between or before class. In the dead of winter, the concept of an aisle is lost. Parka-arms and fleece-jacket edges, plus the usual books, backpacks, purses, and lunch bags have a way of creeping out in search of one another.

The sad truth was, anybody could have extracted the money

from Margaret's backpack at any time, removed a wad of cash, and replaced the pilfered packet. Or she, or one of the other collectors, had miscounted. It wasn't as if we were talking about a school full of mathematical geniuses, even if their hearts were in the right place.

"I've got an idea," I said. "Suppose I have both of you collect all the homerooms' donations, then count the money along with Mrs. Codd every day at the start of first period. I'll write a note giving you permission to be late to my class this week. Would that work?"

They both nodded. "Except that's about the future," Eddie said. "What about whoever took that money?"

The odds of finding that out were slim, but I didn't want to sound hopeless. "We'll keep working on that. Let's find out where the money was when, and maybe that'll show who could have taken it. But meanwhile, when you collect from each homeroom—make sure the class knows who you are and what you're doing."

Eddie squinted. "How would that work at flushing out the culprit? And isn't that kind of dangerous? Kind of setting us up?"

He'd been watching too many crime shows. "This is Philly Prep," I said. "Not exactly those mean streets. You're taking the money directly down to the office. What I was hoping to do was let whoever's been siphoning off funds know that he or she can't do it anymore."

"Oh," they both said softly. Stopping the crime didn't sound as exciting as catching and punishing the culprit.

"If, in fact, somebody at school has been doing that," I added. This time, they merely looked around at their classmates sauntering and bopping into the room, and either bored with me, annoyed by my approach, or simply acknowledging that we'd exhausted the topic and had run out of time, they mumbled thanks and moved toward their desks. Margaret immediately was all business, pulling her notebook, *A Tale of Two Cities,* and a felt-tipped pen out of her book bag, then shoving it in the general direction of the floor under her chair. So much for anything ever being under constant surveillance.

The ninth graders were still in the semi-cowed phase, still slightly tinged with the shame of being the babies of the bunch. Some began copying the vocabulary words into their notebooks while others were still finding their seats. They'd done such things in September and October with a worried, dogged obedience, listening attentively to any cues and clues that would help them survive the next four years. By November, they were picking up a little attitude, and now, with winter break looming, the more precocious among them were practicing how to look bored with and slightly annoyed by anything that goes on in a classroom.

Now, they did what was requested, but with frowns and sighs. With each passing moment that we neared vacation, the enchanted autumn's mellowness evaporated.

Once they'd copied the words and I'd read them the sentences in which they were found, and together they'd tried to decipher meaning from context, we moved on to a class discussion of the many tantalizing threads at the start of the novel, including the opening segment with its famous lists of opposites and contrasts, "It was the best of . . ."

That, of course, made me think of Dennis-the-Jerk, but I forced him out of my consciousness, replacing him with starving French peasants and long-lost fathers. We had to talk about history, something my classes never comfortably accept as having any relevance to the English curriculum. Of course, the ninth graders were still too timid to say so directly, so we had a reasonably good talk about the era, the simmering violence in France, the way Dickens foreshadowed a future of great bloodshed, and conditions in England where the coach's passengers feared the messenger might be a highwayman. To my enormous relief, when they understood that the book's story began in 1775, they correctly surmised what the "messages . . . from a congress of British subjects in America" were. Some history had sunk in.

We talked about violent times when the accepted order stops being automatically accepted. " 'Jacques' was the revolutionaries' code name for one another. Four hundred years earlier, the peasants had revolted, and the royals dismissed them as 'Jacques,' a common name. Calling all of them that one name was meant to show they weren't unique human beings, just a mass of ordinary nothings. The revolutionary peasants adopted the name 'Jacques' for themselves, and four hundred years later, the time of this novel, they're still using the name."

That idea of making a taunt a proud slogan intrigued most of the class, though I did see a bit of side action at the rear of the room, as a folded note was flicked to the floor, swooped up by the boy across the aisle, who read it, flicked a glance my way, then lowered his eyelids in exquisite boredom and shrugged. The body language saved him the time and energy that holding up a gigantic sign reading: WHO CARES? would have expended.

I concentrated on the ones who did care, at least a little.

As she was leaving the room, Margaret came back to my desk, dragging Eddie behind her. "We were just thinking," she said, "that it's kind of our own *Tale of Two Cities,* isn't it?"

"Isn't what?"

"Here. Philadelphia and New Orleans."

It was, I thought. Here, and at home.

"That's why the money's so important," Margaret said. "So thanks for helping us. And that other city." Then she winked and smiled and pulled Eddie out of the room.

They were definitely a couple, even if he didn't know it yet. And Margaret should think about running for elected office.

At noon, having gotten through the French Revolution and S.A.T. preparation the next period, and the subjunctive-and-gerunds hour after that, I walked out to the front steps, where reception was better, and phoned Mackenzie. "Change of plans," I said. "Turns out I promised—or at least Sasha says I did—to be in Bordentown this afternoon. Cleaning out—tossing—Phoebe's

treasures so that a house-buyer can see the actual walls and surfaces."

He had no problems with it. He'd use the time to study, and
that would be fine, as long as I didn't "rescue" any throwaways.
He was probably relieved. He needed the time, always needed it.
I knew that, in addition to hitting the books, he'd be on his cell to
Louisiana, and thanks be for the toll-free calls. And when he
wasn't phoning, he'd be online, trying to help via e-mail. I knew
Sasha wanted the great detective, not his lowly apprentice, but no
matter how she might feel about it, I'd do the actual legwork for
this labor of love.

He was still talking, sounding down. He'd spoken with his
mother's eighty-five-year-old cousin, who had not only lost his
home but the land it stood on, which had become a permanent
wetland. Nobody could think of a good solution, although the
eighty-five-year-old had been chuckling about the ridiculousness
of it, Mackenzie said.

Shortly after, we clicked off and were back in our separate
worlds. I walked into the school's large entry hall bucking lunchtime traffic, and the folly of my direction was proven when a
navy, hooded parka barreled into me.

"Sorry!" he said.

"Jonesy?" I said when I could see his face.

"Yeah. Sorry." He looked at the door. "Didn't see you."

"Those hoods make it hard," I said. "I didn't get a chance to
say good-bye on Sunday, to thank you for coming."

He looked as if he were dying to say, "And your point is?"

"Well," I said lamely, "I guess this is my chance. It was nice of
you to come."

He shrugged. "I didn't exactly have an option."

"Did you know Phoebe Ennis?"

He sighed. "Kind of. When I was with my dad. She was
around when I got to his apartment." He shrugged. I am constantly amazed by the acute discomfort teens who brag and lie—

I hope—about their own experience and prowess show when touching, even peripherally, on the subject of their parents' private lives. I nodded and let the subject go.

Besides, the tide of humans was against me, and I was keeping him from wherever he'd been headed, and I wasn't sure why. I could have asked him why he was voluntarily going out into the damp cold, but that would have sounded so geriatric. Besides, he'd probably have told me, and I already knew the answer: frostbite and freedom were better than any heated schoolhouse. "Nice to see you again," I said.

"Yeah." The parka hood nodded and moved off.

I turned and went into the office to speak with Opal about the hurricane money. Also, of course, for the thrill of reading the blather that had made its way into my inbox since morning.

I was still surprised, each time, by the sight of our newest school secretary. Today, as always in my experience, she was smiling, the first surprise, given past experience. She was a tiny woman, and she seemed still smaller when she stood behind the divider. "Yes, dear," she said, "can I help you?"

Helpful. The second surprise.

Opal looked freshly minted from a child's storybook. The reason I'd grabbed for the stupid "sounds like Miss Odd" was that otherwise, when I thought of her, the name Miss Tiddly-something popped up. Her gray hair was pulled up and back in a bun, tendrils escaping and waving around her round face no matter what she did. She wore aptly-named granny glasses—she had "one dozen grands," she'd told me with one of her smiles—and long-sleeved dresses, the skirts mid-calf. She was efficient, cheery, and did not seem fazed by the student body or worried about our school's depressing secretarial turnover. She'd been retired from a lifetime of exemplary office work when a relative of a friend of a school parent called to say Philly Prep once again needed a secretary.

She had an air about her that suggested she'd likely as not

whip a freshly baked pie from her computer. "So glad to be busy
again!" she'd said when she was hired. "I thought I'd go insane sitting home. There is just so much gardening and lunching and
book clubbing and grand-sitting that one woman wants to do.
And Mr. Codd being home as well, well, oh my!"

That had been only a matter of one week ago, but she'd bustled in and gotten the hang of the system within minutes.

All the same, hurricane money was probably missing.

"You know a petite ninth grader named Margaret Burbidge?"
I asked her.

She nodded. "Mite of a thing, isn't she? Cute. And proud of
this hurricane project, isn't she? She's been in here, along with
that sweet young man—"

"Eddie Schneider?"

"Yes. Him. I think he's sweet on her. The two of them have
been in asking about how much we have so far. Nice that young
people are concerned about the welfare of strangers." She smiled
again, and there was no way I could envision her siphoning funds
out of the collections.

"I think they'd love to be still more involved, and it's good
training. I was wondering if you could help them out. They're
going to be collecting all the funds—going from classroom to
classroom—each morning, and so far, they've been doing the
math in their heads. Eddie's head, actually. A guesstimate, I'm
sure, but they're concerned about how they're doing with calcu-
lating the total sums turned in to the office and wondered
whether they could be here when the count is made."

That sentence emerged with such loops and convolutions, I
hoped it made sense. And then again, I hoped it didn't. I didn't
want Opal to suspect for a moment what had been suggested.

"The count would be made under your supervision, of
course. That might help them get things straight." That was
about as non-threatening a way of framing their suspicions as I
could come up with.

The lines that always crisscrossed Opal's face rearranged into confused hatch-marks, but she nodded. "Of course! But I do that final count during first period, and they'll miss a bit of class."

"It's okay," I said. "It's my class, and it's only for this week."

I thanked her and went to pick up my mail, though I wasn't sure why we called it that. It was seldom actual letters. "Picking up my junk," "picking up recycling-bin fodder," or "picking up today's detritus" would all have been closer to the truth.

Opal was looking beyond me, through the open doorway into the hallway, where the exodus had subsided, those students with this lunch hour presumably now wherever they intended to be. "Funny how things change," she said. She waited for me to respond, even though I'd thought it was a rhetorical comment.

"Yes," I said, flipping through a Xeroxed news story about a young man who'd conquered a physical disability, near-starvation, homelessness, and a precocious bout of alcoholism to go on to win a college scholarship. The headmaster, Maurice Havermeyer, who was maintaining his record for never once coming up with a good idea, had scrawled across the top, "Good story to inspire our youth!"

I could just imagine the response. The young man in the article deserved praise and respect. He would not get it if I read this story to my classes. They'd be intrigued by the alcoholism, not the recovery.

"In my day, it meant you were a bad boy. The kind your mother didn't want you to associate with."

I untangled Opal's sentence. Two boys were involved. One bad, one told not to associate with him. Or perhaps one bad boy and one girl whose mother didn't want her associating with him. But I still didn't know what she was talking about.

She saw my puzzlement. "Gambling!" she said. "A 'poker-playing man,' they'd say, meaning a gambler." She shook her head and pursed her mouth. "Code for up to no good in my day." Then her features relaxed. She must have been a pretty, delicate young woman, and she was still attractive, even with accordion-pleated skin. "Nowadays, it's a fad! It's fashionable. Look at these boys, the crème de la crème!"

Hardly. We were a school filled with intellectual skim milk, not cream.

She sighed. "I know I'm out of touch with this modern world because Mr. Codd watches the poker tournaments on TV, too. Loves them, and I'm sure those boys do, too. Besides, who knows better than the administration—"

I was proud of myself for not informing her that pretty much everybody knew better than our administration.

"—and obviously, Dr. Havermeyer and his board aren't perturbed by it."

"By poker playing?" Poker held no interest for me. I'm not great with numbers, and I can't remember what was played or what to do about it. I thereby infuriate everyone else in the game, and bore myself. So I responded to Mrs. Codd out of politeness, not interest. "Why would they be?"

"Well, the way our boys—it is almost all boys—play so much. Noon, and after school, and for all I know, into the night."

"Here? In the building?" How had she noticed and understood so much in a week, and why hadn't I?

"Not inside the school." She shook her head. The silver tendrils swayed with her motion. "Our archididascalos forbids it," she said, then she chuckled.

"Mrs. Codd—"

"Opal, please!"

"Archididascalos?"

Another chuckle. "I like a little sparkle in my sentences, so I'm studying up. Need a better vocabulary now that I'm here in a place of higher learning. Need to set an example."

"And archididascalos?"

"School principal. Dr. Havermeyer."

"I've never heard that term before."

"Few have, alas. And amazingly, it's not in every dictionary, but it is a perfectly good word."

Perhaps so, but I didn't see the point of a word that obscured meaning rather than clarified it. Perhaps that was evidence only of my ignorance.

"Put his foot down, as I understand," she said. "The woman who was here before me? That lovely young woman?" She paused, brow creased.

"Harriet Rummel," I prompted.

"Yes," she said with another of her smiles. "She was so kind to stay a day and train me, and she told me the rule about no playing in school. It's the gambling part, you know, not the playing itself, that's so worrisome."

"Times do change," I murmured. I felt mildly queasy about kids rushing off to play poker in the cold. Queasier still that I'd been unaware of it till now. Still, I knew watching poker on TV or playing it online was almost a mania, and I wasn't surprised. Or particularly interested.

"Harriet was a sweet young thing, wasn't she?" Opal Codd said. "And so deeply in love. I do hope things worked out for them."

Our last secretary had been engaged to a man who was so preoccupied with finding himself and following his bliss that he was rarely to be seen. They'd been engaged for over a decade, and still, he was lost. He'd thought he'd found himself at taxidermy school, but after nearly completing his course of study, he apparently had been chastised for misstuffing a wildcat. "You're a clown," the instructor had said, and he took it to be an omen and a portent.

Harriet followed him to Florida, to Clown School, sure that once there and settled in—and while she continued as always to support him—they would wed.

I'd liked her, the poor deluded woman, and I hoped against hope that even at this very moment, she was walking down the aisle with a man in a fake, red ball of a nose and oversized clown shoes.

Four

I tried to get out of school quickly, not out of any urgency to get to the job with Sasha, but so as to beat the traffic over the bridge into New Jersey. Bordentown was about thirty miles away, and could be a quick enough trip or a nightmare commute.

I hit gridlock at the front door, with students hellbent on getting out of the building, and I once again was jostled by parkas and mufflers and lined leather gloves.

"Sorry!" a young male voice said. That same word, that same voice—time-delayed echoes in these hallowed halls?

"Jonesy?" It was indeed. He looked horrified by the sight of me. And frightened, too. "We have to stop meeting this way," I said.

Not only did he not find my remark witty in the least, but

the boy next to him looked perturbed. Almost angry. "Meeting?" he said. "Why?" His eyes flicked over me dismissively and fixed on Jonesy. "Why would you?"

I disliked his rudeness—why would he be that incredulous about somebody meeting with me?—but wasn't surprised by it, or by his stupidity. I disliked him. "It was a joke, Griffith," I said. "An old joke."

I knew he didn't like having his entire first name used, and that he wanted to be called "Griff." Otherwise, people thought of his father, Griffith Ward, host of a popular local TV talk show, occasional guest reporter on the evening news, and former movie actor. His movies had been dreadful, and his talk show was nothing if not ordinary, but he was a man of great charm and that seemed enough to draw in interesting, or at least famous, celebrity guests. As for his string of forgettable films—Philadelphians forgot about them.

I liked him, too, or whatever I knew of his public persona. But his son was another matter. He had charm, but only a thin veneer that barely covered a smug, arrogant, and slow-witted personality.

I felt wretched admitting that I did not like Griffith Ward the Younger. I entered teaching intending to and believing that I would respect and fully appreciate each child's individuality. If asked back then, I would have reacted with sincere horror at the idea of a teacher's disliking a student. I might even react with the same horror now.

And yet, here we were.

It didn't happen often. Not that negative emotions were never in play. I was often-enough annoyed, also vexed, irritated, miffed, put out, riled, and chafed by students' behavior. But that was different. That was justified, at least to me, and transient.

My feelings about Griffith Ward the Younger and his ilk were deep-set. He didn't like being confused with or compared to his father, but he didn't mind trading on his father's popularity. The faculty considered it a laughable prank when he declared himself a candidate for Junior Class president, a position that held little responsibility, but a strong promise of reelection as Senior Class president. That, too, meant little in the grand scheme of real power, but it was a test of popularity, and participation in student government looked great on college applications.

Eventually it didn't matter if he was taken seriously or not. He became the candidate of choice when his father, with superb political timing, presented the school with two summer internships on his show, and invited his son's entire eleventh grade classmates to a special day's taping at the studio. A day that featured a rock star, plus the chance for many in the audience to speak on air.

That was it. The new and future class or school president was a shoo-in. How could you not like that vacant, happy, glad-handing jock? I wouldn't mind the complete lack of intellectual interest, not as much as I do, if he were not so arrogant. If he didn't strut around the school with a smirk on his face. If he weren't always surrounded by a group of toadies. Jonesy, I could see, was one of them.

"A joke," Griffith said with a typical sneer. "Yeah. An *old* joke. Got it. Sorry. I should have known."

He made it sound like an insult. Or maybe it was.

"We'll be late," he told Jonesy. "Hurry up."

And they were gone, and so was I, none of us up for long farewells or even civilities. Good thing that neither Jonesy nor Griffith was particularly verbose or glib, because that meant they left me with time to get over the bridge without a single snarl. I pulled up outside Phoebe's house in little more than a half hour, and felt as if I'd done a good thing.

The neighborhood she'd shared with her fifth husband was unprepossessing but pleasant: small vintage homes from before one of our wars, each with a bay window in the living room, almost all with tieback drapes and sheer curtains, and all with a square of green lawn neatly divided by a path to the front door. A few owners had tinkered with the symmetry, turning garages into rooms that almost looked as if they'd always served that function, but the look of the street was settled, comfortable, and unpretentious. It was not the sort of neighborhood I'd have expected Phoebe to wind up in, given her dreams of grandeur. I wondered if she'd been surprised to find herself here.

I pulled into the driveway behind Sasha's car, and as I slammed my door shut, I sensed movement to my left. A woman stood framed in the front window of the house next door. She held back a sheer curtain, and as I caught her eye, she nodded at me. I nodded in return, happy to know she was there. A solidly nosey neighbor is always a good thing and makes my job easier.

I knew Sasha was waiting for me inside Phoebe's house for cleaning and tossing detail. But she also wanted me to find out more about Phoebe's death, so why delay when a friendly face snooped? I went toward the neighbor's house. "Hi," I said when she answered the bell. "I hope I'm not interrupting you."

"Not at all. Saw you drive up. It's always good to keep an eye out, I say. You selling something?"

"No, I'm with Bright Investigations, and I wonder if—"

"Hah!" she interrupted. "That's a good one all right. Don't suppose anybody's going to come to the door and say they're from Stupid Investigations. Or Dim Investigations."

I nodded. "It is a silly-sounding name. Only it's the actual name of the owner. Ozzie Bright." I didn't add that his I.Q. didn't fit his surname, either.

She looked somewhat abashed.

"I was wondering if you had some time."

"You sure you want me? You're parked in my neighbor's driveway, not mine." She had the throaty tones of a devoted smoker. "Not that I watch all the time, or anything—don't want you thinking I'm that kind of person. But I happened to see you pull up."

"I'd love the chance to speak with you," I said. "And I'm parked next door because I need to visit that house, too. I'm—"

"Investigating. Brightly."

I chuckled, and she looked pleased. "My name's Amanda Pepper," I said.

She nodded sagaciously as if she'd suspected that name all along and I'd just confirmed her hunch. "What is it? Problems with the will?"

"Umm." I tried not to lie in these situations, and most of the time, being noncommittal prompts people to provide the information I'm withholding.

"Bequests?" She looked interested and a bit hopeful.

Once again, not lying but not answering, either, had worked. "Umm," I said again.

"Oh. Right. You can't talk about it, probably. Client privilege, whatever. Right?"

I hoped I looked as if I secretly agreed, but was unfortunately sworn to silence. Then I sighed and cleared my throat. "I was hoping you could answer a few questions, the kind a neighbor might know. I'd only take a few minutes of your time."

The word "bequest" was probably still playing in waltz-time in her mind, and she opened the door wide, and invited me in, first putting out a hand. "Ramona Fulgham here."

I handed her a business card and she ushered me into her house, which was tidy, organized, and devoid of personality. It could have been a display in a furniture showroom for the surface-phobic. Nothing was allowed to remain uncovered. Bits of a dark blue sofa peeked out from under a ribbed white bedspread. The TV screen it faced was almost as large as the wall behind it, except it had a long runner atop it, making it look as if it were wearing a headscarf. The dark wooden coffee table was covered with glass, and the carpet beneath my feet had a plastic runner over it. Ramona Fulgham gestured me to an uncomfortable-looking chair with doilies protecting its already plasticized arms and back.

I hadn't seen crocheted doilies since my great-grandmother was still alive and carefully protecting every hard-won thing she owned against human stains. The net result then and now was to make me feel as if I were a dirty wild thing trespassing on the premises.

I sat down gently on the side chair, which was as uncomfortable as its contours had suggested, and Ms. Fulgham seated herself in a corner of the sofa. It was a perfect vantage point to see the comings and goings of the neighborhood, should the TV provide inadequate entertainment. The glass-covered end table next to her was carefully arranged for her convenience with a copy of *TV Guide*, a large ashtray, a waiting pack of cigarettes, and a teacup and saucer. This one corner of the room reflected its owner, after all. "Mind?" she asked as she lit up.

Unfortunately, she hadn't found a way to cover the air, and the stale cigarette smell of the house was so overpowering, there'd been a danger of secondhand smoke even before she lit up. "No, of course not," I said. "It's your house."

"Well, thank you kindly. I like your attitude, but some people are so damned self-righteous, and I was raised to try to be polite." She exhaled a plume of smoke, then eyed me. "So," she said. "I don't know what's under dispute, but let me make something perfectly clear. Phoebe gave me the eagle. I admired it, it being the American symbol and all, and she gave it to me. Flat out, no strings, and for keeps. She had so many beautiful things."

I shook my head. "No," I said, "that isn't . . . there isn't a question about your eagle."

By now, she'd gone to a corner shelf and retrieved a porcelain bird five or six inches tall. "See?" she said. "It's got this little flag in its talons. I thought it was cute, but I didn't mean for her to give it to me. She did, though. The next day, walked over here and gave it to me. Could have knocked me over with a feather, you could have." She considered her remark, and laughed. "Funny, that, isn't it? Feathers when I'm talking about an eagle."

I smiled and nodded, then assured her there was no problem with the bird. Meantime, I wondered when the gift had been bestowed and whether Phoebe had given other things away. Wasn't that supposedly a sign of suicidal plans?

"Well, if not that," Ramona Fulgham said, settling into her sofa corner, the eagle in one hand, and a cigarette laden with ash in the other. "If not that, then what is it about Phoebe Ennis?"

"I'm not at liberty to be precise, but there's some question about identifying a recent visitor to her home, so if—"

"Hah!" she said with no mirth. "No surprise. Which one?" Her laugh produced a brief coughing spell, after which she laughed again. Despite the chortling, Ramona did not seem to be expressing joy or approval.

"I take it there were many visitors?"

"Many? Many? Lord help us all! It was . . . well, far be it from me to speak ill of the dead, or to imply anything bad about the poor soul, but I was surprised to hear she was depressed enough to kill herself. Unless all those people were psychiatrists making house calls!" She laughed and coughed again. "Otherwise, it looked to me as if she was having quite a good time, going out or having company in, nearly every night. But I'm not saying anything was wrong; they might have been relatives. Or people paying their condolences." This last was said with eyebrows raised, to make sure I understood that she in no way believed what she was saying.

"So these—these visitors—were a fairly recent occurence?"

She shook her head. "Not while she was married, of course. Not the men, at least. I'm not implying anything of the sort. At least, not that I know of. But I am a widow myself, and I know how terrible it is to lose a husband, so I was surprised by how quickly she, um, bounced back, shall we say, from her state of grief."

"She's been a widow for a while now," I murmured. "Didn't Mr. Ennis die last January?"

Ramona looked stern. "Not even a full year yet. She's been going out and having visitors for months now, too. But far be it from me to criticize anybody's method of handling grief. We all have to find our own ways, so I'd never say having all those people over and going out so much was improper and unseemly behavior."

Of course she was saying precisely that. She was apophasing—mentioning something by saying it wouldn't be mentioned. I knew that thanks to Opal Codd. Sometimes her ridiculous words were actually useful.

"You must understand," Ramona said with great earnestness, "losing a husband and being on her own wasn't exactly a new experience for her, the way it was for me, so maybe . . ."

I let the idea of Phoebe's suddenly-single-again expertise pass me by. Then I said, "About how many people would you say visited her in the past month?"

Ramona slowly shook her head and looked thoughtful. "Men and women? Because women visited, too. Don't mean to imply only men. Women friends. I'd see them arrive, all fixed up, and Phoebe would be in her finery—she really knew how to dress, although she gave up on wearing black real quick, at least in the daytime. I mean she wore black, but she wore it the way women dressing up always wear black, not as a widow. But when the women came, they'd go out together, mostly. On the town, you know?"

"Any idea of how many?"

"I couldn't say. I'm not the type to spy on a neighbor or keep track. The houses are close together, but I'm not always where I would know if somebody came. But I'd say a person every day, just about. As far as I could tell. But I don't know if there were repeats. Who is this person you're looking for? An heir? Maybe if you described him or her, I could think back and remember something. I believe she had a son."

I sighed. "Do you know where Phoebe and her callers went when they left here? Women or men? Any special place or places?"

"How would . . . ?" She shook her head. "I only meant they were all dressed up and I never saw her in church, so I assumed . . .

I surely didn't mean anything else. Probably just cheering her up. A widow needs her friends, I can tell you that, and I know from bitter experience. Trust me. The world of couples certainly forgets all about you."

I murmured sympathetically. "Would you consider yourself one of Mrs. Ennis's friends, then?" I asked gently. "Did the two of you ever go out on the town?"

She set her mouth in a tight, small circle and shook her head. "I tried. Tried to be a good neighbor. After all, I felt like somebody who could understand her trials, being in the same situation and all. I tried, and she was polite enough, but not close, do you understand what I'm saying?" She stubbed out the remnant of her cigarette. "Some might call her uppity, or a snob, too good for the rest of us here. All her talk about her ancestors and such, even though she admitted she wasn't one thousand percent positive. If you aren't, then why mention it, is what I wondered. Napoleon, did you ever hear such a thing? Her family was from Ireland! She told me that herself, so where would they come to Napoleon, even if her imagination wasn't running wild? I was too polite to note the inconsistency there, mind you, and in any case, who really cares—besides her, I mean? I'm not a name-caller, mind you, and all that talk—who did it hurt, is what I say. She thinks of herself as something special, well . . . who does it hurt?"

"When was this that she talked about her ancestors?" Ramona had said they didn't go out together socially, and I couldn't envision even Phoebe seeing this woman in the driveway and abruptly spouting her mishmosh of genealogical theories.

"One time, a few months ago, her husband had passed and maybe she was lonely. But in any case, she invited me and two other neighbors in for tea. You know she didn't live here that long before he died, so nobody really knew her, and I thought this was her effort to finally really move into the neighborhood, you know? I thought a cup of tea—" She flicked a finger against the teacup on the end table. "In fact, would you like one? Where are my manners?"

I demurred, thanking her, reminding her that I'd barged in on her and that, in any case, I wasn't staying long. I hoped that would speed up her memories and get us to the night Phoebe died, but not all hopes are realized.

"Tea, I thought. A cup. How would I know different? But she meant the whole shebang. Like the Queen of England might have in the afternoon, with the little sandwiches and cookies. And pretty china, I have to admit. And she talked about having inherited the set, which was quite grand, but it wasn't clear if that was from the mister who just died, or an earlier husband, or her own family. And afterward, when we talked, we all had noticed that the silver service was monogrammed, but it wasn't clear whose initials they were, unless the big 'B' in the middle of a lot of curlicues was one of her husbands' initial and it was a souvenir from that marriage. Of course, you know she was married more than once, don't you?"

I nodded. I also knew who the "B" in the alphabet of mates had been, although I would have said that Charlie Berg, Sasha's father, would be more likely to want plastic implements. Disposability was high on his list of priorites, certainly when it came to wives.

"So one of those marriages, maybe. It seemed rude and insensitive, given her recent widowhood, to ask why I knew her as Phoebe Ennis, and her silver had the wrong monogram. I mean what if she bought it secondhand somewhere?" She paused to light another cigarette, this time not bothering to ask if I minded.

"The thing was," she continued after a deep drag, "she suggested that she was descended from royalty. That was the very way she put it. Royal blood flowing in the veins, the whole thing. She said it as if it was a joke: Haha, look what it's all come down to. And she said it was something her grandmother—who wasn't all the way right in the head by then—had told her, but you know, she also sounded like she wanted us to believe it. Like she did, anyway, and like it mattered. I mean this is the United States of America. We don't have royals here and we don't want them, either, so what was that all about? That's when I noticed the eagle with the flag, and commented on it, kind of a small reminder of what makes this country great. It was almost a relief, seeing something patriotic in her house after that la-di-dah talk."

I mentally noted that the giving away had been relatively recent, since the tea party was after Phoebe was widowed.

"Unfortunately," Ramona said, "the other two women she invited, Sally Molinari and Neva Sheffler, they tend to be judgmental, something I try never to be. Nice women but dreadful talkers. Not mean, not really, not on purpose, but they do like a bit of gossip, so they told everybody she was hoity-toity, putting on airs or maybe a little crazy. I mean, what royalty would live on this block? That's the kind of thing they said. It wasn't right, if you ask me, because we had been drinking her tea and eating her little cakes. Not right to bite the hand that feeds you, as they say. If you can't say something nice, keep your mouth shut. And also, royal blood doesn't mean you are still rich. It's about the past. It doesn't have anything to do with now. I've seen the movies, the ones showing how after the Russian Revolution, all those bigshot aristocrats were down and out in Paris."

I tried not to smile, not so much at Ramona's insistence on her charitable heart, but at the image of those émigrés. It was an image I remember Phoebe invoking all those years ago, when she was married to Sasha's dad. Not that she said she was the missing czarina, but she identified with the threadbare former rulers of the universe. The wheel goes round, she'd say—too often—and where you wind up, nobody knows, and life was one long game of roulette. She hoped that what had gone down had to come up. Something like that.

I had seldom paid attention to her genealogical flights of fancy, her supposed past. I was too enraptured by the ones having to do with my future, like her ridiculous assurances that I could have been a famous dancer if I'd started lessons sooner. Even then, I knew her words were pure nonsense. Along with every other little girl in my neighborhood, I had taken ballet lessons early on, and I was the one at recitals turning the wrong way or falling down. "No, no," Phoebe would say, "there's still time. Modern dance, that's it. You'd be elegant." And then she'd find another glamorous and unlikely future for me—astronaut, secretary of state, courtesan.

"I hope I'm not sounding harsh, or mean-spirited," Ramona said.

"Not at all, not at all." I murmured further understanding and approval of the high moral ground on which she stood. "I was wondering if she—" I began, but Mrs. Fulgham was not finished.

"Some people don't bother to consider the mental anguish somebody else might be going through, and why she might make things up, or exaggerate. I understand, because I've gone through it myself."

"Of course," I said. "But I was wondering—"

"Not that I myself made things up afterwards. I need to make that clear. So easy to misunderstand each other, isn't it?"

"Of course," I said again. "In fact, just so I'm clear—those other women, Sally and Neva—are they in the neighborhood, too?"

She nodded vigorously. "I thought I said—sure, they live on this block. Well, if you count all four sides of it. Sally's over there, across the street." She pointed toward the living-room window, aiming her finger to the left. "First house from the corner," she said, "and Neva's house is behind Phoebe's. Their backyards touch, so to speak. Both been here for a long time, too."

"Was Phoebe friendly with either of them before the tea, do you think?"

Ramona's head pulled back a minute amount, but enough to convey the idea that I'd insulted her. "She wasn't unfriendly, if that's what you're saying. And I'm sure—I mean a back-fence neighbor, you talk to sometimes. It's summer and hot, and everybody's barbecuing, but I don't know if there was more than that. And Sally?"

She shook her head. "Not more so than Phoebe was with me, and I was right next door. She wasn't a neighborly type, if you don't mind my saying so. Standoffish, you know? Didn't let anybody get too close, even if somebody tried. But it takes all types, and a man's home is his castle, and a woman's, too. And she made that tea for us."

I wrote down both the neighbors' names and nodded. "Thanks. This is helpful. About those other neighbors—"

"If you're wondering because she left something to them in her will, well, I'd be surprised, is all." She crossed her arms over her chest.

I'd almost forgotten my supposed mission. "Why is that?" I prompted, though I was sure she'd be surprised—and angry—because she hadn't been left anything.

She lit another cigarette again without asking, and inhaled deeply. "I mean," she said in a cloud of exhaled smoke, "her possessions were quite special. Heirlooms, some of them, but even the ones that weren't had meaning for her. Her treasures, she called them, making it a joke, but underneath, I think they were. The things she collected—beautiful things, and so many. I can understand why she was proud. They were all souvenirs of her life, her adventures. Everything had meaning for her.

"I was so touched when she gave me the eagle. Do you see how beautifully it's made, with every tiny talon clear as can be? And the flag with its ripples? And when you'd compliment something, she'd tell you all about where she found it and what was going on with her at the time. That little eagle had been a gift during the Vietnam War. A suitor, or maybe one of her husbands. She said his name, but I don't recall it. So every single object was a treasure to her, because they held her memories." She inhaled, looked down, shook her head, sighed out the smoke. "And what else do we have, when you get down to it?"

"Yes. So true," I said, leaving the politics of why the other neighborhood women should not, by Ramona's rights, have in-

herited any of those memory-treasures. "I guess you must have
been in her house several times, enough times to learn about the
different pieces."

She shrugged. "I'd stopped by, as I said, after she lost her husband. Brought a cake one time, asked her to go to a church social
with me another. She declined, invited her over another time,
but she couldn't make it. So no, not that often."

"And about those other visitors, the ones you didn't know.
Did she talk about them with you? Tell you their names, or how
they came to be in her life?" She did it for whoever was associated
with a pathetic-looking, flag-waving eagle, I mentally reminded
the universe. For heaven's sake, she could do it for the humans in
her life as well and make my mission easier.

"You mean that day when we had the tea?" Ramona asked.
"Did she talk about her other friends that day?"

"That day or any of the other days when you stopped in, or
had a little chat outside."

"No. Never."

Nice that she'd needed to know which date I was talking
about in order to say no, never.

"Not that I mentioned taking note of them to her, you see. I
didn't want her to think I was prying, and if she'd wanted me to
know, she'd have told me. It's only that I'd hear the automobile
door and think it was somebody for me—the houses are close, as
you can see. Her driveway and carport are right beside mine, and
almost in my living room. Otherwise, I wouldn't know. They
were quiet, the visitors. And most times, they went out somewhere else. No carrying on. I didn't mean to suggest any such
thing."

"No, no, of course. One last question: The night she passed
away, were you home?"

"It was a weeknight, wasn't it? Which night, do you recall?"

"A Thursday evening." Unless happenings were a lot more
dramatic on Hutchinson Court than I had reason to think, it was
difficult for me to believe this woman wouldn't recall in minute

and excruciating detail where she'd been, what she'd seen, and
what night of the week it had been when her secondary source of
entertainment, her next door neighbor, had killed herself.

"Oh wait, of course. It was a Thursday. Yes, I saw her briefly.
She was all gussied up. High heels and lots of jewelry, and I must
say, though events proved otherwise, that I would *never* have suspected that she was feeling low. She was cordial and seemed quite
contented."

"What was she doing when you spoke with her?"

"Taking the trash to the curb."

"In her high heels and jewelry?"

Ramona Fulgham grimaced. "What are you going to do
when there's no man of the house? I remember because she said
she always forgets until it's too late at night to want to go outside
and take care of it. I understood, because when your husband
passes away, things like that become sad reminders of what he
would have done. Not that I would have wanted to take out the
trash in my dress shoes, or with clean hands and all. Don't want
those smells on us, do we? I try to do it in the afternoon if I'm
going out at night, like I was that night. But then, I'm not—I was
not, I guess—Phoebe Ennis. To each his own."

Again I agreed, and waited while Mrs. Fulgham spent a moment looking as if she were remembering all the glorious Thursday nights that somebody else had taken the trash can down to
the curb. "Did she in any way mention her plans for the
evening?" I finally asked.

"Not in any detail, not with anything specific. But I do recall
she said something about having a surprise visitor. Just like
that, she said, or maybe I said something about how pretty she
looked, and she said, 'Ramona, I was all prepared to have a quiet
night home alone, but in fact, I have a surprise visitor this
evening.' And she winked at me, and I knew that was my cue to
keep my mouth shut, so I said I hoped it was a good surprise, and
I didn't ask anything, and she just winked again and didn't say
anything more."

"She didn't make it clear whether it was a male or female?"

Ramona Fulgham shook her head. Then she raised her eyebrows. "But . . . that wink, you know. And the good earrings—those diamond studs of hers. And the shoes."

"You think it was a man, then."

She raised her eyebrows once more and didn't bother to say anything.

"When she went out with her women friends, did she dress differently?"

Ramona's eyes widened, then she frowned, squinted. And then she sighed. "I suppose you're right. She pretty much looked like that no matter who was coming calling." She frowned again.

"And I suppose you didn't have a chance to find out who, in fact, it was. Didn't you hear the car pull up?"

"It was Thursday!"

"I don't understand."

"Bingo night. I saw her because I was getting ready to go—waiting outside for my ride. It was Theresa's turn to drive, and she's always on time, so off we went."

"What time did Theresa show up?"

"Seven P.M. sharp, like always. Takes fifteen minutes, then you have to buy in and find a good place. Theresa and me, we like to sit at the table right in front of the caller. Easier to hear, you know, and Theresa's beginning to have problems with that. And we have regular friends who sit there, too, so there's a little talk, catching up on everybody's doings. It's fun, and then, you're ready to roll at seven-thirty."

I couldn't think of anything else to ask Ramona, unless it was about Bingo. Interview over with no real information except a deeper conviction that people can use a staggering amount of words to say nothing.

Despite my impulsive decision about the stiletto heels, I was convinced that, as Gertrude Stein had said about something else, there was "no there there." And if there was nothing there to be revealed, then maybe this dull interview was actually progress, because it proved my point.

"Thank you so much for your time," I said as I stood up. "I hope you did well at Bingo that night, too."

She smiled. "I'd been on a winning streak, but that night capped it. Won my age times ten. I won't say how much that was, but it's a night I'll always remember."

"I hadn't realized you could win that much. I mean not that you're old—but my age times ten. I hadn't realized . . ."

"Oh my, yes. And much more, depending on the game and the place. There's one coming up that will pay ten thousand dollars. That one's too rich for my blood, but Bingo's a fine way to spend a few hours for not much money. Theresa and me, we go with twenty dollars each to spend, and that's it. So it's a bargain, too."

I hadn't learned much about Phoebe, but the possibilities of Bingo—that was news to me.

Five

I had a long night ahead of looking at Phoebe's detritus, so I thought I'd check out the other two women first. I hoped they were as gossip prone as Ramona Fulgham had insisted she herself was not. I popped in, told Sasha my plan, and popped back out.

We were approaching dinnertime, so I was disappointed when nobody answered my knock at Sally Molinari's house. Lights were on inside, and music played, but either she was hiding from me, which was unlikely, or she was one of the people who worked hard to disguise the fact that she wasn't home.

I walked around the corner, then around again, and counted houses until I was sure I was behind Phoebe's house. Luckily, the architect had been a bit anal, and each house had precisely the same shape and size lot, so that they lined up tidily.

The windows must face each other in the back, I realized. So forget the fence. Unless somebody had huge plantings, a great deal could be observed from the comfort of one's kitchen window, assuming all the houses had the same configuration as Ramona's had. Or so I hoped, although I mostly hoped for definitive proof that Phoebe had, indeed, taken her own life. Mackenzie has taught me that most times, whatever seems the logical and obvious explanation of an event is, indeed, the logical and obvious explanation. It is also generally the truth. As upsetting as Sasha would find that conclusion, it would, at least, be a conclusion and something with which she could deal.

I rang the bell and a teen with long hair answered. He said nothing, but looked at me inquisitively, waiting. I introduced myself, and said I was with the offices of Ozzie Bright, which I'd finally realized sounded better than Bright Investigations, and also left some mystery as to what sort of offices they might be. I asked for Neva Sheffler.

He looked surprised. "Mom?" he asked, then "Mom!" he yelled, facing me. "Somebody for you!" He still looked surprised that anyone new would appear at the door for his mother.

A woman with salt-and-pepper hair came out of the back of the house. "Yes?" she asked, but before I could answer, she looked at her son. "How many times have I asked you to come quietly and tell me if somebody's at the door?"

He shrugged and sauntered off.

Once again, I offered up a string of words in lieu of an honest explanation of why I was there.

"Phoebe Ennis? Why would you be—what is it you're doing again? Investigating what?"

"There's some confusion about the disposition of her estate," I said. It wasn't exactly a lie. There was the division of the profit on the house to be settled, and I at least was confused about how that would work out, given Dennis-the-Jerk's personality.

"Really? Then how could I possibly help you?" She waved me in and I looked at the same architectural bones I'd seen in Ramona's house, but here, bright solids in rust, yellow, and deep green brought the room alive. And rather than being covered and hidden and protected, the furniture showed the comfortable scars of being used. I admired the spray of autumn leaves in a low vase on her coffee table.

"I waxed them," Neva said. "Remember pressing leaves in elementary school? It's the same idea. Lasts a long time, too." Then she smiled expectantly, and held the expression. Enough of meaningless pleasantries, it said. High time for me to make some sense of my presence.

"I was wondering if you knew Phoebe Ennis well, given your location here—her back-fence neighbor, if that isn't too old-fashioned an expression."

She shook her head. "We've got backyards, and we've got fences. But we've got dryers, too, instead of those clotheslines our mothers had, so you don't get that casual back and forth while those ladies clipped and shook out and unclipped and folded, the way my mother said she used to do."

"So you and she had no chance to become friends."

Neva Sheffler raised her eyebrows, pushed her chin forward, and shook her head gently, side to side, as if evaluating what the word "friend" meant and, more specifically, meant to me. I had to wonder why such an innocuous question required such deliberation. "You realize there was quite an age difference," she finally said. "I knew her husband more than I knew her—not that I knew him in any real way, either. But I'd see him in the garden. He seemed to like to go out there with a book and sit in the sun, and if I was out puttering, we'd exchange pleasantries. Pity about his dying. Much too young to go."

"And Phoebe?"

"Pity about her, too, of course," she said. "She was even younger, and to be in such despair . . ."

"I meant, did you get to know her at all?"

"We talked," she finally said. "Now and then. Also mostly

after meeting by accident, pruning the roses, raking leaves, or bumping into each other at the market. That kind of thing."

"But you had tea with her one time, too, I understand."

She laughed. "You've been talking with Ramona. She's the one can tell you every detail of what's going on around these parts. She has so little to think about, I swear, she has every minute of her life emblazoned on her brain."

"She says she didn't know Mrs. Ennis very well."

Neva compressed her lips and did a half nod to the right, as if to say "Who did?" "She was a woman of mystery, I guess. Besides, she wasn't here long enough to really dig in. It takes a few years to become part of a neighborhood. And if she had, it wouldn't have been with me. We're different generations. In fact, I'd be the least likely person in the whole neighborhood, because they're all either her generation, or young marrieds. These seem to be starter or finisher houses. In any case, nobody around here's my age. My husband walked out on us seven years ago, and probably if he hadn't, we'd have moved to a bigger place, too. But I didn't have that option. Hard enough to take care of Jimmy and his sister, and pay the taxes on this place and the daycare when his sister needed it, and to hang on to a job with the economy going all to hell and . . . On the other hand, there's lots of babysitting opportunities for Lizzie. She's the only teen in town." She shook her head and sighed. "Jimmy could sit, too, but he doesn't want to. Instead, he blames me for the lack of kids his age. Everything's my fault."

"The teen years are rough, but they do grow up," I said.

"Yeah. Right. And become men! Some improvement! He'll become like his father, who created the whole mess."

"Not necessarily," I said softly. "I don't mean about his father creating the mess, but about his turning out like him. You'll see."

"I don't mean to be rude, but how would you know? You don't know him. Besides, you look barely out of your teens yourself."

I smiled. Poor woman had too much on her plate. "I am well out of them, and my twenties as well. I work with teens every day, and then, when I go out and see the teens of the past, I realize that they do grow up and out of it."

"An investigator who works with teens? Why? I'm confused now. You a social worker? Looking for a runaway, a juvenile delinquent, what? And what would that have to do with Phoebe Ennis?"

My incredibly big mouth and tiny brain. "A special program," I improvised. "I'm part of an outreach program for a few months, but it's not the usual thing I do. This is more what I do."

That seemed to satisfy her enough for her to let me continue. "I was wondering, whether you saw or met any of Mrs. Ennis's friends?"

She shook her head. "Look, to make things perfectly clear, here's the big difference between me and people like Ramona and most of the other people her age around here. They're retired or never worked outside the home. Me, I work. Every single weekday, I'm gone. And on Saturday, I'm gone, too. That's when I have to do every chore, buy the kids whatever, sometimes go to their games, stock the pantry— And on Sunday, I'm near death. Sometimes we get in the car and go see my folks, who are two hours away, but mostly, I hole up with the papers and coffee and try not to move a muscle. So I don't know what goes on outside my home. Besides, I'm not interested. Right now, that sulky teenager and his sister are the only people I'm watching, and let me tell you, they're enough."

"I take it, then, you did not meet any of her friends," I said quietly.

She sighed. "Not really." She frowned and thought. "Well, maybe once. Late this past summer there was, you know . . . By accident—I was in the yard, and she was in hers, with this woman. It stuck in my mind because it looked at first like two friends having lemonade or something stronger at her white, wrought-iron table. I always admired that table. But then I realized—I mean you could see from the way they were sitting, all stiff, and rigid-like—that it wasn't any casual, friendly talk in the garden. But that was months ago."

"Could you get any sense of what it was about?"

She shook her head. "I wasn't about to go hang over the fence. I didn't even say hello. It would have been rude, and why would I interrupt them, anyway? I went about my business and went back into the house."

"The other woman, do you remember her age, or what she looked like?"

She shrugged. "A redhead. Not naturally, but a pretty good dye job. Probably around Phoebe's age, so what would that be—her fifties? A little older? She had that cared-for look. A little on the plump side, but well maintained. I don't know anything about brands and designer things, but everything she was wearing—her skirt, which was filmy and long and patterned, and her blouse and even her hair—it all looked like the things I'd like to buy but can't afford. The stuff that looks easy and casual but costs a fortune? She looked that way. And she didn't look like she'd live in our kinds of houses. You know what I mean?"

I thought I did, and I was glad I'd been deputized for this interview, not Mackenzie, who'd have been privately breathing fire at the woman's vagueness. But I knew what "being taken care of" looked like, and Phoebe's redheaded business partner Merilee had that look. And was, in fact, quite pampered, at least till recently. Until late summer when she might well have begun an ongoing feud with Phoebe.

Of course, Phoebe could have known any number of slightly plump well-maintained women, and might have been at odds with one of them for reasons having nothing to do with her death.

"And I saw a couple of men going to her house. I can see her driveway from here, but all I can see is that a person's there, not how they look. They were just . . . men." She stood up, and gestured for me to join her as she walked through the small dining room into the kitchen. And we both stood at the window, looking out at darkness, although there were lights on in Phoebe's house.

"See? If I'm washing dishes or cleaning up and somebody happens to be parking their car and the headlights catch my eye, then I can see something. Maybe. But nothing like features at this distance."

It felt like an itch inside my skull, being this close to information, and getting none, and believing ever more strongly that there was none to get. Phoebe's driveway, partially obscured by plantings, was simply too far away. "In business suits? In jeans?" I asked, flailing wildly for anything that might pass as information.

"Yes."

"Both?"

"Yes. Separately, of course."

"Could you tell"—I knew she couldn't. I knew the answer. I didn't know why I nonetheless felt compelled to ask—"if anybody made a repeat visit? Or if the suit and jeans guys were the same person?"

We stood in her kitchen, and I could see the beginnings of dinner on the counter. I'd interrupted a busy woman who was being more than patient with me.

"Would you like coffee or something?" she asked, perhaps thinking that's why I had glanced around the tidy room. I declined and thanked her, and asked again about repeat visitors, although Phoebe had told Ramona that the visitor her final night of life was a surprise, an unexpected person, so my questions became ever less potentially useful.

First Neva shook her head, looking a little impatient with me, and I couldn't blame her. Then she frowned. "Well, actually, they weren't the same. I mean not all of them, though maybe somebody came back more than once. First of all, I couldn't see, or didn't happen to see most of the time. Lately, he'd have had to be wearing neon or something, because it's been dark, or at least dusk. Anybody could have been there. And second, one of the visitors was quite tall and thin. I remember that. Another one was rather stocky. So more than one man visited her."

The nice thing was that unlike next-door neighbor Ramona, back-fence neighbor Neva did not try to make something shady out of Phoebe's visitors, who could have been, after all, insurance and medical people, or old friends—even former husbands.

"I don't know who they were or what their business was," Neva said, as if she'd been reading my mind. "I do know that at least one was a date. A fix-up, she told Ramona. And I think Ramona was mad because she wanted to have been fixed up."

"Mad at Phoebe?"

Neva shook her head. "Maybe. I think Ramona's been angry with Phoebe since the woman was widowed, but I'm not sure Ramona knows it. She seems to resent Phoebe's having—well, having had, a life. But this time, she was jealous maybe of Phoebe, but mad at Sally, who did the fixing up. Ramona told me—the side of my backyard fence touches the side of hers, too, you know. She said she'd known Sally for twenty-two years, and she thought this was a real breach of friendship. After all, eligible men are few and far between, and here Sally had been hiding away a perfectly good cousin, then had given him to a relative stranger!" Neva laughed and shook her head slowly. "Those widows. They're really something."

"I have to ask: Did the fix-up work out?"

She shrugged. "As I say, Phoebe and I weren't confidantes."

"Thanks," I said. "I know you're busy, and you've been really generous with your time."

She shrugged. "I don't think I helped, and I still can't imagine what all this is about Phoebe's will. Wasn't that what you said?"

"Her estate," I said.

Her eyes widened. "You mean her stories were true? That day we had tea, she talked about her treasures, but my grandmother was the same way, loving her carnival prizes and calling them treasures. Of course, in both cases, they were ordinary five-and-dime knickknacks. At least most of them were. I thought she was kidding, or I just understood it to mean that they were treasures to her."

"Did she by any chance give you any?"

Neva's eyebrows elevated, then she nodded. "Is this about that? A sort of inventory? Because I'd happily return it to the estate. Maybe somebody would actually want it. I didn't and don't."

I shook my head. "No, thank you. I'd only heard she was . . . generous."

"She certainly was with me and I think she gave something to Sally, too. Kind of sad, which is why I kept it, even though I keep it in a closet now that she's gone and can't drop in and see that I'd hidden it. I'd said I liked it because it felt imperative to compliment something in her house. She was so proud of her so-called treasures. I think she gave us things because she was trying to make friends, fit in."

As she spoke, she moved toward a door to the side of the room, which, once opened, turned out to be a closet. She bent down and dug back and pulled out a gilded equestrian statue, or statuette, as it was only about six inches high. An equally gilded warrior, sword held high, sat atop the horse. The poor creature was a ludicrous, diminutive hero, proportions out of whack, and not at all as elegant or triumphant as surely the artist must have intended.

"A little garish, don't you think?" she asked. "A little stupid? And when we had it one week, it fell onto Lizzie's foot and broke her little toe. But what could I say? We were in her house, and Ramona was *ooh*ing and *ahh*ing—it's all so weird because Ramona thinks of everything as dust collectors, and Phoebe's house was the central collection spot of the universe. But it felt necessary to join in and compliment her collections. And then the next day, there she was, with the horse I'd happened to choose to praise."

She held up the horse, which looked ridiculous in her well-worn living room. "Sure you don't want it back?" she asked.

"No thanks," I said.

"I'm going to take it to a flea market or Goodwill."

"As you choose. Nobody's asking for it, but about that fix-up, that man . . . ?"

"Ah," she said. "She obviously left something special to somebody you have to find. I wish the thing she'd left was this stupid horse. My grandmother, collector of carnival prizes, would have loved it, if only she were still alive. But in any case, you should talk to Sally Molinari," she said. "She's the one who did the fixing up. She's on Phoebe's block, across the street from her. If he mattered to her, whoever he is, I hope she left him something more valuable or good-looking than this thing, or the rest of the things in her living room. I mean all the work and trouble and expense that's going into hunting for him. Hope it's worth it. And if he has a yearning for this horse—it's his." She laughed again. "But don't bother trying to find Sally tonight. It's Monday, so she's visiting her married daughter over in Philly. It's a regular thing. You could set a clock by it. She takes the bus over, then the son-in-law drives her back here around ten o'clock."

"I'll try her another day," I said, and with more thanks, I bid Neva adieu, and set out around the block once more.

I turned at the bottom of her short walkway and looked back. Neva Sheffler was still standing in her doorway, the light behind her silhouetting her form and the golden horse and rider in her arms, as if still silently hoping I'd take it.

Six

I found Sasha surrounded by open cartons. When she saw me, she rolled her eyes. "This is so intensely not fun," she said. "Somebody should have done an intervention. She must have spent every free minute on the shopping channel, eBay, or in catalogues. And that's before she left home. I think she had a standing worldwide order for anything with frills and furbelows. And what is a furbelow, anyway?"

"A flounce on a skirt—or ornamentation. Know how I know?"

She shrugged. "English teacher."

"Nope. New secretary. The day she commented—complimented the furbelow of my blouse, she also told me she was a gobemouche. That, my dear, is somebody gullible or, literally, one who swallows flies."

Sasha stared at me, expression guarded.

I laughed. "That's precisely how I looked. It isn't easy understanding Opal. That's her only real flaw. She's semiprecious, like her namesake." No response. "Right. We were discussing Phoebe's treasures. Did you make any headway?" I couldn't see any visible reduction in the clutter.

Sasha sighed and shrugged. "How could I? You said not to toss anything till you got here. Big excitement was that Dad phoned me on the cell."

"Really? Your father?"

"I e-mailed him when Phoebe died. I don't know the protocol about dead ex-wives, but it seemed the right thing to do. She was a part of his life for a while. And then I didn't hear back, and I figured that's just Dad being Dad. Then he phoned today."

"From—where is he?"

"Still in Spain. He'd been traveling and not picking up mail, so he gets an excused absence."

This time, I thought. Only this time. The man was the definition of unreliability.

"He told me things about Phoebe I'd never known, or else I forgot them. She didn't talk about them." She suddenly grinned. "All I remember were snarls and sighs, but I guess they had a brief period when things went well enough for confidences. What he said helped explain her to me. The weirder—the more idiosyncratic—parts. Like this." She waved her hands in all directions.

My gaze followed her motions and landed on a bookcase top crowded with zebra effigies in wood, glass, and china. I turned back, my hands folded, ready to learn the origins of all of Phoebe's species.

"First of all, she grew up dirt poor. Her mother and grandmother both worked in factories—the grandmother something with wire manufacturing, and her mother in a chemical factory. I knew she hadn't had money, but I didn't realize how poor they actually were. It was the kind of working poor where every penny counted, and there was never anything extra except, sometimes, maybe more than sometimes, bar tabs. But first among the missing extras was her father, including any idea of who he was. I hadn't known about that.

"It's not that big a deal nowadays, maybe, but back then, there was this incredible stigma, and it marked her for life."

I didn't need reminding of how things must have been. My mother, product of that generation, was still slack-jawed and aghast at how things worked these days. When I was still living at home, she'd read the latest headlines and say, "Movie stars pregnant and unmarried!" with shock and horror on her face. And she'd tell me again about how in her day, even a major star like Ingrid Bergman was about ruined when she became pregnant "out of wedlock."

She still talked about girls getting "in trouble," and had told my sister and me many stories—warnings—about girls disappearing from school for a year, supposedly going to live with relatives elsewhere, but in reality, going into a home for unwed mothers. "And everybody knew," she'd say with a tsk and a frown. Scandal. Shame. "Those girls' reputations gone forever—right down the drain," she would add with a meaningful look at her daughters.

All those phrases with no place to put them. Was there a home for reputations, scandals, trouble, and all the other out-of-date terminology?

"Kids made fun of Phoebe at school. 'Bastard' was one of the first words she learned. Some of her friends' mothers wouldn't let Phoebe play with their kids, like she had a contagious disease, or she'd be a bad influence." Sasha's words drifted off, and she looked as if she was seeing a fifty-year-old black-and-white schoolyard snapshot.

"And that accounts for her collections in what way?" I prompted when the pause threatened to become permanent.

She blinked, as if I'd startled her out of the reverie, then she nodded. "Apparently, her mother decided that giving her this illustrious, if mysterious and cloudy lineage, would make up for how the world was treating them. Her grandmother, who was admittedly losing it a little at that point, backed up the story and embellished it as she went along. So as if by magic, they were no longer common folk. They were the descendants of courtesans, and, her grandmother would say with a wink, 'notice that the word *court* is part of that word. We were at court, child. Famous, independent women beloved by royalty.' "

"Oh, for Pete's sake."

"It helped Phoebe hold her head up high."

"Held up high and full of delusions," I said. "Didn't you mention any spare change going toward a bar tab? I take it Phoebe's mother or grandmother drank?"

"I think both, a little. Maybe more than a little. Why?"

"Because they were so grandiose. I get it about giving her a sense of a past, of credentials if you will, but they could have done the same thing without stretching it to ridiculous lengths. Why courtesans? Why not inventors, artists, poets—"

"Please! How would that play at recess? Somebody calls you a bastard and you say, 'Maybe, but my great-grandpa was a poet, so how do you feel about that, mister?' You think the ignorant bully would slink away, head down low?"

"Nonetheless, their kind of talk sounds like what must happen late at night at the neighborhood bar. Instead of 'I could have been somebody,' 'I *was* somebody,' or '*some*body was somebody.' "

Sasha stood up and walked in a tight circle. The room did not have enough clear space in which to pace. Aside from being overfilled with furniture, the shelves and surfaces were so covered with collections, nobody wanted to bump into anything. As she passed the bookcase, she paused, and lifted a zebra, holding it in her palm while she studied it. "I thought about that, too, before you got here. But what would it be?"

"How about this? If you're going to lie anyway, why not be simple and logical and say her father died. Even say you were married, but he died. We have enough wars. Make him a casualty of one of them. Wouldn't that be logical?" I thought of two generations of women spinning ludicrous stories to cover their embarrassment about their unorthodox reproductive behavior, and I felt sorry for them.

"Logical and boring and suspect."

"Right, and the idea of generations of New Jersey–factory workers being the irresistible inamoratas of royalty makes lots of sense. At least she could have come up with a lie that reflected a democratic country. Hadn't she noticed we don't have kings?"

"I agree it's a stretch."

"Stretch? Nothing's that elastic. The logic in it snapped the first time her ma mentioned it. Anyway, how did they supposedly meet their princes?"

"They were courtesans. That would make any babies born to them very possibly the children of the royals, or something like that, wouldn't it?"

"Courtesan's a fancy word for—"

"I know it and you know it, and so what?"

"I just think that you have an illegitimate kid in New Jersey in the forties, there are easier stories to weave than one involving a royal court. I mean sooner or later your kid's going to think it through and know it's completely insane and that your mother still wasn't married to your father, no matter who he was."

She shrugged. "I think Phoebe was torn between wanting to believe their stories, and knowing they weren't real. And I think that's why she was so obsessed with finding her roots—a totally impossible task, once her mother was dead—and finding out everybody else's as well."

"And the tchotchkes?"

"That part's from the poverty, I guess. Simply wanting nice things, even if she didn't have a clear concept of what that meant.

There was apparently also a lot of talk about treasures they'd had, or lost, or didn't recognize or—"

Life was too short for drunken old wives' tales. "What's for me to do?"

"There's a carton there for you with everything from her desk, including her laptop and backup files. I couldn't see anything interesting, but I'm not the trained investigator, and I didn't look very hard. Maybe there's more somewhere else, but I went through the house opening drawers and doors and looking under beds, and in the garage, and I think that's about it for paper and electronic records. Except for old tax forms, but I can't see how they'd help find out who poisoned her that night."

"Nobody knows that somebody—"

"Okay, the alleged—"

"—by you alone—"

"—poisoner." And then she stood up straighter and squinted at me. Her face darkened, as if a light had been turned off. "You're humoring me, aren't you? You're just going through the motions."

"I—no—I—"

"You think I'm crazy. Deluded the way her mother and grandmother were."

"Of course not, Sasha, but in truth, aside from the discomfort of sitting on spike heels, which you have to admit is a pretty weak piece of evidence, I don't get the sense—"

"How long have you known me?"

"For Pete's sake, you know precisely the day, the year. Seventh grade. You were still Susan, having not yet discovered your inner Sasha. Do the math yourself. If we're thirty-two—how old are seventh graders, and really, who cares? A very long time is the answer."

"And has this friendship endured despite my being incredibly stupid about people?"

"Honestly? Yes."

Her eyes widened, then she furrowed her brow. I couldn't believe she'd asked me that question or been surprised by my response. "You're talking about my taste in *men*," she finally said.

I nodded.

Her mouth turned up at one side in a crooked grin. "Point taken. I am incredibly stupid about sexy men. But I'm not stupid in general, am I?"

I shook my head.

"I *knew* her. She was not suicidal. She wasn't the type."

"Anybody can be pushed to—"

Sasha's turn at head-shaking. "Even if that's true, nothing was pushing her that way. She was sad about her husband, but she was also one of the most resilient people I ever knew. She was looking forward to online dating, to trying new things. She was not in a place where she'd up and off herself."

"How about the whole fracas about the business? The charges of embezzling or stealing?"

"That was ridiculous! She knew it was, and Merilee knew it was, too. They would have made peace if she'd had a little more time. It's what she expected. They were in a bad patch because of Merilee's divorce."

I must not have looked convinced.

"Listen, Manda, I know a dozen people I'd believe might commit suicide. They're moody, they sink into long depressions. They have constant, mind-grinding stress. Phoebe wasn't like that."

I must still not have looked convinced.

"Okay," she said. "Here's what I mean. It's my gut impression that you're pretty much okay right now. Maybe it's bugging you to be here, helping me with something you don't believe happened, maybe you're stressed with two jobs and Mackenzie with years of school to go, and maybe you're really worried about his family, and the floods and what's going to be—and even with his stress over it all."

I was feeling worse and worse as she enumerated my woes.

"But you're not devastated. So if you died tonight, and to-morrow somebody told me that you'd committed suicide, and the evidence pointed that way, could I believe them? Would it be rational of me to insist, kicking and screaming, that you were not suicidal when I saw you today? That it was not your person-ality to solve something that way, that I did not believe you'd done it?"

"You feel it that strongly?"

She nodded.

"Then I'll believe it, too." I tried my best to truly mean it. "On your side of the ledger, I now know that she was expecting a visitor the night she died. A surprise visitor. That's why she wouldn't have told you."

"All right! You're good. How did you find that out so quickly? Who knew that?"

"Next door—"

"Oh, Lord—Ramona Not-That-I'm-Prying-But? I should have known. Phoebe used to laugh about her. She said that all Ramona lacked was a periscope aimed at the bedroom and a phone tap, but she wasn't so sure about the phone tap."

I settled on the sofa with the carton of papers and ancient-looking floppy disks nearby. "For all her snooping, the only thing that registered, or that she was willing to share, was a parade of mostly men coming in and out of this house. Ditto for the woman who lives behind this house."

"The problem is that while Ramona loves to pry, she's so self-involved she barely sees what's in front of her. Her ideal situation would be spying on herself, because that's what interests her most. Or so Phoebe said. Basically, Ramona was horrified that Phoebe was socializing after her widowhood. She'd thought Phoebe would quit her job, join Ramona's Bible-study group, play Bingo, all those sorts of things. She was disappointed and disapproving that Phoebe wasn't interested."

"Except the woman in the back said Ramona was also jealous, because another neighbor fixed Phoebe up with a date, and Ramona apparently thought she was ahead of Phoebe in line for men."

"Would she kill her perceived rival? Is that what you're saying?"

"I have no idea what I'm saying. But do you know anything about that man? That's the most specific information I've gotten about anybody so far."

Sasha looked into some middle distance. I imagined a small Rolodex file spinning card by card in her mind, name after possible name, the memory of conversations long gone searched for names, and found wanting. "Nothing," she said. "Can't we go ask the neighbor who fixed her up?"

"Tomorrow. She's not home today."

Sasha's features softened, the muscles in her face relaxed. "Good," she said. "Besides, if she was still interested in doing some hunting online, he couldn't have been Mr. Perfect. She was a serial monogamist. If she'd found him, she wouldn't have looked any further. Until she decided to lose him again, that is. But there'd be a marriage in between. So that fix-up date probably fizzled pretty quickly, or she'd have been engaged again. Unless, of course, she rejected him and he was the surprise visitor-killer that night." She looked concerned for a moment, then sighed, and shook her head. "Hungry yet?"

"Well, I guess . . . I was going to look through those papers, and it's early, but . . ."

"Then, if you can hold off a minute, look at this." She turned and lifted a clear glass bowl of matchbooks and handed it to me with a flourish.

"Matchbooks," I said. "Just what I always wanted."

"For the case!"

"Did Phoebe smoke?"

"Not really. But matchbooks mean something, don't they?"

"They mean she collected them, too, Sash."

"In the movies, they're always a clue." She was actually serious. Nobody in the movies found three dozen matchbooks in a glass bowl. "They could lead you to where she maybe picked up a date," Sasha said. "The one who was here that night."

"There was only one glass of wine," I said.

"Sure, but maybe he was AA, or . . ."

"I promise to follow up with the matchbooks." I emptied the bowl into the carton. If Sasha weren't so desperate, she'd recognize they were no more than another of Phoebe's acquisitions, like the rows of tiny glass bells, or the flowers made of woven horsehair, and whatever else was on the tables, shelves, and windowsills of this house.

"I picked up a barbecued chicken and salads," Sasha said. "You can look at things and eat at the same time, can't you?"

I could indeed multitask. We relocated to the kitchen, which looked less used and functional than Neva's had. In addition to cooking necessities, Phoebe had another collection on the countertops: roosters and chickens made of china, tin, painted wood, and plastic. I peered inside the refrigerator, a better clue to its owner than a matchbook, but Phoebe's had been cleaned out, except for the eternal half-filled bottles of condiments. I didn't know who'd cleaned the fridge out, or why those bottles were left. What was to become of an inch and a half of teriyaki sauce, a small bottle of horseradish in cream, six bread-and-butter pickles, and nearly empty containers of mustard, ketchup, and mayonnaise?

But the archeological digging was still fine on the outside of the refrigerator. Angel magnets held calendars, reminders of doctors' appointments, snapshots, newspaper clippings, and cards from local purveyors of driveway repair, delicatessen, and aromatherapy.

"Whoops," Sasha said. "I forgot all about that junk."

I carefully relocated the surface papers to one of the boxes Sasha had handed me, and made a pile of the fat, thin, ethereal, silly, and cherubic angels.

Sasha munched salad greens and watched me. "Whatever else, Phoebe answered the age-old question," she said.

"I give up."

Sasha gestured at the box on the floor. "Hasn't mankind always been tormented by the question of how many angels fit on the front of a refrigerator?"

Seven

We settled in to dinner while I half-heartedly clicked my way through Phoebe's laptop. "You may have been right about The Shopping Channel," I said. "She had a real problem. Her bookmarks are for online shopping sites and auctions. Look at this—kitchenware, antiques, home furnishings, linens, toys, music, books, art, more antiques, household goods, table coverings, pottery, accessories, original art from—"

"I am not surprised. Think about it. Even her business was about turning dogs and cats into tchotchke collectors—or tchotchkes themselves."

"Her shopping included the male market. Lots of fix-'em-up sites are bookmarked, but how would I know if she'd enrolled in any of them?"

"Believe it or not, I have never done online dating."

"I don't believe it."

"True," she said, nodding for emphasis. "Never."

"Wait a minute. It's not about guys or arranged or blind dates with you, is it. It's about computer illiteracy."

"Call it what you will," she said, finishing off a drumstick. "But the truth is, I don' need no stinking Internet."

"Yet," I said.

"Yet," she agreed. "Besides, we're talking about Phoebe, and she was waiting for those photos I took. I think that means she was waiting to officially sign up and put a picture of herself on there. Wherever 'there' is. Maybe those bookmarks were more a case of checking out the possibilities."

There'd be time to find out later. Meanwhile, unless something leaped out wearing neon script that said "This is important!" I wasn't going to find anything worthwhile, so I moved on to the word processing program. "Oh, wait. Listen to this. It's in a file called *Shopping*. I thought it would be an inventory or something of her purchases, but I think it's more a list of future, ah, acquisitions, or a rough draft. She was a funny lady, wasn't she?"

Sasha looked wistful, and nodded. "She was fun," she said. "But what are you talking about?"

"She was getting ready for those photos and a lot of shopping." I cleared my throat and read, "Interested in a feisty forty?"

"An ad? Her ad?"

"A draft of it, anyway."

"Forty? Phoebe?"

"—who loves games, hates dishonesty—"

"Forty!" Sasha repeated. "And she hates dishonesty?"

"—interested in art, history, genealogy, movies, sports—"

"She hated sports," Sasha said. "She'd leave the room when my dad watched football, and never went to the games with him. How stupid is writing an ad like that? What if it works? And he loves sports and wants somebody forty?"

"Funnier still if they'd both lied, and they wind up at game after game and are both secretly bored out of their skulls. Anyway, the list goes on. She's also interested in cooking, old music—"

"I hope she included shoes on that list of interests," Sasha said.

"—and knowing someone deeply and—"

"Stop," Sasha said softly. "No more. It's too sad." She shook her head and said nothing else.

I agreed. "Maybe this is more than we need to know."

"Sad," she repeated. "Lying in a rough draft. Lying to herself. There's something funny about an ad called 'personal' that isn't close to the truth of the person, isn't there? An ad supposedly designed to find your soul mate—and you aren't truthful about your own interests?" Sasha's voice was still muted.

"Everybody fudges in these ads," I said. Sasha looked at me intently. "As far as I've heard."

"Oh," she said quietly. "I thought maybe you . . . nah."

I tried to get into Phoebe's online financial account, but I didn't have her password. I'd have to leave finding it up to Mackenzie or Ozzie. There wasn't all that much else. I could go to all the sites and see what she'd bought if I figured out her password, but I couldn't see the point.

"There's a calendar program on here," I said. "That could be helpful. Who was she expecting to see that last evening of her life?"

But it was password protected, and I felt stymied and annoyed at having to make everything wait until I found a computer genius to decipher the password.

I ate my last slice of chicken breast, and looked at the stainless flatware for a moment before I remembered. "Sasha, what was Phoebe's maiden name?"

She thought for a moment. "Something weathery. Summer? Winter? Rayne? River?"

"River isn't weathery. It's geologically."

"Got it— Breeze! She said it had once been French and something like deBreece, but the kids made fun of it and called it "debris" and then called her 'Trashie.' So her mother, who had also hated the name, dropped the 'de' part and changed the spelling. Or so the story went."

Another "B," so the monograms on the silver could have been from a better day for the deBreece family. Or— "Did your father and Phoebe have sterling silver flatware with their initial on it? Kind of ornate?"

Sasha's forehead wrinkled. "Can't remember," she said. "Maybe. I do remember her setting what another woman called 'quite a table.' The expression stuck because I found it so weird back then. And I do have a memory of helping Phoebe polish spoons that drove me crazy for all the little creases and crevasses in the design. So maybe . . . but all the same, I wouldn't think so. When it comes to spending money on wives, as opposed to spending it on fiancées or dates, Dad can be frugal. Why? Did you see something?"

"I heard about it, didn't see it. Ramona mentioned it. You didn't run across a set of monogrammed silver? It should still be here."

"Maybe in the dining room. I didn't get there yet." She went to look while I made notes and read a clipping I'd taken off the refrigerator. Apparently, *Antiques Roadshow* was coming to New Jersey, and Phoebe had wanted a chance to be part of it.

Poor woman, so sure the world would appreciate her "treasures" as much as she did.

The laptop glowed, keeping its secrets. Meanwhile, I played with various spellings of "Breece," "Breeze," "Debrise," and "debris." Caps and lowercase. Frenchified spelling or Anglo-Saxon.

"Here's the silver, and I do remember it." Sasha came into the kitchen carrying a large wooden box. "I hated it back then. So clunky and heavy-looking, but aside from needing to be polished, it's really nice."

She was right on both counts. It was lovely indeed, and polishing it would be a bitch.

"You should definitely keep it. It's beautiful." I typed another combination on the computer. "Eureka! 'Breezy' did it. It's her password, and I'm in!" I scrolled to the calendar function, then to the month of December. Sasha pulled her chair over to mine, and tilted sideways so she also could view the screen.

That Thursday had only an "M."

"Her damn shorthand!" Sasha said. "It drove me crazy. 'M.' Great. Why couldn't she for once write something out?"

"It's something," I said. "It's a start. We can go through her address book and find people with that initial and—"

The doorbell rang.

"Nobody lives here," I said. "It's got to be somebody selling something."

"Or good old Not-That-I'd-Pry-But from next door," Sasha said.

I shut the laptop down, just in case it was Ramona, and put it into the big carton I was taking home. At least partly it was because I didn't know if going through Phoebe's private records was the right or legal thing to do. I already felt embarrassed knowing about the false picture of herself she was planning to use as bait.

Sasha and I both went to the door, as mutual protection from whatever we imagined the winter night might reveal, but when it opened, we saw only a tiny twenty-something woman with a mane of dark blond curls that could be described as midway between Botticelli tresses and a fright wig.

She stood in the doorway, the overhead light reflecting off high-heeled boots that covered her calves and disappeared under her suede skirt. She had a burnt-orange-and-forest-green scarf flung artfully over one shoulder of a tight fur jacket. Real fur, I thought, judging by the way the light hit it. The jacket wasn't even practical, covering a fraction of her body, and it seemed a cruel waste of a soft creature who'd had first dibs on that coat.

She carried a briefcase that looked too expensive to hold mere paperwork.

"Not a neighbor," I said softly.

"Saleswoman," Sasha said. "You were right."

The petite woman with the huge hair opened the storm door with her eyebrows raised as a way of asking permission, and once there was no more glass barrier between us, only frigid air, she spoke. "I am so glad to find you here! I was afraid the house would be empty. I'm Toy Rasmussen!" She smiled and nodded, as if sure we'd be delighted with that information.

"Miss Rasmussen, we were having dinner, my friend and I," Sasha said. "Whatever it is will have to wait for some other time. And, in fact, I'm not the owner, and the house is actually empty in a manner of speaking, so I can't buy or rent whatever you're selling." She backed up a step to close the inside door.

"No, no, no!" the little woman said with a joyous expression that didn't match the situation.

Definitely a saleswoman, no matter what she said.

And what she said was: "You've got me confused with somebody you don't want to see—but you *do* want to see me! This is where I belong. You're Sasha, right? Sasha Berg?" The twinkly woman tapped a long pink nail against her cheek. "Dennis told me you'd be here off and on, but I wasn't sure when that would be, and he forgot to give me your contact info! I was simply going to leave my card, but this is so much better! Nothing like a face-to-face, is there? So lucky to find you here and all!"

"Dennis?" Sasha echoed.

"Yay-uss," Toy said, pulling a card out of her briefcase. "Dennis Allenby. His mother owned this house—poor soul, she's gone now—and the house is going up for sale."

"Yes, I know that."

"Of course!" she said with a laugh that sounded like water running over stones. "Dennis didn't explain your exact connection with the property, but he did say you'd be glad to help me out. Are you a relative as well? I thought Dennis was an only child, but my condolences in any case. Sometimes friends are as close as family, and all losses are painful. What a pity she was taken too young and so suddenly."

There are few things more offensive to me than totally insincere sympathy. My personal ad would say, "Loves games; hates cloying, fake new best friends." I'd rather the person skipped it altogether, or said outright, "I don't care one whit about what's happened to you. I'm here for other reasons, which have to do with making money. I'm here for me." I might be able to be friends with that person.

I wanted to demand that Toy explain why she considered it a pity that Phoebe, a woman whose name she didn't even know, had died. I expected Sasha to challenge her, but, "What did he tell you?" she asked instead.

"Dennis?" She laughed again before going on. "He agreed with what I told him and am here to tell you. I am the best stager in the tristate area." This laugh, like the others, sounded like a tiny chandelier's crystals. She dug into her soft briefcase another time, and whipped out a second card, placing one on each upturned palm, as if they were offerings, and we each took one. Her business cards showed an open theater curtain on each side margin, and between them, a flat line with a sofa on it, and TOY'S STAGING: THIS TOY'S FOR REAL in a fake scriptlike font.

I was freezing. It was not a night for open front doors; yet inviting her in seemed a worse option. Once again I thought about other things I could be doing. Better, more interesting things, like doing absolutely nothing, but in my own home.

"So, long story short," she said, "he hired me to come stage his mother's house, and here I am, at your service!" Again her laugh tinkled forth like a child's xylophone, then it stopped abruptly, and she pointed one leather-gloved finger at me. "We haven't been introduced, but you know who I am, so who are you, may I ask?"

I wanted to say no, she couldn't ask, but Sasha had better manners, so she introduced me, and tried to explain what we were doing there; and finally, in a resigned tone, she said, "Come in."

"Well, my oh my," Toy said as she just about leaped into the house. She pulled off the fur jacket and dangled it from one hand. "She certainly liked . . ." She pivoted, surveying the living room. "Everything. Didn't she, though? A distinct personality lived here, I can tell, but it means I've got my work cut out for me." She twirled once more. "Some of this is quite nice, but . . . really. Not for this setting!" She lifted a box with a tableau on it in inlaid woods. "Nice but too small—and too muchness! Way too cluttered. No room for people to imagine their lives in this room. It's too full of hers."

"You'd think a person intelligent enough to have the where-withal to buy a house would have a little imagination, wouldn't you?" Sasha stood, arms crossed at the chest, looking not at all happy about the twirling, trilling woman. "I mean they're buying the place from another human being, so why be shocked if its contents reflect who that person was? After all, they aren't buying its contents. They don't have to match the buyer's personality."

"People . . ." Toy said, letting the idea trail off into whatever negative meaning we wanted to give it. "Imagination . . . *you* can't imagine . . ." The mini-chandelier laugh sounded at her word play. "When you've dealt with as many people in transition as I have . . ." she said in her airy voice. "Well, what can I say?"

She could say a lot, most likely, but so far, she'd said nothing.

"May I?" she asked as she edged toward the dining room.

So this is what became of my students who could not get it straight that they should be called on before they spoke. The ones who raised their hands only after they'd said their piece.

Sasha closed in on her. Phoebe's house was not large. It took only a few steps for Sasha to be next to Toy, or more accurately, to loom over her. There had to be a foot's difference in height, though I thought that if psyches and determination were duking it out, it might be a draw. "First tell me," Sasha said. "You 'stage' the house?"

Toy shook her great yellow mane in a nod.

"The entire house?"

"Attic to basement, if need be," she said. "We're a full-service staging operation."

"And that means what?"

Toy made a sweeping motion with her hand. "Pare down, arrange what's left, bring in accessories, flowers, paint the walls, replace the furniture, make sure the grounds are inviting—whatever it takes to give the place some juice, some feel, maybe even some pizzazz."

"But no personality," Sasha said.

Toy, despite her name and diminutive stature, was in no way intimidated by my friend Sasha's dark mood or six-foot height. "No *specific* personality—and no idiosyncratic personality. But more than that, no clutter! You want the buyer to walk in and feel at home, to say, 'Yes, this is where I belong.' And you don't want them to think it's a dark place, a cramped place, because the former owner stuffed it with too much!" She waved at her surroundings, almost like an orchestra conductor, then turned toward the dining room. "You want them to have space to breathe, to imagine themselves in here. To imagine putting Aunt Sadie's enormous breakfront right there and the gigantic flat-screen TV over there. To let them imagine cluttering it up themselves."

"Specifically, what are we talking about?" Sasha asked. "What does what you're saying entail?"

"Up to you, and in this case, Dennis, too, I suppose. We can do anything and everything. Make that garage look useable. Replace gangly houseplants with smaller, tidier-looking ones. Replace, recover, redo the furniture if need be—and your budget allows. Trust me, it's money well spent. Staged houses sell for more and sell more quickly. I have charts and statistical evidence I'll show you. They're right outside in my car. You'd be amazed!"

We shook our heads. "No thanks." She wasn't going to carry literature with her that made her profession seem less than a basic necessity of life.

She was alive with energy and excitement about making this home look better. I would not have been surprised if she suddenly broke into song, or tap-danced.

"What do you do with the things you pare down?" Sasha asked.

Toy lifted both carefully sculpted eyebrows. "*You*—or Dennis—do whatever you want with them. Take them, give them to charity, keep them as souvenirs, burn them, store them. If you have no interest in so doing, we'll dispose of it all for you, but there is a charge for hauling it away."

She did a few more slow pirouettes, opening her arms in the Evita pose, embracing the house with her vision as she spoke. "My concern is what this area will *say*. Right now, I'm envisioning it empty, and then I will slowly envision filling it back up. Think of this as my stage. Literally. As if you were in the theater, and the curtain went up and you saw this house up there; and it was set up and painted and decorated so that before the play even started, before anybody walked onstage, you'd know that this was a good house, a happy house, a house to be proud of, though not pretentious."

Sasha turned and looked at me, deadpan, then turned back to Toy, who continued her narrative with great gusto. "Right now," she said, "it's filled with tiny things that don't make a statement; they chatter. The feeling is decidedly busy, busy, busy! No breathing room. One or two significant pieces would be much more effective than all this clutter. As for the disposition of what's in here now—well, I don't have it in writing but Dennis for one didn't sound that interested in any of it." Without asking for permission, Toy walked around the dining room. "Oh my!" she squeaked, sounding like a startled Disney mousekin.

"What is he thinking?" Sasha whispered to me. "He tells me to take care of things, then he sends *her* here? Doesn't he trust me? Or did he tell her to throw everything of his mother's away? I haven't even had time to think about half of it. Plus, God knows what she charges, and am I supposed to pay it out of my half because I'm taking care of this sale? I won't; but even if it's out of both of our shares equally—who wants this?"

I felt it wise to stay out of this altogether.

"Well, some of these pieces might work," Toy said when she'd recovered from the shock of Phoebe's dining-room collections. Every surface was covered, but not the way Ramona's had been. No plastic here, only objects. Lots and lots of them. The center of the dining-room table had a wide runner on it holding candle-holders. Some were beautiful, some were silly, but you didn't have to be a professional stager to know there were too many of them. If all had been in use, the house might explode from the heat they'd produce.

"I wouldn't keep much," Toy now was saying, "that's for sure. Maybe that breakfront, and we could put a few important pieces in it if there's anything that—"

"I know, makes a statement," Sasha muttered.

"—sings to me," Toy said. "And let me check out the kitchen, not that we can do too much in there, unless Dennis is up for some remodeling. But even something like colored place mats, and clean counters, and—"

"I'd have to be up for it, too," Sasha declared loudly from the living room.

"Sorry!" Toy trilled. "Of course I meant both of you."

"I vote no remodeling," Sasha continued. "Also, I need a whole lot more information before you talk about painting and finding things that sing to you. Furthermore, I haven't heard from Dennis, and he should have let me know. He put me in charge of this house, and I'm not ready to sign off on expenses and decisions I know nothing about."

"But," I whispered, giving up on my decision to stay out of this, "You don't want to do this yourself. You were complaining about it when I got here. This place is a mess—not dirty, but I've never seen more clutter."

Sasha's mouth tightened. "Don't give me common sense, Amanda. If there's one thing I hate when I'm pissed off it's logic!

Why did he hire somebody behind my back? Doesn't he trust me to do a decent job? His high-handedness is the point!"

"The man's a jerk. Why be surprised when he does something jerky?"

Toy came back into the living room. "I've promised Dennis a solid guesstimate ASAP. So as soon as I've seen the rest of the house and crunch some numbers, I'd be happier than happy to give it to you, too; and then you and Dennis can decide whether it's worth it. I can tell you right now—it absolutely is. Without me, this house won't sell for what it's worth. Not close. With all due apologies to the deceased, she wasn't thinking about market value, curb appeal."

"Right. She was thinking about living in it," Sasha said, "about having it appeal to her own self, not the curb."

Toy was already on the third riser of the staircase, ignoring us. "May I?" she said as she went upstairs. "The bedrooms are relatively simple to freshen up. Shouldn't take me but a minute to evaluate."

"What are you really afraid of?" I asked when Toy was out of earshot.

"She lived with us—I lived with her. Some of her memories are mine, too. I don't want some stranger stomping through everything."

"Then, instead of deciding what has to go—let's go through the place tonight, or however many other nights it takes, and tag each thing you want as a keepsake. There has to be less of those than there are of the get-rid-ofs, and it shouldn't take that long. It's not that large a house. Do you think there's lots you'd want to keep?"

Sasha shrugged. "Not really. I remember some things from way back when we were, officially, family. They had sentimental attachments for her, so now they do for me as well. But I really resent Dennis, and this makes me wonder if he wasn't the surprise visitor that night."

"Are you honestly saying he killed his own mother?"

"I wouldn't put it past him." She looked serious, and the expression on her face and what she was suggesting frightened me. "He's screwed up most of his life and he's still not exactly a roaring success, and the money he'll get from this house is going to matter to him a lot. Not that it won't matter to me—it definitely will, and I'm probably poorer than Dennis. But even so, it won't matter in the same way. There's always something desperate about Dennis."

I thought I understood at least enough of what she was trying to say.

"No love was lost between them," she said. "You heard the way he talked at her memorial service."

"Good thing is: He's in Chicago and we're here. Take all the time you need to go through this house. Then, maybe, Toy can get rid of the things you don't want. Let her worry about getting Dumpsters and trucks. We can start taking the small things home with us tonight."

"Well, well, well," Toy said, clunking down the stairs in her boots. "You aren't going to believe this place when we're finished with it. It will be a doll's house, a little showplace. It has decent enough bones. Now we have to give it a chance to shine. A little powder and lipstick, or if you will, a little face-lift. Let me work up my estimate and get back to you. I think I could have it ready by tomorrow, but I may need to get into the house one more time first. Maybe during the day? With good light? Then meet here and talk over each idea?"

"Fine," Sasha snapped. "I'll see you at five P.M."

She made it sound as if the appointment were for a duel.

Eight

"We didn't make much headway, or maybe there isn't much headway to make," I said to Mackenzie. "Sasha's digging in, literally and figuratively, but after yesterday, I'm calling quits to the sorting and packing up. Friendship goes far, but sifting through junk in search of other people's memories gets old fast."

"Who names their kid Toy?" Mackenzie asked. "But aside from her name, I don't see why hiring her is such a big deal. It's the smart and easy thing to do. As long as Dennis divvies up the spoils properly, including the cost of staging, then let the Toy girl make the place sell."

"I'm sure that's what's going to happen. It wasn't really about that. It was about staking a claim, about rights and privileges.

About Sasha having Toy appear versus Sasha making the decision to hire her herself."

"Interesting what things are really about versus what we say they're about," he murmured.

Milky winter morning filtered through the skylight. When I'd looked out the windows of the loft that faced the street below, I'd seen people huddling and bundled, and I was glad I had the car again today. "I couldn't find anything interesting so far," I said. "I'm pretty sure she wasn't far enough along with on-line dating for there to have been some unknown crazy person who did her in. She probably was waiting for that new photo."

Mackenzie finished his coffee and stood up. "You know this is hogwash, don't you? Phoebe killed herself, on purpose or accidentally. We don't know the reason and she didn't choose to share it with us. Her business was failing, her partner accusing her of all kinds of evil behavior, her husband was dead, she'd done the marriage thing too many times already, and her only child was a creep. So maybe she was simply tired of it all, or she drank too much and mixed it up with pills by accident. Inventing a conspiracy, a crime, isn't an appropriate way for Sasha to mourn."

"I promised."

He cocked his head and raised an eyebrow. "You know what Napoleon said?"

" 'Not tonight, Josephine'?" He winced. " 'Able was I ere I saw Elba'?"

"You know what Napoleon said about promises."

"I'm fresh out of Napoleonic quotes."

"He said, 'If you wish to be a success in the world, promise everything, deliver nothing.' "

"Are you sure *he* said that? Most of our politicians could have; and why are you quoting Napoleon so early in the morning?"

"Because I want to impress you with my learning, and because I thought it was apt."

"I am impressed. Incredulous, actually, that I say the word 'promise' and that you've got that quote at the ready, right on the tip of your tongue."

"Well," he said with a wink, "might not have been there a week ago, but I'm reading this terrific biography and I just read that line."

"You're reading for fun? I thought you were up to here with schoolwork and moonlighting and your family's woes and—"

"I am. But sometimes I need a break from the here and now. Don't you? You've been talkin' about *A Tale of Two Cities*, which got me to thinkin' about the Revolution, the Terror, and how little I really know about how Napoleon came to power—or much of anything, except for word games like that Able/Elba thing you said."

"Promise everything and deliver nothing. Does that mean you won't really check the databases for Sasha?"

" 'Course not. I'm too tall to have a Napoleon complex. I'm checking out as much as I can about Phoebe, and Dennis, and the late lamented Mr. Ennis, too, just in case he left dangerous enemies behind. Any lawsuits, debts, prison experiences—"

"Phoebe?"

He shrugged. "So far, zilch, but I'm not finished. Oh, I'm also looking at exes, living exes, and I did see that Allenby, the original husband—"

"And father of Dennis."

He nodded. "—who is still alive and well and living in New Jersey, has a bit of a credit-rating problem. I looked at his history and it's like a roller coaster, and I'm willing to bet, without anything concrete to substantiate it yet, that Ex Number One has a gambling problem."

For a moment, I was thrilled—we'd found something. But one moment doesn't go very far. One exhalation later, my elation was history. "I don't see what that could have to do with the way she died," I said. "I wish I did, but I don't."

"Neither do I. Unless we find out he inherits something."

"She didn't have anything worthwhile except the house. Unless Dennis did it for the love of his daddy."

He smiled. "Dennis may have done it for the love of himself. He has his own checkered history."

"Sasha told me he's screwed up a number of times."

"Including one brief arrest for brawling, and once a charge of domestic abuse, although the charge was dropped. And financially, he seems to have made teetering on the edge of catastrophe a lifestyle. Sometimes he's had major assets, and then the bubble—one or another kind of bubble—bursts."

"Is it all legal?"

"Far as I can see. Legal but risky. There have been civil suits, especially when he apparently had friends invest in his schemes."

"Sounds more likely that somebody would kill him rather than the opposite."

"Profits from the house might save him from bankruptcy. I need to look into that more, but suffice to say he isn't in great shape as far as income is concerned."

"And his father?"

Mackenzie shook his head and went to get his coat. "I only mentioned Harvey Allenby's problems to dazzle you—to show you that I'm on the trail, the track, the whole superhighway. I'm not ignoring my obligations. I'm not breaking my promises, no matter what Napoleon advised. But maybe my fantastic work will convince you that you don't have to make this your number-one priority, and you shouldn't expect much in the way of dramatic results." He turned toward the pegs where we put our coats, and stopped. "And what is this?" he asked mildly, bending to retrieve a painting that I'd propped against the wall.

"Sasha wanted me to have it. She said it was one of Phoebe's favorites, and she'd already taken several other paintings. After Toy showed up, instead of thinking about tossing things, Sasha went through picking out things that had meaning for her. This was one of them. I thought it was nice enough. No, actually, it *isn't* nice enough. I'm not fond of it, but I thought not accepting it would hurt Sasha's feelings."

C.K. held it in one hand, moving it back and closer, staring. The fruit in the foreground was against a midnight-dark void, as if beyond these pomegranates lay nothingness. The silver pitcher next to the fruit reflected light from nowhere. I didn't like it at all.

"Okay," I said. "Granted. It's not nice at all, but maybe not repulsive?"

He looked at me with as little expression as he could allow.

"Okay. Kind of repulsive," I acknowledged. "The frame's probably worth more than the painting."

He raised one eyebrow. "To whom?"

"I don't know. It's so fancy, I thought . . ."

He carefully put it back on the floor, propped against the wall.

"I know," I said. "I was thinking the same thing myself."

"How would you know what I'm—"

"—the loft's huge, with tons of wall space and we like light colors, an airy feeling, so the reason this painting's on the floor is that there isn't a single inch where it would look right. Aside from being mildly creepy, it's going to look like a splat, a splotch, a dark hole on our walls."

"We've been married too long," he said.

"Two months? Too long?"

"When you finish each other's sentences, or don't even need the sentences to know what they're thinkin' . . . one of the ten warning signs you've been married too long."

"What are the other nine?"

"Can't remember," he said, "except that not being able to remember the warning signs is another of the signs." He shrugged on his coat. We were both in the process of wrapping ourselves in coats, scarves, and gloves, and when finished—twice the size we'd been before the cocooning began—we turned and double-checked that we had everything we needed. "Think she'll be upset if she doesn't see it when she comes over?" C.K. asked.

"I'll find a wee corner somewhere," I said, and we were off to our schools.

"Morning, morning, morning," Opal Codd said. "Ugglesome day, isn't it? Subboreal, and all that faffling!"

"You rehearse these greetings, don't you? Don't tell me those words come tripping off the tongue." She insisted that I, as an English teacher, must know all the obscure words she spouted. And if I did not, which was a sad commentary on the state of knowledge these days, then I must, at the very least, have a great joy in being introduced to them. For, she'd told me, this was the very heart of education. "Never stop learning, that's my motto," she'd said.

She was right, but there were so many things to learn, I wished she hadn't decided to master words nobody used. Nonetheless, I did my best to act thrilled with each new incomprehensible entry.

"Ugglesome," she said in her precise manner. "Horrible or frightful. Subboreal, cold but not freezing. Faffling, blowing."

"Thank you! I really like ugglesome, too!"

"One out of three is pretty good," she said.

The contents of my mailbox were ugglesome. Notice of a faculty meeting to discuss "recent disruptive activities including prohibited gambling in or around school property." The poker games must have prompted this, but what did it mean that "around school property" was no-man's-land? I wondered how wide an area "around" encompassed. I also wondered how the school could patrol and enforce the rules of its "around" area.

I wished I could have hauled Havermeyer in for a few remedial English sessions.

There was more. A notice to be read to our homerooms that the drama club's winter production, scheduled for February, would be *The Man Who Came to Dinner* and that auditions would begin after school today. A note from a student explaining why he had been unable to do his homework. The reasons were so convoluted, involving the woman with whom his mother co-shared a job, and that woman's fuel pump and an accident that had blocked the expressway, and—I gave up. Another notice about holiday parties and assignments over winter break. Maurice Havermeyer was apparently in favor of minimal parties ("food residue and similar detritus abandoned and left in classrooms over the winter break presents serious sanitation issues to the maintenance staff") and maximum assignments ("bearing in mind the possibility that our students' families may be relocating the students during the break, so access to encyclopedias and specialized research resources may not be possible").

I have long suspected that our headmaster lived in an alternate academia, where Philly Prep students would spend their winter break agonizing about being in Belize instead of a world-class reference library. Or, in fact, would do any assignments over winter break even if they were spending it in a world-class reference library. Or, in fact, would remember during winter break that they had assignments.

And yet year after year, Maurice Havermeyer issued the same daffy, optimistic warnings. Perhaps he could be that way because he almost never interacted with the actual breathing students who populated the school, preferring the scholars of his imagination.

I tossed the notices into the trash and made my exit.

Either Jonesy Farmer spent most of his days near the front entrance, or his timing and mine had been synchronized, because I once again found myself nodding to him. But not before I'd noticed his hunched posture, as if he was holding a secret to his center, perhaps protecting it from Griffith Ward and a third cohort beside him, another of the subspecies that make me believe the word "spoiled" is appropriate. There was something soft and gone to rot in these boys, and part of what seemed missing was the true joy of youth, the excitement, the sense of adventure. They seemed jaded, old in bad ways before their time. In class, they tilted their seats back in eloquent body language that said they'd rather be anywhere but there. They traded signs and signals only with each other and did not participate in group discussions. In the great sea of students, they were the undertow, pulling us down if we allowed it.

Opal would have blamed gambling for their woes, and would expect me to seize this opportunity to say something to them. Reform their degenerate game-playing.

But what would I say? Half the country was enraptured with poker: poker as spectator sport on TV; poker as online Internet gambling; and, presumably, old-fashioned, sit-down-and-play-with-your-pals poker.

I suspected that lots of factors—more than I could guess at—were responsible for their missing parts, and criticizing, let alone trying to change what they did on their own time outside of school, would be rightly seen as none of my business or concern, as picking on them.

There would be some truth in that.

I sighed. I wasn't doing too well with my like-every-child decision, was I? Not when it came to The Griff and company.

The position of the trio prompted me to active eavesdropping, a talent I admit with no shame. Knowledge is power. Understanding anything more than what they willingly shared was, if not power, then perhaps comprehension of my students. Especially given that they shared next to nothing.

So before he was made aware of me, I'd caught a snippet of Jonesy's conversation, if conversation it was. "—can't," he said. "You have to wait. . . ." His voice was low but urgent. "Give me a little—"

"Now!" That was said with such force, I didn't even have to eavesdrop. Several other students turned to look at Griffith, who dropped back to sotto voce. ". . . know how." I missed the rest of the sentence until I heard, "—again?" As usual, Griffith looked smug, imperious, his posture slouched in a way that made it clear whatever was bothering Jonesy in no way troubled him. His buddy, Casey, the yes-man with arms crossed against his abdomen, nodded every time Griffith spoke.

"I can't!" Jonesy said.

"No choice," Griffith said.

The toady shook his head, emphasizing Griffith's dictum.

"But not—I—I didn't mean—"

"Didn't mean what you said? Interesting."

I was close by now, lingering, pretending to have something wrong with my briefcase. I was intrigued by how Griffith made his flat statement reverberate with the sense of a massive, threatening subtext. Without moving a muscle, his words pushed and shoved Jonesy.

I wished for a cartoon character's ear that could telescope out, the better with which to hear, as I caught only snips. The word that most surprised me was "honor," but as I tried to move closer, fiddling with my briefcase as a delaying tactic, Jonesy spotted me. He put a hand on Griffith's arm as he said, a little too loudly, "Hey, Miss Pepper."

Griffith turned and grinned at me. "Hey," he said with complete ease. He looked a little goofy, but certainly not like the threatening bully I'd thought I'd heard. I felt a rush of shame. I wondered why I had such well-developed antibodies to his hail fellow well met charisma. His peers certainly found him charming. Why did I suspect his charm, resent his breezy self-assurance? Was I jealous? Upset that I hadn't had that smooth patina, that easy self-confidence, when I was in high school?

"Morning, guys," I said, and I moved toward the staircase. With difficulty, I controlled the urge to look back, to see if and how their body language changed when I moved out of sight. I wanted to know whether their cryptic discussion continued. It had certainly not seemed resolved.

The day ahead rolled through my brain, hour by hour, as I walked up the stairs. A grammar quiz in one class, vocabulary work in another, oral book reports in my two sections of seniors, and more of *A Tale of Two Cities* with the ninth graders. In a larger school, with thousands of students, large staffs, and the need for many English classes at each level, I might have taught five sections of one grade and faced only one daily preparation. Sometimes, and this morning might have been one of them, that sounded like a dream, a way to avoid the frazzle of my multi-preparations, an easy slide into home each day.

Other days, and this might be one of those, too, I wondered how those teachers managed to make the fifth presentation of the same material feel fresh to the students, and more importantly, to themselves. By the end of the day, did they even know what they were saying or were they like telemarketers with a memorized script?

All things considered, I didn't begrudge the rigorous schedule. I wheeled through a lot of emotions at Philly Prep, but boredom was seldom on the list. Still, I kept returning to that throwaway line from the morning, when I'd asked Mackenzie about his extracurricular reading, and he'd said he needed a break from the here and now. "Don't you?" he'd asked without expecting an answer.

I should have said an emphatic yes. Too often of late, I thought I was approaching the telemarketer side of the teacherly scale. Saying what I should, but with too little heart, and sometimes mind, in it. The larger problem was that I didn't know what to do about it, but a break from the here and now sounded perfect, if only I knew what that could mean.

And there was almost no emotion, let alone passion, invested in settling what happened to Phoebe Ennis. However, I'd told Sasha this would be my final session in Jersey, and knowing the end was in sight eased the strain. I'd try to speak with that other neighbor, ask around to see if anybody else on the block had noticed anything, and take care of whatever other investigating there might be from home or at the office. Whatever I did was pure formality in any case. Wouldn't anyone who'd noticed anything odd have already told the police? And if they had reason to keep it to themselves till now, why would they tell me?

When I reached the top of the stairs, I could no longer resist. I went to the banister and looked down, and saw Griffith and Jonesy high-fiving and nodding.

Ah, the dramatics of high school. Standoff one minute, best buds the next. All was obviously well, and life would roll on, and I had been reading much too much into overheated adolescent dialogue, my reaction compounded by my unprofessional and baseless antipathy toward Griffith.

Margaret and Eddie popped heads into my room before class. "We've got all the cash," Margaret said. "Are we still on for counting?" Eddie asked.

I gave them a thumbs-up. "Mrs. Codd awaits you," I said. They beamed, first at me, then at each other. I was positive they'd be running a Fortune 500 firm in the foreseeable future. They'd run it now, if someone wasn't sure to quibble about age requirements. "See you in a while," I said, and they were gone.

The class discussion went well. I asked a difficult question, demanding enough sophistication to move beyond pure story and consider what Dickens was saying through his characters. "Was he trying to say anything about the French Revolution, or revolutions in general, or other things?"

And at a surprising gallop, we were off and running. At first, they weren't sure of their ground, didn't trust their own impressions, but after a while, they gained confidence and were surprisingly insightful.

"Too violent," a boy said.

"But it was a revolution!" another shouted.

"Yeah, but the good guys turned just as bad as the bad guys in the end. Killing everybody who disagreed. Going out to watch people beheaded like it was a football game."

"So is Dickens against changing the social system in France? Does he think it was fair before the Revolution?" I asked.

They had a hard time letting each other speak. They remembered the aristocrat who flipped a coin at the man whose child he'd just killed, the starvation of the ordinary people, the worker. When Eddie and Margaret returned, a late entry together that might normally have set off suggestive noises, they were barely acknowledged. I considered this proof of an academic triumph.

"Then, what might he be saying is wrong, or not a good way to go?"

And eventually, we got to the idea of vengeance versus forgiveness, and to Madame Defarge's role in the novel.

"She was going to kill the little girl," somebody whispered. "Just because her *grandfather* had been evil. He was, but now she'd become evil, too."

"She watched people die and she kept on knitting. Served her right when she shot herself."

"That's called poetic justice," I said, and as I explained the Aristotelian origin of the term, they didn't flinch. They didn't flinch when I used the word "irony" either and high-fived when we mentioned the ironic twist of fate that had Madame Defarge shooting herself while trying to kill Miss Pross.

I turned to the board and wrote Shakespeare's famous phrase, "Hoist with his own petard." They didn't flinch then, either.

When I explained that a "petard" was a small bomb or firecracker (and, they were delighted to know, it also meant "an exhalation of intestinal gas") and "hoist" meant lifted up, they smiled and let that bit of the literary canon slip into their systems.

We were having such a pleasant time, I hated to dampen their spirits with their homework: writing their own opinions of what Dickens was saying about the French Revolution, or about France versus England, or about English conditions at the time. "Think about today's discussion. Lots of good ideas were mentioned. Use them or come up with your own. You can have any idea in the world, and any opinion, but justify it. Back it up. Give examples and let me understand your thinking."

Now they looked insulted, as if I'd tossed that coin to them as I killed their babies. It was possible that we were about to have a revolution in the classroom. "Come on," I said. "You've spent this period having all kinds of ideas and giving tons of examples to back them up. All I'm asking is for you to—"

"*Write it!*" a freckled boy's agonized voice made his point conclusively.

"It can and should be brief. If you write down a guide for yourself, what the point is that you want to make, why you feel that way, you're just about home free."

"In writing? Tonight?" The freckled boy had not been convinced or swayed by my performance.

"Yes. You can't go through life text-messaging every idea with abbreviations and signs. Imagine if the revolutionaries we're reading about couldn't frame an argument, couldn't make their points."

They didn't believe me. After all, cell phones had been invented in order to eliminate the need for written exchanges.

"Write it *tonight*? Really?" the freckled boy said in a still louder, more incredulous tone.

I nodded.

They sulked and sighed, and I smiled and wished them well. It really wasn't fair. They went off, overburdened, abused children.

Between classes, I called Marc Wilkins, he who blamed his midlife crisis on Phoebe. I'd Googled him last night before I staggered off to bed, and today I hoped to use the information to see how he'd react.

He made sense as "M." Phoebe would have been glad to see him, sure she could make things right between them. His claims sounded like a madman's to me, but maybe he really believed them, believed that she'd embezzled, or kept fake financial records. Maybe he'd come to find what he'd lost.

He taught writing at the University of the Arts, and according to the online class schedule, he had office hours right now. I crossed my fingers and prepared to lie and flatter him sufficiently to get him to see me today.

Nine

"Thank you!" I said. "I can't thank you enough for seeing me on such short notice. You'll never know what this means to me. Everything's been happening so fast, and I know I'm late about the application process, but I just found out—"

"Whoa!" Marc Wilkins said, not unkindly. We were in his office, or rather, an office he shared with two other lecturers who either used the room on different schedules or were out to lunch. "Ruby, is it?"

The smile he gave me clearly signaled that before this session was out, Marc Wilkins was going to make a pass at me.

"Yessir, Ruby Osgood." I have no idea where the name came from, but I did not want to risk the chance that he'd listened attentively to his wife's chatter and had somehow heard of me, or Sasha's friend Amanda. I was being overcautious, but given that every other sentence I was likely to say to him would be a lie, why not my name as well. "I'm so lucky you were here today and—"

"How can I help you, Ms. Osgood?" He was a good-enough-looking man, well maintained. Sasha said Merilee claimed he had been left a small trust, which cushioned his teaching and writing income. If so, it was all the more infuriating that he was being so petty about the failed business and Phoebe's role in it.

I looked down at my hands. "I've never had the opportunity to go to college, but all of a sudden, I do. And this is where I want to go, and you are the person I want to study with. Uh—with whom I want to study!"

He lifted and cupped my hands in his. "Why me?" he asked softly.

I extricated my hands as gently as I could. "Because my godmother knew you and thought you were so talented. Loved your book, and your movies." According to the website, he'd written the scripts for two films I'd never heard of, *Warbucks* and *Once Upon a Mesa*. My never having seen them meant very little since I saw so few movies. He'd also published a book he called a novel. It was about an unhappily married writing teacher at an urban university.

"And it's my godmother who's making all of this possible," I, or Ruby, said. "Unfortunately—this is very sad, and I don't mean to trivialize it—it's because she died and left me money that I can afford to quit my job and study full time now. I had no idea she would ever do such a thing—I didn't even think she had any money! I know it's so late for me to be trying to find out about applying, but truly, I just found out about my inheritance and so—here I am! I so want to write for the movies!"

"And you came to me rather than to the admissions office because . . . ?"

"I thought you could tell me how to make myself the best application, and what I'd need—because, like I said, I'd heard of you, and I'm at a loss as to how to proceed."

He smiled and patted my upper arm. I smiled back and twisted slightly to dislodge him. "Phoebe, that's my godmother," I said. "She admired you and your talent. I'm sad that it took her death for this to happen."

"Phoebe. That's an unusual name. You say I knew her? Or she said she knew me?"

I nodded vigorously. "Phoebe Ennis." I waited, with what I hoped was an expectant smile on my face. When instead he bit at his upper lip and lowered his brow, I resumed babbling. "Maybe you knew her under a different last name. She was married five times. Isn't that incredible? The last names of her husbands were alphabetical, starting with the 'A' husband, and then the—"

"I think I remember her. In fact, I'm sure I do. She knew my wife more than she knew me. I'm sorry to hear that she died."

"You didn't know?"

Now he raised his eyebrows, as if I'd just said an amazingly naïve thing. Then he said, "No. I'm afraid not."

I nodded. "You must have left before she . . . before she did it."

"Left where and did what?"

"You must have left her house before she killed herself."

"What? What in God's name are you talking about?"

"See, that's one of the stories I want to try to write. Her life was such a . . . Well, it was a mess, kind of. And yet she is doing this for me. A kind of redemption, don't you think?"

"I don't know what to think. I don't know what you're talking about. I have never visited this woman. I don't even know where she lives."

"Really? I wonder what she meant, then. I spoke with her that very day. I think about it a lot, because maybe I could have done something if I'd heard the despair she must have been feeling. But honestly, I couldn't tell at all. She hid it well. I was going to ask you if you could tell, but you're saying—"

"Please. I don't know what you're talking about. You have me confused with somebody else."

"I don't know. I thought she said Daddy Warbucks was coming over. I could swear that's what she said, and didn't you write a movie about him? About his early life, before he even met Annie? That's what she told me. Sounds so clever."

Bless the Internet.

Either he was the "M" who'd visited that night, and she might have said that—or he'd think my imaginary Phoebe meant it symbolically, that she was referring to the man whose money she had funneled into her hands, her unwitting benefactor. And now mine.

"I'm sorry," I said when he continued to stare at me. "I'm probably mixed up. She said something about being pleased, about Daddy Warbucks. It turned out to be such a bad night for her, and for all of us who loved her, that I probably got all confused about her exact words."

He sat forward in his desk chair, his hands clasped. "Let me get this clear. She left you enough money for four years of school?"

"Even better. Four years of tuition and my living expenses. Amazing, isn't it? Like a fairy tale come true."

"And you want to write about this? About her?"

"Well, yes, because she was amazing, and I'm interested in character. On getting great characters up on the screen."

"You need a story as well, you know."

"See? That's exactly the kind of thing I need to know—exactly why I have to come here and learn all this!"

"It could be interesting to write it as a mystery. Where did this woman get that money?"

"Great idea because yes, it is a mystery to me! I mean she was a widow, and she'd never had a good-paying job, and her husband didn't leave her much. Everybody I've told was stunned, too."

He grew pale and his skin had a sick sheen. "You might want

to consider a twist in your plot about the magic money," he finally said. "If it's ill-gotten gain, your inheritance might be in jeopardy."

"Ill-gotten? I mean that could be interesting in a script, but it wouldn't fit her character. I can't imagine how . . ."

"Things happen," he said. "If the money was stolen, for example, there'd be a victim with, probably, a desire for revenge."

"Stolen! My godmother would never—that's just not possible!"

He took a deep breath and leaned further forward and patted my knee. "Let's consider this your first lesson. You must exercise your imagination, envision how anything could happen. That's what will make you a writer."

"But—but—"

He shook his head. "I'm glad that you're interested in getting an education. If you take care of the application process promptly, you aren't too late. The directions and requirements are spelled out online, or you can go talk to the admissions people now. I'm flattered that your godmother admired my oeuvre."

I controlled the urge to gag.

"And I wish you much luck. I also wish I could write you a recommendation, but it would be worthless, given that we've just met. Aside from that, I am afraid there is nothing I can offer you but my best wishes, and the hope that I see you in my class next year."

I left, thanking him for his time.

Marc Wilkins was a letch and a liar. It was stupid to lie about knowing Phoebe, let alone knowing she was dead. Only somebody as naïve as my imagined Ruby Osgood would be too dim to check him out and know that his wife Merilee and Phoebe were in partnership in a business he'd underwritten. What was the point of a complete lie?

Marc Wilkins—and his oeuvre—stayed on the list.

* * *

I was meeting Sasha at five, but I didn't want to drive to Jersey at all, and I didn't want to sit in Phoebe's cluttered rooms and look at more teddy bears or souvenir spoons. We'd moved through the house yesterday with amazing speed. It was easy, after all, to decide about the large objects, the ones that would be Toy's primary focus. And even the abundance of what Phoebe would have called "collectibles" was no real chore. No sentimentality was attached to the perfume bottles, though Sasha thought they might appeal to an antiques dealer along with a dozen or more enamel boxes and a group of milk-glass vases. The paintings in their ornate frames were mostly unlikeable—including the one Sasha had so generously given me—and we left their fate up to Toy.

Our decision-making ability accelerated with the hours, and by night's end, the house was close to inventoried, at least as far as things to be saved, sold, or forgotten were concerned. I went home with the painting and the carton holding Phoebe's laptop and all the contents of her desk. Sasha had gone home with three cartons' worth of Phoebe memorabilia, including the silver.

We could have called it quits yesterday, and I thought we should have, but Toy was coming over around five for that last walk-through, or showdown. I was to be moral support in case of a clash of wills or, more likely, a clash of budgets.

Once in my car, I hesitated, debating between going home for an hour or going into the office for the same amount of time. But the thought of Ozzie Bright's office made me remember that my other act of Sasha–friendship required closure. I had to finish, to Sasha's satisfaction, the futile investigation of Phoebe's cause of death. So Bordentown it would be.

The weather was nastier than it should have been at this point on the calendar, with a raw wind blowing off the Delaware, and I wanted to be home, curled on the sofa, or standing by the range, making soup. Even marking papers seemed preferable to spinning wheels in Bordentown, and nothing was helped by the traffic creeping over the bridge.

Nor did I have any hopes that this interview—if it

happened—would reveal anything worthwhile. Why would Phoebe have been any more forthcoming with this neighbor than with the other two in her tea-party trio?

I might not have been overly enthusiastic about meeting her, but as soon as Sally Molinari opened the door, she behaved as if she'd been waiting for me all her life.

"Hey!" she said with a big smile. "Glad to see you!"

I hadn't said a word. Not an introduction or an explanation of my presence, and she had no way of knowing who I was. I had a fleeting moment of fear that she was part of a cult and I should refuse her overly friendly greetings, but then I decided that I didn't mind being prequalified as good news. What would school be like if all the students greeted me this way? And meant it?

I explained my presence, heavy on the word "investigator" and intimations of an inheritance "confusion."

She nodded and smiled even more, waving me into her home with one hand as she held the door wide open with the other. "Yes, yes," she said, "I read mysteries and I know lawyers hire investigators, use them all the time, to sort things through." I didn't contradict her because what she said was true, even if it didn't have anything to do with my presence.

"Come in, come in, make yourself comfortable," she said. "Poor Phoebe, of course I knew her, and there—sit there. It's a comfy couch. Or here, on this chair. Or anywhere, really."

She'd pointed to the sofa, then a wing chair, and I settled on the latter, already feeling a bit exhausted. The living room and what I could see of the dining room behind it, the mirror image of Phoebe's layout, were filled with heavy pine and maple Early American pieces, with a rag rug on the floor, a dry sink on one wall, rush-bottomed chairs in the dining room, and everywhere, brass accessories. Even what I was sure was a TV cabinet had been engineered to appear to be a Colonial hutch. Every wood surface looked lovingly waxed or polished, and the phrase "controlled comfort" popped onto my mental screen, even though I wasn't sure what it meant.

Sally plumped a sofa cushion before sitting down on the one next to it. She was an ace homemaker.

The coffee table in front of her held a wineglass and a fraction of a second after she sat down, she popped back up and retrieved a second goblet and a bottle of red wine. "Yes?" she said, already pouring.

"Thank you." It seemed the polite thing to say.

"So sad about Phoebe." She settled back into the cushions. She was a solidly built woman with a pretty, though wrinkled, face and a flush that suggested her late-afternoon drink might not be the first she'd had today. "I thought we were going to be such friends! I thought we were well on our way!"

"Her death was a shock to you, then?"

Her mouth formed an "o" like a comic-book character. "Shock? What's beyond that? I thought I'd die myself when I heard not only that she'd died but that she'd killed herself! I didn't think she could be that unhappy—I mean, I thought I knew her. At least a little. We went out together a few times. You want to be a good neighbor, don't you? And she was a nice woman so it wasn't any real effort. To the movies, that kind of thing. I knew she'd been newly widowed and was probably feeling raw— I know how that feels—so we only saw comedies, and old-time comedies, you know? None of the dirty sort that's popular now. Nothing that would upset her in any way. And she seemed fine. Sad, of course. And her with her only child living so far away and no grandchildren to brighten the picture. I felt sorry for her, but I wasn't worried about her. She seemed a person who'd rather be happy than not. And she was pretty enough, and kept herself up, so if she was going to be in the market for a man again—and she did seem the sort to need to stay in that market, didn't she?— then she probably wasn't going to have all that hard a time. Unless she was hyper-picky of course. The pickings for older women are not exactly luxurious."

While I was trying to extract anything concrete and helpful from the verbal avalanche, Sally stood up again and retrieved a porcelain shepherdess in wide skirts and a white apron, a crook held in one tiny porcelain hand. "She gave me this. Generous woman, but she said she had so much—maybe that was a sign, then? Isn't that what they say? People up and give things away? Divest themselves?" She put the shepherdess into my hands, being careful to avoid cracking the crook. The little statue was cold and heavy with a vapid expression on its face, as if she were playacting at being this bucolic lassie and was bored with the performance.

It didn't belong in this room, and in truth, I couldn't think of a room I'd like where it might belong. Luckily, Sally didn't seem to expect me to say anything about it.

"Person thinking about suicide starts giving things away," she said, retrieving the shepherdess and carefully putting it back on a knickknack shelf in the corner. "But these—she gave things to other neighbors, too—were such . . . well, they weren't personal things. She certainly had personal treasures she adored, and she delighted in showing them to us: little paintings and figurines and things she'd had passed down from her grandma. But she didn't give those away, far as I know, and that's what I would have considered a sign—important, valuable, personal things, wouldn't you? So how do you tell a gift of friendship from a cry for help? Should I have known? Did I miss it altogether?" She refilled her wineglass and raised an eyebrow, held the bottle at the ready to do the same for mine. I smiled and shook my head. "I'm still fine," I said.

I wondered if she was this garrulous when not sipping wine. "As far as I can tell, nobody saw any signs indicating that serious a depression," I said. "You really shouldn't blame yourself for whatever—"

"I tried, you know." She sighed from deep within her own narrative, and the best I could do was to simply go along and understand that nothing worthwhile would come of this. I hadn't expected to learn anything, anyway. This visit was a formality. The whole so-called investigation was.

"She was a woman who liked having a man in her life," Sally said. "You know she was married a whole lot of times?" She shook her head in incredulity.

I nodded.

"Well, I valued our friendship and I think she did, too, and I'm not sure I would have thought of it on my own—there are so few available men around for women our age, anyway, and I'm one who is completely happy with her own company and so the idea didn't pop right into my brain. But one night, we were having coffee after the movie—decaf really, at our age—and my cousin's brother-in-law walked in—former brother-in-law because my cousin's sister passed on, and he's a widower, too, poor soul, lives with his sister, who's a widow—and he saw me and said hello. And then, the next morning, he phoned me and asked about my 'companion,' who'd obviously impressed him. So that's how I played cupid, or matchmaker."

"They went out, then?" I asked.

"Ooooh, yes," she said with semi-drunk exaggeration. "Ooooh, yes indeed."

"The date," I said carefully. "How did it go? When was that? How was your matchmaking?"

She rolled her eyes. "It was nothing short of a catastrophe!"

Things were finally interesting. "Oh my," I said in the mildest voice I could master. "What happened?"

She shook her head, her mouth pursed. "What didn't? She wasn't quite ready when he arrived, and he's a bit of a priss, I'm afraid. A man lives alone for a long time, and he hadn't married until he was fifty-one, a confirmed bachelor, and oh, how happy my cousin's family was that their daughter had finally found somebody! I always wonder how that marriage went, when he finally took the plunge. He wasn't the easiest—but then, neither was she, and then poof! Over within two years!"

"You're not suggesting that . . . well, that somebody helped it end sooner than it might have?"

"What?" She blinked. "Oh! Oh my, no! She got some weird virus, and an infection and—no, no. I didn't mean to suggest that at all!" She looked slightly suspicious of me now.

I nodded and smiled. She forgave me and resumed her wandering interminable narrative.

"And nowadays, he and his sister just rattle around a big house and I don't think they speak to each other all that much and he's just not used to—to going with the flow, you know what I mean? People get older and get stuck in their ways. Women, too. Probably has happened even to me!" She laughed incredulously, checked the level of the wine in the bottle, and excused herself, returning quickly with an opener and a new bottle.

So much for that glimmer of an actual potential murderer.

"But that's not all," Sally said, her glass refreshed, her enthusiasm unquenched along with her thirst. "He took her to a seafood restaurant. A good place, but she must have eaten something that didn't agree with her—that can happen, even in the best of places—but all the same, what could put more of a damper on things than that? I mean she didn't throw up on him or anything, but she came close; she was queasy, and he thought she was making it up, just to avoid him when he tried, well, you know. What men try."

"Did they . . . did, um—I can't believe I forgot his name!" I said.

"Gregory's?"

"Right. I am so bad with names," I said briskly before she remembered that she'd never mentioned it. "I meet people and zip! Their names are out of my head."

"You know Gregory McIntyre?"

"Not well," I said, "but I'm bad with everybody's names." I was sad that she seemed to have slipped beyond a clear memory of what she'd said and hadn't said before I could get anything solid from her. I checked the time. Fifteen minutes before I was meeting Sasha, so I might as well plug on. "About when was this catastrophe of a date?" I asked.

She sighed, and wrinkled her forehead. "You want a specific date? Like on those cop shows?"

"Not necessarily. As close as you can get, though. Summer? Near Thanksgiving? Or Labor Day?"

More forehead gymnastics. Then a big smile. "Right around Halloween, because Gregory came to visit me and I still had the pumpkin outside, but it was getting mushy-faced, and that's when I heard about the being-sick business and all." She sat back on her sofa, and looked as if she'd just conquered a huge impediment.

"So did Phoebe and Gregory try a second time? When maybe she wouldn't have an upset stomach?"

"I think so. I know he wanted to. In fact, he never used to visit me, and I thought he came over so as to be on her street, you know what I mean? Maybe just happen to drop in?" She frowned. "I think in fact he phoned from here and maybe they made a plan but then she . . . I don't know if it actually . . . Why can't I remember? She was busy, I think that's what she told him first, and you know, that wasn't necessarily an excuse. That woman was always on the go. Had a job, of course, and we all know that owning a business is the worst kind of thing for having free time. I know because my late husband owned his business and . . ." She may have noticed my expression. She cleared her throat, and pushed herself back on track. "Gregory wasn't her only gentleman caller, and then there were the women, too, or at least one woman I saw. That one nearly ran me over! Came screeching into the street, and if a car can be angry, that one was. And she just screeched to a halt, banged the door shut, and stomped into Phoebe's house."

"Do you remember anything about her?"

"Red hair. Long, straight red hair completely inappropriate for a woman her age, know what I mean?"

I did, and I knew to whose head that long red hair was attached.

"There's a time and place for everything, and middle age isn't the time to have hair down to the rear end like a teenager. Skirt was too short and her high heels nearly sank into the grass by the curb. That's all I remember, I was almost in shock with nearly being killed by her, and she didn't even look at me or apologize or anything. I never did find out who she was, because the next thing I hear is about poor Phoebe."

"Wait—do you know which day you saw this redhead with the big car?"

Sally laughed. "You're bad with names, and me? Rotten with numbers, and that includes dates." She shrugged. "I have no idea."

I nodded, gave up on that tack. "So we don't know if Phoebe and Gregory ever arranged a second date."

Sally shook her head. "I worry about the whole situation, about that one terrible evening, and worry that maybe she set too much stock by it. Pinned too many hopes on Gregory. And then, when it was such a disappointment, especially since she herself was the cause of the date's fizzle, so to speak, not that she could help being sick. I'm not saying that, but maybe it set her off, made her so depressed—"

"But you said he wasn't the only man in her life."

"Kids don't count."

"What are you saying? Her son visited her?"

She shook her head.

"Little children?"

"Jus' an expression. Too young to be anything serious. I think. Not that I knew who or anything much."

I wondered how Sally filled her long, solo evenings. Mondays she went to her daughter's house, but there were six other nights in a week. She said she was content with her own company, but I feared she was more content with a wine bottle as companion.

"You know, I'm old-fashioned. Once I was a widow, I stayed a widow, so don't listen to me! But I really hoped that Gregory . . . and maybe they did get to have another date—nobody tells me much unless I ask. And I did ask, but I don't think Gregory gave me a straight answer." She wrinkled her brow again, looking confused and disoriented, perhaps surprised that her memories weren't crisp and sharp.

"Does Gregory live in the neighborhood?"

She shook her head. "In Cherry Hill, with his sister, in this house that is much too big for them." She shook her head again.

"Do you happen to have a phone number for him?"

She looked surprised by the request, then took a moment to think it through, and nodded, standing rather unsteadily and saying, "I'll get it."

"If you tell me where . . ." I began, but she shook her head again, and wove her way into the dining room.

Gregory's second date could have been that final night. He wouldn't have been ready to tell Sally he'd been there. But then, Phoebe's visitor could have been her furious business partner, whose red hair had been long enough to put up into an elaborate French braid the day of the memorial service. Or one of her inappropriately young dates. Who were they—if indeed there were plural young men—and where did she find them?

And why the devil did she want to find men online if she was already overloaded with them?

"Still and all, fate stepped in, didn't it?" Sally said, returning with a cracked and battered address book, which she handed to me.

I didn't know what she was talking about.

"One way or another, they were simply not meant to be." She sat back down, although it wasn't quite a matter of seating herself as much as it was allowing herself to descend onto the sofa pillow.

"I only meant to make everybody happy," she said with her whiny and sentimental undertone growing stronger by the second. I flipped through the book to the "Mc"s and copied Gregory's address and phone number.

"The woman killed herself! I didn't exactly make her happy, did I?" Once again, the slightly puzzled, worried expression. "I really liked her, too."

"You can't blame yourself if she was depressed, or if the man you fixed her up with didn't turn out to be Prince Charming."

She sighed and seemed to have run out of words and steam. I checked my watch. "I'm so sorry! I've been keeping you, and I only meant to stay a minute. You're too good of a hostess. Thanks so much for the wine, and for the address." I put the book on the coffee table. "I nearly forgot I have another appointment in two minutes."

"Only tried to make her happy," she repeated.

I showed myself out and crossed the street to Phoebe's house. The cold air was a shock at first, but it cleared my head, and I thought how silly it was to be circling around the idea of this pathetically-rigid-sounding blind date suddenly murdering Phoebe. Drugging her wine—to what purpose? Or looking for whatever Sally considered a "kid" visitor. Or trying to believe that Merilee would screech up to a house in which she was about to commit a very low-key kind of murder.

Nobody had murdered Phoebe.

I felt a little better, as if I'd finally been allowed to put down an unwieldy and heavy piece of luggage.

Sasha's car pulled up as I reached the house.

"Perfect timing," I said, my breath a frosty fog. Sasha shivered while she unlocked the front door.

"No Dumpsters yet, at least," she said. "But I thought she'd be here. I thought we agreed. . . ."

"I love you, dear friend, but you do have a tendency to overstate things. Nobody's talking Dumpsters. She isn't rebuilding the house, just removing excess items and sprucing the place up. So probably, there will be a truck or two taking things to Goodwill. You have to admit, there is too much stuff in this house. I for one am glad that somebody else is going to do the scut work of making the place presentable. That way I don't have to volunteer to be a good friend and help you with it. Don't make the situation out to be so dire."

"She's supposed to be here. We have an appointment."

I looked at my watch. "You're five minutes early. Cut her some slack. She's probably stuck in traffic."

Sasha grumbled as she opened the door and entered. Then her voice became an angry shout. "It looks worse than ever!"

I was ready to suggest that maybe Toy had been playing with ideas, tentatively rearranging a few things, but then I glimpsed the room, and the words died in my throat.

It *was* worse than ever. Much worse. We hadn't left tables turned over, lampshades hanging crazily from broken stands. We hadn't pulled out cabinet doors and buffet-table drawers and left them open.

Neither would Toy have done that.

I felt a chill much more extreme than I'd felt outside. "Sasha," I whispered, "Sasha, I think—"

"Don't think," she said from the dining room. "Come here."

I did.

Toy lay the way her namesake might, when it was broken, head twisted in an unnatural direction, arms splayed, booted feet pointing outwards.

Except, of course, real toys don't bleed.

Or die.

Ten

"Get out of the house," I whispered.

Sasha stood there, paralyzed, staring at Toy's small body, which lay like a marionette's might, arms and head at the wrong angle. Then Sasha bent over and touched her at the neck, where the pulse should be, and she had the same results I'd had one minute earlier. Nothing. No pulse. No life.

"Sasha! Out!" I said, pulling at her sleeve. "Whoever—there might still—out!"

She stood up but remained speechless. I felt like a tugboat, leading a steamship into safe harbor.

Outside, shivering, I pulled out my cell and dialed nine-one-one.

"She's dead," Sasha whispered.

"I think so," I said.

"She's still warm," she said in a hushed voice. "Still warm. That means—"

"Yes. That's one more reason to be out of the house."

"I'm freezing."

"Yes, but this just happened and—"

"She looked so . . ."

I nodded, unable to find the right words any more than Sasha was. And I knew we were both thinking the irrational but irresistible thought: But I just saw her last night and she was fine. Such a sudden, unexpected, irrevocable cancellation of what we so take for granted needed those denials. Surely if I saw her last night and she was animate, this couldn't have happened to her in the interim.

Surely if Sasha arrived ready to do battle with Toy about possessions and priorities, then Toy could not be dead, violently, abruptly, dead on the very floor of the house under dispute.

"In Phoebe's house!" Sasha looked at me and bit at her upper lip. I again knew what she was thinking before she said it. "Because . . . this—it's too much, the same house. This must have some connection to Phoebe."

I didn't want to allow that idea back into my head. I'd resolved the issue of Phoebe's death fifteen minutes earlier.

"Two dead women in this one house. This is a quiet neighborhood. This doesn't happen. This doesn't happen in neighborhoods that *aren't* this quiet."

I agreed, but I didn't want to think past that, to what that meant, so I waited as patiently as I could for the police to arrive, and luckily, it was a blessedly brief time.

They were all business, moving into the house at the ready, searching it thoroughly, finding nobody on the premises except poor, broken Toy. After checking the carpet for whatever they check it for, they allowed us back in and kept us standing close to the front window, an area that looked relatively untouched, while a square-headed, burly man who identified himself as "Collins" asked us questions as his fellow officers dusted and photographed the area, moving in and out the front door.

We explained who Toy was, and luckily Sasha still had her business card, as I'd forgotten her last name and the name of her company. We explained what staging was, and who had hired Toy, and why we didn't know much about her, and how we'd already removed sentimental objects.

I say "we" said all that, and we did, but I did most of the talking because Sasha was in some other place. Not quite in a state of shock, but unable to truly be present. Her mind had shut down on the scene, and words came only with great difficulty.

And so I also said, with Sasha nodding and adding the occasional word, that no, we didn't have any idea who might have done this, or why.

Sasha tried again to plead the case for Phoebe's having been murdered. "Don't you see?" she asked. "Too much for coincidence, don't you see?"

I took over, filling in the many blanks she'd left, but it didn't matter.

"All in good time," Officer Collins said in the most patronizing tone possible. He wanted to talk about Toy Rasmussen. She had definitely been murdered. He did not want to cater to a freaked-out witness's half-baked theories about a death that had already been determined to be a suicide. "I assure you, we'll look at everything that's germane to this investigation."

He didn't have to say that Phoebe was not germane.

I could see how mistakes geometrically expand and build upon themselves. Nobody—including me, including Mackenzie—would listen to Sasha's convictions the first time. We humored her rather than believed her. So Phoebe's death had been officially "solved." Now she was a closed and tidily disposed of non-case that would not therefore be relevant to this new occurrence.

"Why were you here if you hired her to clean out the house?"

Collins asked. I was pretty sure it was the second or third time for that same question.

"We hadn't officially signed anything. I didn't know the price or her plans. She was going to stop in during the day and decide whether anything major—like painting or whatever—was necessary, and how much of the furniture would stay. That kind of thing. We were going to talk it over this evening. Right about now, in fact."

"What was your precise relationship to the deceased owner of this house?" he asked—definitely again.

Sasha had to repeat her unorthodox family history and what part Phoebe had played in it. "She was my stepmother for a few years. I lived with her and my father. My mother was married to a Norwegian at the time. I didn't want to move to Oslo."

"How is it, do you think, that you came to be the person who stumbled upon both of these women's deaths?"

Sasha was agape, shaking her head in disbelief. "You can't think—please!"

"Officer," I said, "we didn't harm this woman. We came here and found her and phoned you. Would we do this if we'd had anything to do with the crime?"

His look and his silence made it clear that my question was not worth answering.

I could see intricately worked criminal machinations on our part playing through his mind. We'd murdered her, then gone away, then returned and phoned the police, hoping it would make us appear innocent. And what the devil—maybe he would find out that the first woman was murdered as well, and pin both on Sasha, the demon of 570 Hutchinson Court. A serial killer for anyone unwise enough to come into or own this house.

Collins wasn't going to let us pull this fast one on him.

Because of Toy's fate, I now believed Sasha's theory about Phoebe's death, but that gave us two inexplicable deaths. The living and dining rooms had been trashed. What was somebody looking for? What could somebody want?

And which of those visitors, those semi-known outsiders, would know about Phoebe's possessions—the one or ones worth this horrifying outcome? I certainly didn't. Sasha didn't.

I spoke out of turn again, but it was so clear what must have happened that I couldn't understand why Collins wasn't operating under this theory. "It seems to me that somebody came here thinking the house was vacant, and wanted to rob it. And they interrupted Toy, whose presence couldn't have been anticipated."

"Where were you the past two hours?" he asked. "You first," he said to Sasha, showing how much he cared about how anything seemed to me.

Sasha explained her job, the corporate client she'd been with earlier. She named the company, its CEO, and much more than Collins seemed to welcome. "They'll tell you I didn't leave till four-thirty-five," she said.

"How can you be so precise about the time?" he asked, a touch of scorn underlying his words.

"I checked it. Obsessively. I was running late. I was going to keep my friend waiting."

"Your friend Toy?"

"My friend Amanda," she said with great precision, pointing at me in case he was as stupid as he seemed. "Amanda didn't have a key to the house, and it's cold out."

"How did you know that Toy wouldn't be able to let her in?"

Sasha's mouth opened in surprise, then worry. She looked as if she now doubted herself, and I had a bad moment when I feared that she had no answer for him, but I was wrong. "I . . . I didn't, but I wasn't sure Toy would still be here then. She was supposed to be, but I don't know her well enough to know how reliable she is."

He scratched his head. "So I don't get this part. How long's the owner—this Phoebe Ennis—been dead?"

"Three weeks," Sasha said. "Just about."

"And who's lived in the house since then?"

"Nobody."

He grinned, an unhappy expression that suggested we'd both just fallen into his diabolically clever trap. "So how come, it just happens by coincidence that the same day you are both here in the neighborhood, plus this lady, this stager, after all those weeks when nobody was here, that somebody decides to burglarize the place—or make it look that way?"

Was that actually a question?

"You know anything about her insurance?" he asked Sasha, ignoring me.

She shook her head. And then she looked directly at him, allowing her irritation to register. "Why would this help any insurance claim? And who would it help?"

"The people who'll inherit from her." He turned to me. "Are you also involved in this woman's will? I'll find it out, so no reason to play around with the truth, in case that idea crossed your mind."

I wanted to shake him, or be like one of those women in old films who slap men's faces. They always seemed to get away with it and, though it always surprised me, I could now feel how satisfying it could be in the right situation. Instead, I swallowed my growing anger, and shook my head. "Only a friend. And Sasha is right. I didn't have a key, so I guess my whereabouts are irrelevant since I could have been anywhere but inside this house."

But I suddenly felt sick to my stomach. The words: "Are you also involved in this woman's will?" echoed in my head, and I could see myself—see the imaginary Ruby Osgood blinking her eyelashes and talking about all the money her godmother Phoebe had left her in her will.

Had I goaded Marc Wilkins into coming here to find proof that Phoebe had robbed him?

Collins was looking at me with a *gotcha!* smirk. "There are such things as having the person inside the house open the door," he said.

"What?" I had completely lost the thread.

"Not having a key. So what? Where were you? Outside shivering for how long?"

"Barely any time. Sasha wasn't late. I was visiting with a neighbor before that."

"Oh, yes? Which neighbor?"

"She's an investigator!" Sasha said before I could think to stop her.

He looked suddenly alert and annoyed.

"I work at a P.I. firm," I explained. "I'm training. Sasha asked me to see what I could find out."

"About Phoebe's death," Sasha added emphatically.

I nodded.

"This neighbor?" he asked.

"She lives up and across the street. Sally Molinari. I don't know the address, but it's the house with yellow shutters." I thought about Sally's intense relationship with her wine cellar, and wondered if she'd even remember my visit, when the police checked my story. And if she did, I was in trouble, since she thought I was working with a law firm about Phoebe's inheritance.

I was one great investigator. While I was sitting across the street, somebody, possibly somebody I'd goaded into doing it, was in this house, murdering Toy.

"How'd you get here?" Collins asked me.

It seemed a stupid and obvious question. "I drove. My car's outside Sally's house. A VW bug."

He frowned. Maybe he didn't approve of my having such a relic of a car. "You drove separately, correct?" he asked Sasha, who nodded. "Alone?" he asked.

She nodded again.

"Then how did she"—his head inclined toward the dining room—"get here?"

"I don't know," I answered. "She had a little sports car last

night." I thought back, tried to remember looking through the
open door, down to the street. "A BMW, I think, but I'm not
sure."

"Where is it?" he asked.

I realized that it hadn't been in the driveway or on the street.
That's why we'd assumed nobody was there. Collins had asked a
good question.

He waited.

"Maybe somebody dropped her off," Sasha said. "Somebody
was going to have to haul things away. Somebody with a truck, or
a big car. Maybe they'll come to pick her up. Or else they were
the one who . . ." She let the obvious idea drift off.

He called someone over and handed him Toy's business card,
and sent him off to call her office and coworkers, see where they
were and where they had been. And then he turned back to us. I
was beyond uncomfortable by now, standing near the front door.
The house hadn't been sufficiently insulated, and I kept my coat
on to protect against the chill coming off the window next to the
door—the inverse twin of the window through which Ramona
Fulgham had watched me.

Ramona! "There's a woman next door," I said. "She watches
the comings and goings here. She'd probably know if a truck was
here, or whatever. Whoever. You need to talk to her."

Whoops. I had overstepped my bounds with the "need to"
and his expression showed it. He didn't "need" to do anything he
didn't want to do, and he did need me to understand that.

"We're already on that," he said after he'd silently made his
point. "It's what we do. Question potential witnesses." He looked
as if he was stifling a yawn. We bored him to tears.

I tried to ignore him and, instead, once again looked at what
had been touched, dislodged, and overturned, hoping to find a
theme, an idea the intruder was pursuing. I couldn't find one. I
knew, from yesterday's inventory, that there was nothing of particular value in either room, at least, not by any means I knew to

set value on objects. Sasha had taken the silver with the "B" monogram. "I can use it. It's my initial, after all," she'd said. But other than that, any valuations Phoebe or Sasha put upon those treasures were not relevant to what the market would say.

The officer who'd been delegated to make the phone call came back in and spoke to our guy in a low voice. My eavesdropping powers didn't work as well as they normally did, or cops were better at being surreptitious than high school students. I couldn't catch what he whispered behind his hand.

The officer turned to us. "She drove the BMW here," he said, peering at each of us in turn, as if he'd catch us in our bald-faced lies about this murder. "Where is it?"

"The murderer must have taken it away," I said.

He frowned. "How did that person get here, then?"

We were both silent. More than one person had been involved. Someone to either drop off the killer, or someone to steal Toy's car while the other drove his own away.

A second officer came over to whisper, turning his back to us and making himself inaudible.

Collins nodded, sighed, and when his fellow officer was gone, he looked at us with no expression and asked, "Which of you drives the SUV?"

"As I said, my VW is across the street," I muttered.

"I drive a Prius," Sasha said, her scorn for SUVs audible though not spoken.

I expected a lecture on buying American, perhaps even incarceration for not doing so, but Collins just sighed again and let the matter drop.

A person didn't need to be Sherlock to figure out why there was interest in an SUV. I was sure Ramona would have been more than happy to describe every movement in and out of this house to the policeman. "Not that I was watching, you know," she'd say between details. So somebody with an SUV had been there at some point in the day. Could be a person with whom Toy worked. Could be half the populace. I never knew why anybody, driving in the flat, temperate city of Philadelphia required four-wheel drive and a massive carriage. But they did. Even Philly Prep parents were gifting their children with these behemoths, because, they said, they were "safer." Perhaps they were, for their drivers, but when I was in my ancient VW, low to the ground, surrounded by dinosaurs that blocked my view of signs and lights and on-coming dangers, they certainly made my driving more hazardous.

Who was it? For a moment, I was glad to think it was some-body with whom Toy had worked. But almost instantly, I realized that wasn't probable if the two deaths were connected, and I had to let the thought back in, had to admit and believe that they had to be.

"So," Collins said after yet another conference, this time with a policewoman. "A question: You said the deceased was coming here to make a plan for what would stay and what wouldn't, cor-rect?"

We nodded.

"And she would do this at her convenience, then meet up with you about now. Correct?"

More nods.

"So I take it you didn't leave the house unlocked overnight and into the next day. Correct?"

I didn't bother to nod this time. He didn't need such obvious confirmation, and my head was too full of a sense of where this was going to be bothered with appeasing him.

"So it was locked, then. Correct?"

"Yes," Sasha said, "but what do you want to know?"

"You gave her a key."

Sasha nodded.

"Where is it?"

That was where I'd feared he was going, and I had no answer. Except that whoever had tried to rob the house and had surprised Toy and wound up killing her now had the key.

He hadn't gotten what he wanted and despite two casualties, he was coming back again. Or he had gotten whatever it was, but wanted access to more.

I was surrounded by the police, but I'd never felt as vulnerable as I did right then. I wanted nothing so much as to be home.

Eleven

"Collins was a creep," I told Mackenzie. "And stupid. Why behave as if you suspect Sasha or me? There was no logical reason to do that. It was all about making him feel all-powerful and wise. There's nothing more pathetic than a slow-thinking man pretending to be a whiz kid."

"Now, look," Mackenzie said. "He has to go through certain procedures, and in reality, there could be reason to suspect Sasha if you didn't know her."

"Why? She's going to inherit the stuff. Dennis wants none of it. Why trash the place and why kill somebody you just hired?"

He shrugged and sputtered, trying to justify Collins's behavior. No longer a cop, Mackenzie nonetheless was still overly sensitive to insults against the men in blue. That, at least, was how I interpreted some of his reactions. He felt he was simply being sensitive to the realities of the job. He was closer to the truth of it than I was, but that didn't make me any more eager to hear his defense of Officer Collins. I wanted to stay angry with Collins's stupidity and rudeness, and I didn't want that anger balanced out by my husband's rational thoughts. I tuned him out.

"Somebody drove an SUV to the house today," I said.

"He told you that?"

"Not exactly, but he was so inept, it was obvious the busy-body next door had said so."

"It could be anybody, mean anything. I'm sure people she worked with drove trucks or SUVs so they could carry whatever they needed for the houses. Or cart away things. Or it might have had nothing to do with that house."

"I suspect that Ramona—the neighbor—mentioned it be-cause she saw its driver go into the house."

"Suspect, suspect," he said in a barely audible voice.

I shrugged. "You have to admit—or at least I do—that the two deaths now seem linked, and if so, it's more likely to me now that Phoebe was murdered."

"Wait! I thought those high heels in the tush had convinced you days ago."

"I will ignore the dig," I said.

He grinned. "She must have ignored it, too."

"May we move on? If Phoebe was murdered, would Toy be involved in that? No matter how desperate you are for clients, you don't drug them to death in order to get a job staging their house."

"So what do you suggest? That we pull in SUV drivers?"

"Merilee drives one. Maybe Marc does, too."

"So does half the metropolitan area's population."

I didn't have any ideas how to use the SUV, and I knew the existence of a suspicious SUV was only what I thought had been discussed between the cop, the invisible Ramona, and Officer

Collins. "How about this? Somebody stole Toy's BMW. Why would a murderer do that?"

Mackenzie lifted one eyebrow. He was interested, or at least half interested. "Where was his own transportation? Was that the SUV? I take it that it wasn't in front of the house when you arrived."

I shook my head.

"So he had help, is that what you're saying?"

"It's the only thing that makes sense. And another thing— the one bright point Collins made was why anybody would choose today to enter and rob the house since it's been unoccupied for three weeks."

"For sale sign up yet?"

"Not yet. Not until it's 'staged.' " I realized what I'd said. "Well, I guess that isn't going to happen."

"Maybe they'd been in it a lot of times since Phoebe died. Only today, somebody else was there."

Of course. I pondered that. Mackenzie was silent, looking off at the far wall. I realized that our conversation, since I'd come home, had been completely one-sided. Stumbling upon a murder scene probably trumps most other domestic news, but still and all, Mackenzie had a bundle of troubles on his shoulders, and he deserved more consideration.

His day had not been at all good. "Almost feels as if there's a vendetta out for Louisiana," he said. "You aren't going to believe this, but a tornado hit them earlier today."

I hadn't seen the news and the car radio, never great, was on the fritz. "Are they—" He nodded. "Did it . . . ?" Mackenzie's father had owned a small hardware store for decades before the hurricane. He'd been struggling against the big-box chain stores, but he had a good reputation and a loyal clientele, all of whom would be more than happy to deal with him now—if only he still had a store. But it was half submerged in water and unsalvageable. So with a little help from his friends, and after lengthy, frustrating negotiations with the relevant government bodies, he'd relocated and begun the rebuilding process. When last I heard, the frame of the new place was up and the Mackenzie family spirits were on the rise. "The store?" I finally squeaked out. "Tell me no."

But he nodded instead. "The winds." Then he shook his head. "An' a school that was goin' up, too. None of the schools nearby are even open yet."

The school Philly Prep was going to adopt next semester was one of those still closed. There was no habitable building and its students were scattered, living in several states, waiting to come back to homes that no longer existed. Our funds would be a drop in the bucket—and buckets and drops were not what Louisiana needed these days.

"It's December," he said. "Hard to believe that much time's gone and nothing's happening, or so far from enough is happening, and hurricane season will start again and nothing to come home to, unless you're a fish."

A goodly amount of acreage that had been near water was now under it. Lots of new swamps. Lots of former neighbors with nowhere to build or start over. "It's makin' some of the people who stayed, who are helping, reconsider. Can't blame them. What are their kids going to do? How will they catch up? How's my dad ever gettin' back on his feet? Mom's been doing relief work, whatever she can find that helps anybody. There's precious little she can do for her own self, though. I've never heard them sound so without hope."

I'd never heard him sound that way, either.

"It is supposedly impossible for people to exist in a crisis state for long without their going insane," he said. "I learned that in Psych I a long time ago. I think of it twenty times a day now."

I took his hand and held on tight, and hoped that communicated thick volumes' worth of words. Not only was his family in a long-term crisis, but so was he. It was impossible to stay this way much longer. The man was overstressed, physically and emotionally.

He took a deep breath and smiled, easing the tightness around my heart a bit. "Ah," he said. "All it takes is a world-class, history-book-making catastrophe and its unending aftermath to make you forget to nag me."

"I never do!"

"You do, you do."

He'd been right about people not being able to endure continuous stress. *He'd* gone insane. Nag? Me? "About what? Name one thing—anything! I can't even think of anything you do or don't do that would require nagging."

"If I hadn't softened you up with a reminder of what my parents and siblings are going through"—he held up his free hand to stop the protests already shaping on my lips—"you'd sure as I'm sitting here have already asked me what I'd been doing about Phoebe's case. Am I right?"

"I don't know. Phoebe's case looks completely different now."

"That's nitpicking. Would you or wouldn't you have asked? Even if it had changed and we had to look at all new things."

"Asking a question is not nagging!"

"That's the Amanda variation of nagging," he said softly. "It's an elegant subset of the art of nagging, but it's nagging all the same."

I took a deep breath. "In that case, forget about Louisiana. Forget your ongoing family tragedies! What the devil have you done about Phoebe's case? Anything? No? I didn't think so! I've asked and I've asked and do you ever do what you say you will? Or do you only—"

His eyes were wide open.

I laughed. "That, my dear, is nagging," I said. "I must say it was fun. But I hope you see the difference. I merely ask questions. Fishwives nag. And I didn't even ask questions today because I am compassionate and understanding, and I know you're too busy between school and your family—"

"And Ozzie's."

"And Ozzie's."

"Ah, but I did work on it," he said. "And I found out something real interestin'. And because you were so considerate—"

"And didn't nag. Not today or ever."

"And because you never nag, here it is: Dennis didn't leave town Sunday."

"That plane?"

"No plane to catch, no rush. Far as I know, he's still here."

"How do you know that?"

"You asked me to check up on him so, of course, I did." He gave a golly-gee-whiz shrug and smiled.

It was difficult resisting that smile—or any of his smiles— and it was such a joy to see it because it appeared less often since the hurricane, but I tried to keep a serious business talk.

"Okay," he said. "I was checking his credit rating, which isn't stellar. The man does not have a head for business. I was going over his recent purchases and to my surprise, they were made here, in good old Philadelphia, the past three days."

"Did they include a rental car?" I asked quietly.

Mackenzie nodded.

"How soon can you find out what kind?" I whispered, as if someone might have been eavesdropping.

He winked. "But you just mentioned that Merilee drives one, too."

"But what would Merilee have to do with Toy?"

"That's what sleuthin's all about, darlin'. Who knows how they're connected. That's for you to find out."

"Maybe there was no connection with Toy in the first place," I said slowly. "Maybe the link was with whatever Merilee might have been searching for in the house. Toy was just in the way."

"There you go. That's as good a thought as any."

The blip of excitement I'd felt dissipated. "Even if it's a real thing, it's all we have, and it's so little," I said. "It's tissue thin."

Another cosmic Mackenzie shrug, followed by a wink. "Don't knock tissue," he said. "If that's all you've got holding you up, then it only means you have to build layers of it, pack it tight, and then tread gently. It doesn't mean you can't tread at all."

I wanted to tell him that I loved him, but he was going to have to peddle his folksy wisdom elsewhere. I was a Philadelphia girl. Give me good, solid cynicism any day. You'd think he'd have known it and swallowed the pitiable homily before he said it.

But I didn't say any of that, and as far as I could tell, that was my greatest accomplishment for that day.

Twelve

I resorted to list-making, a favorite desperation method of un-tangling my brain. I headed the page: Who Wanted What?
That yielded nothing but question marks.
New page:

Q: What did Phoebe and Toy's death have in common?
A: Phoebe's house as their setting.

Q: Why would somebody return?
A: To get more.

Q: Of what?
A:

Q: What did he get the first time?

A: Who knows? When Sasha had found Phoebe, she'd had no handle on what might be missing, if anything was. And maybe, as Mackenzie had suggested, the thief had been back several times since, not just today.

Q: What is the point of these questions?
Had anybody looked for signs of a break-in before today? I couldn't think why they might have, so the house could have been used as somebody's personal department store for a while now.
But of what? Why? Sasha hadn't noticed anything missing the night she'd found Phoebe dead, and if the two deaths were connected, and this one looked like attempted robbery, then shouldn't the first one look like that, too?
Shouldn't the silver have been taken the first round?
Or between Phoebe's death and this week?

A: There is no point to these questions. They have no answers. They go in circles. They make me weary.

It wasn't a matter of treading lightly, it was a matter of not having any idea where to tread in the first place. I backtracked instead. I'd done a haphazard job of looking into the carton Sasha had given me, and at the laptop for that matter. I'd only just figured out the password, when Toy appeared. It was time to go through everything systematically. It might be an exercise in futility, but I had no better ideas.

The carton held a lot of souvenirs: theater programs and the matchbook covers Sasha had been so excited about, clippings about art openings, invitations to weddings, cocktail parties, and lots of condolence cards the new widow had saved.

I went through that last group, wondering why I was doing so, because even I didn't believe the killer would send a sympathy card. But perhaps it would expand my idea of Phoebe's friends and acquaintances.

Aside from the souvenir papers, there wasn't much. Her stationery—much of it appropriated from hotel rooms—was composed of stamps, 3×5 cards, a bunch of half-empty ballpoint pens, and a small cache of greeting cards waiting for occasions to send them: two expressing sympathy, two birthdays, one happy new baby, one anniversary, and three blanks. Most were too ornate and sentimental for my taste, but they echoed Phoebe's aesthetics.

And from her refrigerator door: three cartoons that involved dogs and cats, a calendar magnet from an aspirin maker, and the clipping about a local taping of *Antiques Roadshow*. Poor Phoebe, but maybe it was for the best that she hadn't been able to drag her beloved objects into the glare of the experts' scrutiny. Aside from that, there were a few business cards: one from a manicure salon offering special prices for the new year, another from some place named "Extraordinaire!" that sold "fine objects." An image of her home flashed through my mind—the overabundance of "fine objects." The card seemed to signify that even too much wasn't enough, that she was out scouting for more. I found as well a two pounds for the price of one coupon for spaghetti and a promised discount for driveway resurfacing.

A lot of nothing. I opened the laptop and looked at the icons again. I'd only gone through that one "shopping" file in her word processing program, but hadn't looked at her e-mails, and it was time to check out the shortcut icons to three dating programs.

"Need help?" Mackenzie asked. "You've been sighing so much, I thought we were having a windstorm."

My impulse is always to refuse an offer of help, and I can defend that a dozen ways, at least some of which explanations are the truth. But I was spinning wheels, and the more quickly I could get through this whole business, the better, so I stifled the urge to explain why I didn't need any assistance whatsoever or to consider how squeezed Mackenzie's time was and how wrong it was to bother him with this.

I thanked him and accepted his offer.

"What do you know about online dating?" I asked. He pulled a chair close to mine, and watched as I reopened the first of the matchmaking sites.

"Lots," he said. "An' this is good. She opted to automatically sign on."

"And that's good because?" I clicked the link.

"Because she told them to save her password, we can see who she's been talking with—or, at least, the fake names she's been in contact with. We couldn't do that otherwise without a lot of dealing with the sites."

"How do you know so much about this sort of thing?"

With a bemused expression, he said, as if speaking to the computer, not me, "How quickly they forget. Once upon a time, and not so very long ago, I was a homicide detective." Then he turned and spoke to me directly. "Phoebe is not the only dead person who looked for love online."

Phoebe's online meet-a-mate service's "datebook" had messages from a cryptic trio. The first, HM47, said he thought they had a lot in common, judging by her profile, and he was looking forward to meeting her as soon as she got back from London.

"London?" I asked. "She wasn't there. Sasha was."

"Probably a lie she was using to keep anybody from expecting to meet her too soon. A kind of firewall against the impetuous."

"It's dated about a week before she died."

"Could be, could be."

"I hope that forty-seven isn't his age," I said. "She lied about her age and said she was in her forties."

"Must get fairly comic at times when the correspondents meet up."

The second message, from "Sizzler" said, "Your 2 hot! So M I! Why don't we see what spontaneously combusts?"

I hoped Phoebe had not opted to respond to that one.

And finally, a woeful message that should have come with red warning flags attached: "Miserable till you" wrote: "I have been searching forever for my soul mate, saving myself for her, but so far, I've had no luck. But I looked into your eyes in the photo online (wish you hadn't been wearing that hat so I could see more of you) and I finally knew I'd found her. When and where can we meet?" He signed himself just plain "Miserable."

I hadn't been around the block nearly as much as Phoebe, but I knew that the ones who needed to introduce themselves as poor, pitiful me's, the lonely, soulful, nobody-till-you guys, were seldom good news. There was always a reason they'd been lonely for so long. They were, indeed, undoubtedly, miserable.

The other dating programs did not have automatic sign-ins, and I theorized that she'd inspected and bookmarked them for future use. Perhaps for when she had her new, hatless, updated photo from Sasha.

I showed Mackenzie the password that got us into Phoebe's calendar and datebook. I was worried that even if there was something important in it, I wouldn't recognize it. I had only the most cursory acquaintance with Phoebe, and that was mostly memories of two decades ago. I said something to that effect to Mackenzie, and he reminded me that investigators seldom know victims personally, and I should focus on what little I did know.

Phoebe had been a scattered sort of person back when I hung around her household. She'd had many interests, none of which, except the genealogy, lasted long. Record-keeping had not been a strength back then, and it was already obvious that it still wasn't. The "M" on the calendar day she died had shown that people don't change just because they buy a computer. Years ago, Phoebe left unintelligible notes for Sasha in what we'd come to call "Phoebehand" because it so heavily relied on abbreviations and symbols of her own making, including small drawings that were cute but unrecognizable. She always showed up when she said she would, and was mystified when we couldn't understand her messages.

Given that messages here had to be typed out, there were no cunning little people making strange gestures, no objects depicted, no visual puns. But she'd adapted her quirky shorthand to the computer keyboard, and the abbreviations were still there, and still by and large unintelligible to anyone but, presumably, the deceased.

"So where's the PDA?" Mackenzie asked. When he saw my puzzled expression, he said, "This program—it has a handheld part, too. You know. The little gizmo she'd carry with her in her purse."

"*Purse!*" I bent over and pawed through the cartons, in case I'd actually missed seeing something as significant as Phoebe's bag.

I hadn't. "Never got it," I said. Given that most women I know, and certainly I myself, basically carry their lives and brains inside their handbags, I found this incredible, both on Sasha's part and mine. I was sure the missing pocketbook hadn't registered with either of us, and I thought of what would have been in it: money and credit cards, keys, makeup, calendars, address books, phones, receipts, photographs, pens, notebooks—very close to everything that might yield a clue as to what had happened to her. Who had taken it?

My back was to Mackenzie. "Feel free to have any derogatory thoughts you like," I said. "You can even think words like 'inept amateurs'—but please don't say them. I'm saying them to myself."

"I was not even thinkin' them," he said. He had to be lying.

I phoned Sasha. "Phoebe's pocketbook is missing," I said.

"Which one? The woman had a shoe and bag fetish. She had thirty bags at least."

"The one she was using the night she died."

"She wasn't using any. She was in her own house."

"Sasha! The one currently in use. The one in which she kept her wallet and car keys!"

Silence. Then, finally, "That one. I've got it here at my house. Why? Do you need it?" Her voice changed and sounded slightly abashed. "There didn't seem to be anything particularly interesting in it, so I, well, I took it. It's pretty great-looking, actually. Some kind of lizard skin, dyed—"

"I don't care. Keep it, but empty the contents into a paper bag and get them to me as soon as you can, okay?"

"I wish you had a safe drop-off."

There are no doormen in lofts, and while the people in the store on the ground floor were nice enough, I wouldn't feel comfortable asking Sasha to entrust them with something as important and possibly lucrative as Phoebe's pocketbook.

"Tomorrow night?" she asked. "I've got this job I'm trying to finish, and I have a full day, at least, of editing and they want me to help design the layout of the photos and—"

"Okay, if the mountain won't come to Mohammed . . . How about if I come by after school? I'd be there by three-thirty."

"Thanks for calling me a mountain," she grumbled, but so it was agreed.

I returned to the table and the laptop.

"The handheld's going to have the same information as this does," C.K. said. "Might as well give a look right now."

Together we began with the dates at the end of summer and proceeded through the calendar, a month at a time. The datebook showed predictable appointments, albeit in her idiosyncratic shorthand (e.g., "dst" in one place, "hrct" a few days later meant, I hoped, dentist and haircut, in turn). She seemed fond, now and then, of an unnamed treatment ("tmnt") at "spa," though she didn't show a location, so we switched to the electronic address book, but didn't find anything under "Spa."

Back to the calendar, where birthdays were both noted and decipherable because a number in parentheses was typed in next to the initial or initials. There were also many times when only a single initial appeared on a date with no mention of why it was there, let alone who it was. I saw "RaBng" one evening, and after a while, realized it was probably Ramona on the Bingo outing. And another time, "t-hr" seemed to be the day the three neighbors were invited over for tea, either "here" or for an "hour." Maybe both. But unless I already knew about the date, I could make no sense of her notations.

Depressing, daunting, and a waste of time.

However, I did now have the advantage, such as it was, of being able to consider the address book component of the calendar along with the datebook, so we could look at a split screen.

I felt a surge of guilt at wasting Mackenzie's time this way. I could compare notations with names on my own and let him get on with his actual work. "I could do this part myself," I said. "Though it wouldn't be as enjoyable."

"I find honesty very sexy." He pulled his chair closer.

"Let's start with the most logical, important-feeling date. The one the night she died. The 'M.' 'Merilee'?"

"Could be," he said, and wrote it down on a tablet I'd put next to the laptop. "That woman certainly had—or feels she had—reason to be furious with Phoebe. And the searching around would make sense. If she thinks Phoebe embezzled money, she could have been looking for evidence of that, or for the cash itself."

I didn't want to believe Phoebe would have stooped to stealing money from a business she owned, so I focused on the address book side of the screen. "Here, Max Delahunt. Another 'M.' He's one of her exes. He was at the memorial service with his son Lee—Leon, no, Lion—so no 'M' there."

"Could be a nickname, so nobody calls him 'Junior.' Add both of them to the list. And I see here a Sally M."

"The neighbor I interviewed today. She's got a little drinking problem. I'm not sure she could get her act together enough to poison somebody else. And Merilee's husband is Marc. He's furious with Phoebe about the business. "

He nodded.

"And the blind date was named Gregory McIntyre."

Another nod and notation. "Here's a plumber—Mahoney."

"You think her plumber killed her?"

He shrugged. "Maybe he became more than a plumber to her. Remember the modus operandi for that one was moonlight and roses, far as I understood it. Fancy duds, a good bottle of wine. Check out the plumber."

His name was added to the list along with a Susie Moskowitz, "Moms" Whiting, Peter Morris, Morris Peters, Zach Masters, "Moo-Moo" Bedderly, Alphonso "Mike" Carocci, and the mysteriously named "Mighty Joe." And we were not through her address book by a long shot.

"Oh Lordy—there are those people in her online datebook, too. Wasn't one 'M' and numbers?"

"HM47," he said without needing to look at his notes.

I nodded my appreciation of his brain. "You are not just a pretty face," I said. And I remembered one, too: "Miserable. Thank goodness for the obnoxious-sounding 'Sizzler' for not using an 'M' name. And while we're at it, you might as well add yourself to the list," I grumbled.

"You think I killed Phoebe? Why is that?"

"I think your name's Mackenzie, and you're as likely to have offed her as most of the people on that list."

"Except, of course, that I appear nowhere in her address book or datebook—or life. I've never met the woman, which makes me a little weak as a suspect. On the other hand, may I remind you that you are most often referred to as 'Manda'? An' you knew her."

"Point taken, but all the same, this is nuts. What are we supposed to do? Spend the next few years interviewing Phoebe's plumber and Mighty Joe whomever, not to mention Miserable and Max?"

"Well, I think you could use a little bit of logic and begin with, say, Merilee. If nothing else, get a sense of where that whole business was and now is. Would Phoebe's death help anything about the situation?"

"Not her death, but finding the supposedly embezzled funds might. Or even proving she'd done it might make Merilee think that would win her roving husband back. It wouldn't, of course, but I'm only saying she could think it might."

"It might explain tossing the house the second time, too. First time, tidily going through and not finding what she was after. Then returning when she thinks nobody's there. What do you think?"

"Wait a minute—I just remembered. Back in junior high, when she was married to Sasha's dad, Phoebe called her son 'M.L.M.' It stood for 'my little man,' and back then it drove him crazy that she called him even that cryptic abbreviation, because of course people would ask what it meant. Sasha and I would taunt him with it at school, and whenever we felt like it. I remember because I can still see him shouting, 'My name is Dennis!,' his face all red. I guess we were pretty mean, but that was long ago. He's got to have grown out of going ballistic about something like that."

"Probably. But mothers might cling to a pet name like that, and use it as private shorthand for a date with the offspring." Mackenzie wrote "Dennis" and then underlined the name. "That's quite a list," he said. "You'd think a person's circle of acquaintances would be spread more equitably over the alphabet. Not that I've ever analyzed address books that way before.

"Or have we wandered into some strange geographical slice where everybody needs an 'M' in their name?" C.K.M. himself asked. "Do you ever wonder who'd be on our list of likely suspects if, say, we were found dead the way Phoebe was?"

Mackenzie's expression was serious, despite the light in those knock-down blue eyes. "No," I said, and I intended to leave it at that, I wanted to leave it at that, but I felt the words I wasn't going to say filling up the airspace. "That question ranks as the creepiest thing you've ever suggested," I said. "Why would I wonder who among my acquaintances or friends might have a motive for killing me? And thanks for being so diplomatic as to suggest both of us were offed, so that you wouldn't be topping the list of suspects. Why did you ask? Do you know who'd be on your list? Tell me, so I can tell the cops when they ask, you know, instead of saying the usual 'He had no enemies.' "

He shrugged. "It's the kind of thing people like me have thought about. I spent years asking that question after a homicide and nobody ever could think of anybody who'd want the victim dead, as evident as it was that somebody definitely had. Besides, there are a few people currently locked up who might have it in for me. But then, I wouldn't have them listed in my address book, and I wouldn't be setting out wine and cheese for them."

"There was only one glass. Hers."

He raised an eyebrow. "What are you suggesting?"

"She wasn't setting out wine for anybody else. Or her caller was a teetotaler."

"What does it mean or matter if there was only one wineglass by the time Sasha arrived? Is there anybody left alive who has not seen a single TV crime show, read a single mystery? Somebody who wouldn't know to wash and dry his glass? Or just stick it in his pocket and take it with him? Apparently, there was no rush. He—"

"Or she! It was a feminine sort of murder, don't you think? Drugs in your wine?"

"Maybe. But let's focus on Phoebe for a moment," he suggested.

I nodded as he continued, "Unless she or he listened to the answering machine, to Sasha's phone calls while she was en route, he—or she—wouldn't know anybody else was going to show up. So there would be a sense that there was time to wash up, erase all traces, and leave. And, in fact, there was."

"Then, can we assume it was somebody Phoebe would welcome with wine and nibbles?" I asked.

"Was she much of a cook or hostess?"

"Yes. It was part of her grand style, what some might call pretentiousness. She'd go all out with puff pastry and clarified butter and pâté and work in the kitchen all day long. Once or twice, she hired Sasha and me to pass around the platters, and people *ooh*ed and *aah*ed. In junior high, I wasn't overly interested in cocktail party food, though I dearly wanted to get into the cocktails, and hated it that Phoebe policed us even while hostessing. She was worse than my parents about that. And now can I ask you why this matters?"

"Don't know that it does, but the fact is, she had set out pretty mundane things. Smoked almonds and packaged cookies. Kind of a weird combo, actually, and no preparation involved. No imagination. No creativity. What would that mean in her worldview of entertaining?"

"That the visitor is . . . not Mr. Right? Or a first date, a tentative sort of thing. Nothing to scare him off, but also, no desire to lure him in through food. Not that night, anyway. Nobody she wanted to impress."

C.K. considered something privately, then nodded. "Or it could be the neighbor. Doesn't seem the most sophisticated of palates, so why bother?"

"Right. That would make sense. Cookies for her. Or it could be somebody she's no longer sure of, like her partner in a failed business. Maybe she thought they might be able to reach a truce that night, so that would be a surprise, and a good one. But maybe she didn't want to overcommit to that. Or show her hand, her hopes."

"Or maybe it was her partner's enraged husband. Nothing but trouble expected from him, so you meet only the minimum socially acceptable amount of munchies."

This was fun, but I could still see the endless list of people with "M" in their names, and Phoebe's death—and now Toy's brutal murder—remained mysteries. "So where would I start?" I asked. "This list is intimidating."

"Like Alice said, start at the beginning."

"Okay, I'll start with the date Sally arranged, that McIntyre fellow."

"You think she'd refer to him as M?"

I shrugged. "Maybe he called himself Mac for her." I checked the notebook page and phoned him. "I'll make an appointment, check him out tomorrow."

"You want it to be him, don't you?" Mackenzie asked. "Because you don't know him. You don't want to believe anybody you do know could have done it."

It didn't look as if it mattered what I wanted, because after seven rings, I heard a recorded message. "Can't come to the phone right now," a nice-enough male voice said, "but leave a message . . ." All the usual requests and promises. "This is Amanda Pepper," I said, and I gave my cell phone number. "I'm doing some research, and I've been told you could help me on a few points. I'd appreciate it if you could get back to me at your earliest convenience."

Mackenzie looked sympathetic to my frustration—but sympathetic in a deliberate, theatrical way, as if he might soon say "boo-hoo." Then he smiled. "He probably wasn't going to say 'Howdy, yes, I killed Phoebe Ennis,' anyway. So while you wait for a response, you might also want to think about havin' 'M' stand for murder, or motive. Who comes to mind?"

"Merilee," I said immediately.

And one more reason we stayed married is because he didn't add "we roll along," which, I have to admit, played in my head every time I thought of the woman.

Thirteen

Start at the beginning. How wise Alice's advice was, but her theory worked best in Wonderland. In the real world, it left me nowhere. I didn't know the story I had to tell, so how to know where it began?

A school is an excellent place to learn impulse control, as long as you're a teacher. I couldn't phone and say I'd be late, or leave a class to its own devices while I talked with Merilee. I couldn't tell my secretary to hold the calls while I dashed off to find Gregory McIntyre. I had no secretary.

The school had Opal Codd, however, and she greeted me as I walked into the office. She was, as usual, dressed in a blouse buttoned up to the lace-edged neck. Today she was in powder blue, a color that made her seem even more a refugee from a child's picture book.

"Is that your handiwork outside?" I asked her.

"Mine?"

"On the bulletin board?"

"Oh, the pamphlet! Yes. I thought it might do some good. What do you think?"

What did I think of an inspirational pamphlet with an abstract arrangement of playing cards and the words: "Gambling! Gambling? Sure it's fun, but . . ." written in chubby red letters on the cover, and inside, a bullet-point list of the many pitfalls of betting on anything?

I thought it might do good by provoking a great deal of derisive laughter, and they say that laughter is the best medicine. Still, I thought it kind not to say so. "You never know what will touch a teen," I said instead. "But do you think gambling's a big problem? Our problem? You said the card-playing was done off-campus."

She sniffed, prettily, and cocked her head, silently telling me that I was entitled to my—unenlightened—opinion, but . . . "I am not alone in thinking that gambling's not a healthy diversion for young boys. Or for their elders, for that matter," she added. "No matter where it takes place. Or on what. Horses, sports, cards."

"They see it on all those TV shows. I'm sure it doesn't seem like gambling to them, but more like what it is—a game."

She shook her head, the silvery-gray tendrils of hair accentuating her movement. "It's the start of a downhill slide and if nothing else, it's a waste of hard-earned money. That's what I've always told Mr. Codd, not that he paid me any heed." She laughed.

"Is Dr. Havermeyer aware of the situation?" I asked.

"Well, he must be, mustn't he?" she said. "In fact, he can see them in the square from his office window."

I wasn't playing fair with her. She was new and innocent and probably believed that the school's founder and headmaster actually followed his rules. I knew that his only code of ethics was the bottom line, and that meant that he wouldn't willingly rock the boat and possibly topple out a tuition-paying student. And if Griffith Ward, son of not only wealth but celebrity, was in that boat, then an office view of gambling wouldn't matter. Havermeyer would willingly go blind rather than see anything that meant he'd have to take a risk.

Besides, he had a nation filled with poker-loving gamblers to cite as a reason to ignore what was going on. Poker seemed second to baseball as the national pastime these days, positively patriotic.

"Well," Opal said, "I put the pamphlet up because it felt better than doing nothing. We'll see."

I nodded, but perhaps not brightly enough.

"Oh, my!" she said. "I thought I'd cheered you up, but I still see a glum expression! Is this a case of matutolypea?"

"Matu-whato?"

"Now, now—the English teacher! Surely you know what that means! Or are you having a case of the mubble-fubbles?"

Cards weren't her game. Words were. Obscure words that hindered communication. "Honestly," I said. "I don't have a clue for either word."

"You had such a long face, you looked as if you'd gotten up on the wrong side of the bed."

"Which is in itself a puzzling expression. But I digress. I was saying I didn't know what those words meant."

"That's what matutolypea means: getting up on the—"

"Oh," I said. "I get it. But I generally say 'getting up on the wrong side of the bed' when that's what I mean."

"Where's the fun in that?"

"And mubble-fubbles?" I didn't know what it meant but, in fact, it felt as if mumbling and fumbling and fuddled and muttering and muddled had all been compressed and packed into it, and I liked it. Whatever she thought it meant—I had the mubble-fubbles.

"A fit of depression," she said with a big smile.

"Ah. Then no, I don't have the mubble-fubbles, but I like the sound of it. I'm keeping that one."

Her smile looked cartoon-strip wide.

"How did it go?" I asked before I left the room.

"Go? What?" Her eyebrows pulled together above the granny glasses and she shook her head.

"The money-counting with the ninth graders."

"Ahhh. Of course. Splendidly! Our tally was precisely what it should have been, according to their predictions. I'm not sure what you thought I could teach them about bookkeeping. He's a math whiz and she's no slouch herself. And both of them are businesslike and delightful! What a lovely group of students you've got here, and I'm impressed and surprised by the student body's burst of holiday generosity!"

Good. Everybody was happy now. I gathered up my notices and waved good-bye, and didn't stop till I was halfway out the door. "Ms—"

"Opal. Please."

"Opal, why were you surprised by the students' generosity? I mean, today. Why today?"

She blinked, and looked as if, were she a less polite person, she might have told me how far from bright she considered my question. Then she cleared her throat. "Well, it's been months since the hurricane, and grown people—let alone adolescents—just plain forget, get bored, or lose interest in much less time than that. Then, you think we've been doing this for nearly three weeks, and that's enough to bore a young person. But here it is, nearly Christmas, and they open up their hearts and give more than ever. Wouldn't you also be surprised?"

I would indeed have been surprised. Stunned. Dumbfounded. "And this 'burst of generosity' was how recent?" I asked.

"Very," she said with a merry smile and a small laugh. "Like yesterday. All of a sudden, two hundred dollars more than the daily average last week. This jump is pretty significant, wouldn't you say?"

"I certainly would." Margaret and Eddie had been correct. When the money was coming in from each homeroom separately, somebody had intercepted it and siphoned off funds, but I couldn't believe Opal Codd would dream of such an action. Somebody else.

I said nothing more about the sudden burst of generosity. Sweet Mrs. Codd thought the students were angels. Let her hold on to that idea as long as possible. Also, it was easier to ignore what was so evident, to play the game that if I didn't acknowledge a problem, it wouldn't actually exist and I wouldn't feel compelled to do a thing about it. I have learned this loathsome way of "handling" things from my headmaster, so I knew he wouldn't blow any whistles.

Feeling guilty but saying nothing, I managed to leave the office.

Griffith Ward was again holding court near the door. That seemed his spot. I wondered if there were turf wars on our no-campus school. In any case, Griffith owned that corner, and stood in his usual cocky stance in his WWII-bomber jacket. I'd seen the reaction to the jacket days ago—outright envy and enthusiastic claps on the back. He wore it as if he'd earned it shooting down enemy planes, and he wore as well his signature smirk.

I had to retool my thinking. His expression could be described as a benign relaxed smile. Not by me now, but perhaps in the future, when I'd be able to be more objective.

But then I saw him put his hand around the shoulder of a small brown-haired girl. She looked startled. Griffith said something, and the boys in the group laughed. None of the girls, including the one he was holding, joined in the laughter. Griffith said something more. I was still standing at the office door, too far to hear what was said, only able to read their body language, to see Griffith's lips moving.

The girl shook her head.

Griffith cocked his, imitating flirtation, but making it clear that he was only imitating it, mocking it at the same time.

She shook her head again.

He leaned over and kissed her on the mouth, kept his mouth on hers for several beats too long, then slowly pulled back.

She twisted her neck, so that she was looking as far away from him as it was possible while being held.

The boys in the group laughed again.

This time he released his grip on the girl's shoulder. She jumped back, her eyes wide, head swiveling to look at the handful of girls in the group. Griffith smiled, nodded at her knowingly, and winked at his friends.

The bell rang, the group dispersed, and I walked so as to wind up near the girl. "Was that okay with you?" I asked when I was beside her and we were walking up the stairs together.

"What?" she asked, her eyes wide.

"The way—that kiss. From where I was, it didn't look as if the whole thing was your choosing."

She had pretty eyes, a sort of green-gray, with heavy dark lashes, but at the moment, they were vacant, uncomprehending. "I don't know what you're talking about." Her voice was sullen.

"Griffith. Griffith Ward kissing you like that."

She tightened her lips. "Did we break some school rule or what?"

The "we" did not fit my take on the situation, but stupidly, I plowed on. "No. Not a school rule per se, but I thought perhaps he broke a federal rule about sexual harassment."

She looked shocked. "He kissed me! He didn't rape me!"

"But it looked as if you didn't want him to. And you don't have to take that kind of treatment."

"God!" she said, making it a prayer, a curse, a shout of indignation, a cry of incredulity at my stupidity and crassness. We'd

arrived at the top of the long staircase and paused. She looked at me with that special look of horrified awe teens reserve for adults. I knew she wouldn't say what was going through her brain to me, a teacher, but I could almost read it nonetheless. I'd been an idiot. It had all been a game downstairs, and she wasn't "it."

I thought she was wrong. I thought she was either dazzled or intimidated by Griffith's aura, his reflected glory, the fact that he was two years ahead of her in school—anything, everything. But it didn't matter what I thought. "I'm sorry," I said. "I misread the signals. I was only trying to help." I could have said that the school might be liable for charges of sexual harassment. We had programs, we had built sensitivity training into the curriculum, but the impulses that fed sexual bullying weren't going to be quashed by an hour or two in the syllabus.

"I'm sorry," I repeated. She didn't say anything, merely shrugged and nodded, and went off to her class.

"I'm sorry," I said to myself. Not for trying to help, but for most likely leaping to a wrong conclusion. For disliking Griffith Ward so profoundly that I saw malevolence in whatever he did. Day after day I observed him back-slapping, chuckling, and smirking, and I could not shake the idea of a smug Pied Piper. Only he'd let his followers disappear into disaster while he remained in comfort, that smirk still on his face.

At the same time, I knew he'd done nothing to make me feel that way.

His supposed victim had looked at me as if I were crazy.

I was sorry for feeling that way about Griffith, and for thinking that maybe she was right.

Fourteen

The morning did not go well. Lessons proceeded, life went on, but I didn't feel fully present. I'd entered school towing massive weights tied to my ankles: two women dead. Murdered. They couldn't be ignored or removed.

And though the episode with Griffith might well have been a misperception, it added still more drag to every step I took. If I couldn't trust my reactions, what could I trust?

By lunchtime, I knew I needed to do something positive, to move forward, ankle weights and all, so like most of the student body, I braved the cold to leave the building and find food or company—or, for some of them, a poker game—elsewhere. I was going to Top Cat and Tails, and since I couldn't take a place with that name seriously, it should have lightened my mood, but it didn't.

But at least I had a sense of progress. It was important to see whether Merilee could be the "M" who'd visited the last night of Phoebe's life. Her arrival would have been the surprise Phoebe mentioned to the neighbor because they'd been estranged. She would have anticipated the possibility of peace with her longtime friend.

As I crossed the square, I pulled out my phone and turned it on, meanwhile catching a glimpse of the knot of boys, Griffith at its center, at one of the corners. I felt very old, because nothing would have convinced me that it was a good idea to play a game—any game—outside when the temperature was somewhere in the 20s. I wondered if parents would sue us if their children wound up frozen to the pavement.

I headed up Walnut and glanced at the phone, which said I had a message. These days, my mother is also armed with a cell phone, and it has unlimited flat-rate long-distance capability. No longer can I predict when she'll call. It almost makes me yearn for the olden days, when I only worried when the rates lowered after dark.

She's no longer as worried about me now that I've achieved what is "safety" in her cosmos—i.e., I'm married. Nonetheless, what she's done is smoothly shift into next gear. These days, calls touch on which of her lucky friends has become a grandmother. If I remind her that she is already a grandmother to my sister's two adorable children, she says I don't understand.

These days, I often receive envelopes filled with clippings from magazines and newspapers about the joys of motherhood, and sometimes, pictures of admittedly adorable infants, with a note saying, "Just saw this and thought that's probably what your baby will look like!"

I was surprised she hadn't found and sent an actual biological clock that would let me hear my reproductive minutes tick away.

But this message was not a familiar number, and definitely wasn't my mother's, so I walked along and listened first with interest, and then confusion.

"Vesta here, although I'm not sure we've met. Maybe you dialed wrong?" the voice said. "But if not, call me again. I'm home now." Of course her "now" had been a few hours ago, but I dialed the number she'd left because it filled the chilly walk to Merilee's store. By the time the phone rang at Vesta's, I was moving away from the busy center of the city to where the stores dribble away as you approach the river, the railroad station, and Penn and Drexel's campus beyond.

I reintroduced myself and asked her why she'd phoned me.

"You phoned me, miss!" she said sternly.

"I'm afraid—"

"No. You did. I recognize your voice. You left a message on my machine last night. What is it you want?"

I had to stop walking, and think, and then I remembered the call to Gregory McIntyre. It had been a man's voice on the machine, but Sally had said he lived with his widowed sister. "Ms. McIntyre? I was trying to reach your brother. I guess I didn't say that in my message."

"You certainly did not," she said. "Because if you had, I wouldn't have phoned."

"Is it possible to speak with him?"

"Surely. But I better warn you, it's a long-distance call."

"That's all right." Like my mother, I had unlimited dialing. Unlike her, I used the powers so bestowed judiciously. "Whereabouts is he now?"

"In Long Beach. That's California."

The far end of the country. Gregory was on the lam. "Sounds nice," I said, swiping at my runny nose and stomping my feet for warmth.

"Nice for him," Vesta snapped.

"I guess on a day like this, we'd all like to be where it's warm."

"But some of us are responsible human beings. Some of us

have to make sure the pipes don't freeze and the bills get paid." Her voice sounded as if she kept its harsh edge permanently honed.

Gregory might well want to get away from home for reasons that had nothing to do with Phoebe. "Could you tell me how to reach him?"

She did, spitting out each number and then repeating them, at my request, as my cold fingers wrote them on a notebook. "Will he be there long?" I asked.

She harrumphed. "He has a *friend* there." She made "friend" sound like a shameful word. "He sublets a room from the friend, bargain price, so he said he wouldn't be back until it was warm here again."

"Do you happen to know when he left Philadelphia?" I asked.

"Of course I do. Who do you think had to drive him to the airport? Besides, it's the same day he went last year. November fifteenth. Mid-November through mid-March, that's when he's in Long Beach. Doesn't even stay here for Thanksgiving."

Gregory had left town two weeks before Phoebe died. The role he'd played in her life was as one bad date, and he'd played no role whatsoever in her death.

I thanked his sister, and moved on, thinking that escaping to California did not sound like the worst idea.

Both my nose and eyes were running, but I'd reached Merilee and Phoebe's once-hopeful business, its façade festooned with a soft yellow metal awning ("Golden Retriever blond" Merilee had once told me with a straight face), which echoed the color of the Top Cat and Tails logo written in script on the front window. The shop reflected its downhill slide. A sign—in what I had to assume was Labrador Retriever black—said: "Going out of Business Sale: Everything Must Go."

I had a quick fantasy of cockapoos, parrots, and boa constrictors rushing, slithering, fluttering, galumphing into the store to snatch up bargains. But not only were they nowhere in sight, even their doting owners were among the missing. The shop looked empty.

That included most of the shelves, so perhaps the bargain-hunters had already been here. Merilee, with the same suddenly-old-and-defeated look that I'd seen at the memorial service, sat in a slump behind the cash register. The accelerated aging process was a matter of muscles loosening—as if she was no longer inter-ested in keeping her face together. The net result was that her hair looked borrowed from somebody much younger. A bell rang when I opened the door, and Merilee looked up with no expres-sion.

Then she activated herself, wrinkling her forehead for only a second, then nodding recognition. "I know you," she said. "You're Phoebe's stepdaughter's friend, aren't you? You were at the memorial."

"Sasha's friend Amanda, yes. I was walking this way—I'm on my lunch break—and saw the store. You remember, I was in with Sasha in the autumn."

She nodded. Her bulldog, today in a tartan jacket, sat on a nearby chair, snuffling.

"So I thought I'd say hello. Sorry to see that the store is clos-ing," I said. "Are you relocating?"

It was a mean question because I knew the answer, but I hoped my purported ignorance—my appearance as a new set of ears to hear her woes—might get her talking.

"Don't I wish!" The bitterness in her voice was so sharp, my taste buds cringed. "This had the makings of a gold mine. Started off so well." She shook her head as if her thick red hair would erase whatever had happened after that great start.

When she didn't say more, I once again primed the pump. "What happened?"

"Sasha didn't tell you? I'm sure Phoebe told her her version." She looked startled, eyebrows raised. As if waiting for me to admit that I knew what had befallen her.

I'd never cared much for Merilee, and her accusations about

Phoebe had done nothing to make me think more highly of her. So I wanted to be clear that I hadn't come into the shop as her sympathizer. I wanted to make her stop considering herself the center of the known universe, the reference point for all of life's events. I knew it was an impossible task. Perhaps years on the couch could have done it, but not a lunch-break visit to her store. Still, I used the only ammunition I had—and poor stuff it was— which was to let her know that her story was not on everyone's lips, that a person such as I wouldn't know what had happened to her. Of course, by that I meant a lovely, upstanding, non-gossipy person, who had never felt *schadenfreude,* had never delighted even mildly in another person's ill fortune. A good person. An ethical person.

I was not that person.

I was appalled by the thoughts prancing and striking poses in my mind, even though I was hearing them from a distance be- cause I was so far up on my high horse. But even at that lofty altitude, my unbearable self-righteousness was audible.

Yes, it was way past time for Merilee to learn that other peo- ple had feelings. And yes, it was sad and stupid and maybe heart- breaking when your husband decided to swap you for a newer model. But you were breaking the rules of womanhood when you transferred all your fury to your longtime loyal friend and business partner, who had nothing whatsoever to do with your marital woes.

"What happened?" Merilee asked rhetorically. "I'll tell you what happened. Your friend's stepmother—"

"Former stepmother."

"Whatever. They were still close, as if the relationship hadn't ever ended, and whatever you want to call her, she ran this busi- ness into the ground. Never pulled her weight, considered herself the 'idea' person. I know that her husband died and all. . . ." She cocked her head to the side for a moment, granting Phoebe that distraction. "But even so, this was our business. This was my life's blood—"

This was hogwash. Merilee hadn't thought of working until finding an "amusing outside interest" became the chic thing for women in her circle to do.

"—and the capital for it, which is pretty much missing now, was provided by my . . . by me."

Not her. Her husband. She couldn't even gulp out his title, and I felt my first flash of sympathy for the hell she was experiencing.

And then she managed to make me stop feeling anything for her. "It was money left to him, and it's gone. And now she's dead!" She made the words an accusation. "Kills herself! That makes it pretty damn impossible for me to ever prove what happened to the money, and she wrecked my marriage through it, drove my husband into another woman's arms, and look!" Her arms waved at the emptiness around her. "I had to sell the inventory for cost so I can get out before another rent's due. And now—what do I have? Nothing! Absolutely nothing! My whole life . . ." She reached for a tissue and blew her nose.

The bulldog looked up at her, panting and drooling sympathetically.

Even when I was in junior high, still defining what it meant to be a woman, when Merilee would stop over at the Bergs, she'd seemed misplaced in time, one of those 1950s Monroe-wannabe baby-doll women. "Cute and helpless" died out shortly after the dinosaurs as far as I'm concerned, but Merilee didn't seem to have gotten the news. Even "cute" all by itself had a sell-by date, and Merilee was long past it. But until recently, until the dumping, she had played the worn-out, threadbare role for all it was worth.

That helplessness included having her husband provide her with a hobby in the shape of a silly store. Now she reminded me of a child who is being punished by having her toys taken away.

I wasn't going to encourage her bratty behavior. "Surely," I said in as mild a voice as I could muster, "surely you don't really think that Phoebe deliberately wrecked your business."

And the angry child face flashed again. "We—I could have

done well, made a success of this place and . . . and . . . it's a clever store, and people are crazy about their pets. She stole the money—cooked the books—did something! Why else were we so in the red all of a sudden? And then—she could have admitted it. That's all I asked her to do, admit it, but she stonewalled me!" She looked as if she actually believed what she was saying, and it chilled me to think that.

"Merilee, think. Why did you ask her to be your partner in the first place? You needed her retail expertise. You had none. You went into the red when your husband stopped underwriting the place. You were never truly making a—"

"We were! I was! I could have! And why do you think he stopped investing in it? Because she was ruining everything!"

"She" meaning Phoebe? When the other "she" was out there, tapping her stilettos, waiting for the divorce? Merilee had rewritten history whole cloth until it fit her comfortably, and the most necessary part of the weave was casting Phoebe as the devil and the source of all her grief.

I was suddenly sure I was looking at "M." "M" as in mad, misguided, and malevolent. Maybe she'd meant to talk with Phoebe during the first visit, convince her to return the money— the money Phoebe had never taken, of course. And maybe she knew Phoebe had sleeping pills, or they were there—or maybe she used her own prescription. Maybe it wasn't premeditated at all.

But the second visit had been more frantic, and definitely planned. She must have thought that now that the house was empty, she'd find proof of what Phoebe had done, if not a stash of money itself.

Merilee-the-Murderer wept at the many injustices life had dealt her.

I surprised myself by feeling another wavelet of sorrow for her because like the child she was emotionally, she had few resources of her own, a warped image of what the world owed her, and no real coping skills. I couldn't imagine how she'd manage now that she was being forced to grow up. Maybe Marc could provide her with a big enough settlement to allow her to fill her days with weeping spells, such as the one I now waited out.

Or prison would become her big surrogate sugar daddy. No more decisions to make on her own. But no more pedicures, either.

The snuffles and wails threatened to go on forever. I looked at the remaining wares on the store's shelves to fill the time and give me something to do.

"You want to buy something?" she squeaked. Then she blew her nose and cleared her throat. The weeping spell was put on hold.

"I have a cat," I said. "But . . ."

"Prices are really low. Cost." This produced a short renewal of the miseries.

I considered a pouffy cat bed, but rejected it because it was fancier than the one I shared with Mackenzie. I loved my cat, but all the same, that didn't seem right. I looked at leather collars with faux jewels, delicate chain collars that could have served as bracelets for humans, but even if I were ready to spend the week's food money on a necklace for my cat, the fact was Macavity never left home, and detested anything around his neck. "All this is quite wonderful," I finally said, "but fairly rich for my feline. He's kind of a minimalist."

She didn't push or try to convince me that Macavity needed a red vinyl raincoat and matching boots, although I would have liked to watch—from a distance—as somebody tried to get that onto the creature. She was a good salesperson. I could feel her studying me, and following my expressions and sight line, and only when I glanced at a cobalt blue double bowl, did she speak up again.

"Gorgeous, isn't it? I am crazy for that blue . . . although there are other glazes available. All gorgeous colors. And it's very cheap now. See, it's a sample, really. Kibble on one side, water on the other, or stations for two cats, plus the option to have your pet's name in calligraphy around the rim, and in the color of your choice."

I was pretty sure Macavity was illiterate, let alone into calligraphy. Sometimes he behaved as if he didn't know his name in the first place. Could other cats read well enough to appreciate monogrammed dishes? Had Macavity flunked out of "Leave No Puss Behind"?

"But," she continued, "I'm out of here end of the year, and that's too soon for me to have the time or ability to order a personalized one and get it back in time."

When speaking of a cat, should one use the word "personalized"? "Catalized" didn't work, either.

"Of course," she said, "since it's you, if it would really matter, I could do it, and find you whenever it ships to me. You live in town, don't you? I could deliver it."

"How much is this sample?" It was a gorgeous color. I didn't want to further antagonize Merilee by pointing out that cats, if not color-blind, were unlikely to find futures as color specialists. Day or night, the world is interestingly grayish to a cat. But I'm in love with color, and the blast of intense blue would give me pleasure, as long as its price didn't cause pain.

She considered, then sighed, and said, "Five dollars. It sells for forty-seven dollars when it's personalized, but what the hell?"

"Sold."

The idea of a transaction visibly cheered her. I'd returned her to the role she'd chosen—except for the married part of it, of course—and we bonded. Time to get back to the actual point of this visit, although having seen her venomous denunciation of Phoebe—a fury that seemed to have increased with Phoebe's death—I didn't feel an acute need for lots more information, and tried to think of what I did want to know, and how to phrase it, even to broach it. "What did you think about what happened at Phoebe's house yesterday?" I asked as she wrapped the double bowl and put it in a bag that said "Top Cat and Tails." She sighed and patted the bag. "Save this. It's a collector's item now," she said, and gave a weak smile.

Only then did she seem to hear my question, as if the words had hung near her until she was ready for them. "Yesterday?" she asked me, her face blank of expression. "Her house?"

Playing dumb? Or really dumb? "I thought you'd have seen it in the paper," I said. "Or on TV."

"I . . . yesterday? I watched a movie at home last night and I was just so tired, I didn't . . ."

Was she presenting me with a prepared alibi? But, of course, the murder hadn't taken place late at night at all, so maybe not.

"Really, the late afternoon," I said.

She wrinkled her brow. Shook her head. "Same difference," she said, using that expression that has always confused me. "I didn't watch TV yesterday. Too depressing. What could happen to a house? Was there a fire?"

"At the house, not to the house." No response. "There was a murder," I said softly.

Her eyes, which would have been a lovely gray if not quite as bloodshot, opened wide. "A murder, but—who? Nobody lives there anymore. How? The house was empty!"

She seemed so honestly dumbfounded it was hard to believe she'd had anything to do with Toy's demise. On the other hand, she'd had plenty of time to think this through and plan her response. I wasn't crossing her name off the list quite yet.

"A woman was there to stage the house. Spruce it up for sale."

She rocked back on her heels, her eyes comic-book wide-open. "A stager?" Then her jaw dropped, she straightened up, and her eyes managed to pop still wider open. "*That* girl?"

"You know her?"

"I don't *know* her, not really, but if it's her, then yeah, sure, I met . . . what's her name. Or I think so."

"Why do you think you know who it was?"

She shrugged. "How many stagers . . . She had a funny name. Pet? Cuddles? Something not normal. I'm sensitive to names. Merilee got made fun of lots of times, and I remember wondering how it would have been to carry her label around."

Okay. For whatever reason, out of all the stagers there must be in the tristate area, she'd pegged the one who'd died in Phoebe's house. "Was her name Toy?" I asked quietly.

At this, Merilee's face blanched. "Toy," she whispered. "Yes. A tiny bit of a thing, right? Big hair, little girl? Flashy. Just started in these parts like six months ago."

I shook my head. I didn't know, but I wanted to know how Merilee did.

"He brought her here," she said, as if reading my mind.

"Who?" I was afraid she was going to say that Toy was her lousy husband's new squeeze, and that he'd actually dragged her into Merilee's store. I knew somebody to whom that had happened. The husband, as dumb as a post, wanted his about-to-be-dumped wife to understand his choice, and in fact, to understand why anyone in his right mind would pick the other woman over her. He felt his wife's meeting her rival would explain it all.

It didn't. It did, however, convince his wife to find the meanest, most aggressive divorce lawyer in the tristate area.

"Dennis," Merilee said.

"Dennis Allenby?"

"Yes. Phoebe's kid. That's how I met her."

"He knew her? When was this?" I tried to think of how Toy had introduced herself, but to tell the truth, I could more easily remember how chilly the house became with the door open while she made introductions. It had been clear that he'd hired her, but I somehow assumed he'd found her through recommendations.

"Has he known her?" Merilee laughed, though there wasn't much joy in the sound. "You mean that in the biblical sense? They were an item. Phoebe thought there'd be a wedding, but that didn't seem to happen. Long-distance romance and all. But dead? Honestly?"

I nodded. "Back up a second. To when you met her."

"It was here, in the store. What's to say? They were all lovey-dovey then. Phoebe said something later, that it was kaput, or going to be. How did she put it? That Dennis was trying to extract Toy's claws from under his skin. Of course, Phoebe would never blame her son for anything, even though he was a man and behaving just like the worst of them. Extracting her claws had to mean he was finished with her. Or that Phoebe wanted them to be. She didn't like Toy."

"But when you met her?" I prompted.

She shrugged. "That was then. They were definitely a couple. But men don't have long memories, do they?"

I was afraid she was going to cry about her husband again. "Why was Dennis in Philadelphia, then? Was he visiting Phoebe?"

Another mirthless laugh. "Only then, meaning that minute, right here. Only saw his mother when he came into where she was working, and brought the girl. She'd just moved here from Chicago. She was trying to get him to move here, too. I figured he brought her in for his mother to meet. I thought, Finally he's going to settle down. And I figured he thought Phoebe and I would know people, send business her way."

My head felt like a house in which all the furniture had been violently relocated. I kept bumping into things that were out of place.

Toy and Dennis. A couple. From Chicago. Why wouldn't he have said anything? Why hadn't she?

Why was he still here in Philadelphia, when he'd been so adamant about catching his plane home on Sunday after the memorial service?

He had an SUV.

Extracting claws didn't sound a happy ending to the relationship. Had the entire hiring been a setup? A way to get rid of Toy once and for all in a pretend robbery? Had, in fact, Phoebe's death been part of his plan as well? A two-fer that would rid him of his mother, and then his now-redundant lover? And, not incidentally, help him out with cash to pay his creditors.

It was a staggering idea, but not one I could dismiss as ridiculous.

"Dennis is a weird person," Merilee said. "Not in a funny way. And really mean to his mother, too."

This from the woman who had posthumously accused Dennis's mother of having first stolen money from her, and then to further annoy her, to have spitefully committed suicide.

M.L.M. his mother had called him. My little man. "M" she'd written in her datebook. And a social visit from him would have certainly been considered the sort of happy surprise she'd suggested to her neighbor.

I might have stood there, gape-mouthed, for hours, had I not glanced at a remaining piece of stock—a dog-shaped clock with a tail that wagged back and forth with the passing minutes. The minute hand was approaching his doggie brow, and I knew for whom the schoolhouse bell was about to toll.

Fifteen

I hoped my students could hear me above the growls and protests of my empty stomach.

I had returned a brief writing exercise and was asking them to edit their own writing by fixing their pronoun misuse. I spoke loudly and with enthusiasm, which isn't that easy when the topic at hand is the pronoun "it." An entire hour of the pronoun "it."

Most people are unaware of the myriad ways in which the pronoun "it" can be abused, and that's the problem, right there. So there was more than enough to fill the hour. And then to fill another hour the next day, by which time the class would have forgotten 99 percent of what I'd said.

But if I could clarify the difference between "its" and "it's," let alone the idea that the word "it" has to refer to something specific, I would justify my existence, make my small contribution to mankind and know that I'd left the world a better place than when I found it.

After they'd moaned and groaned, and insisted that the concepts were now crystal clear, I gave them a brief in-class writing exercise, the better to use their new pronoun-beefed-up muscles.

Even a cursory glance at the results they handed me at the end of the period showed that "it" wasn't going to be the way I made my contribution to this planet. I tried to be philosophical about it. If teens absorbed everything you had to say the first time around—even the first time around this semester—then the school year probably could be reduced to two or three weeks. There was a reason we had ten months in which to state and re-state everything. And we then gave them two months in which to pretty much forget it, which ensured teachers of further employment the following year.

The repetitive process wasn't discouraging if I looked at it that way. Job security was a good thing. Besides, my own mind wasn't holding on to things as well as I'd have liked it to. I was still embarrassed about my failure to remember that I hadn't seen Phoebe's pocketbook. What else so defines a woman besides her literal "baggage"?

And what else had I forgotten? What was I forgetting this very moment? I knew how to use the pronoun "it," but there was no need to be smug. I did not know how to use what little bits and scraps of information I had.

The juniors walked in casually and found their seats. I could see the faint flush of vacation fever in their postures. Winter break was near, and these youngsters were not into the zen concept of living in the moment, at least not when the moment was at a school desk. Their bodies might be here, but their minds and hearts were already elsewhere, whether or not their holiday plans included travel.

I suspected that my holiday plans would take me—take us— to Louisiana, and sometimes lately I thought we might remove "holiday" from that. I didn't know for how long Mackenzie could—or should—stand being torn between his life in Philadelphia and the devastated land and people he'd left in Louisiana.

A tale of two cities indeed, as Margaret had said.

Mackenzie had been to see his parents twice since the hurricane. I would have gone, but we decided to conserve funds and let him fly twice instead of spending anything on plane fare for me. Besides, when Mackenzie was there, he tried to weave his way through the bureaucracy to find loans and temporary housing for his family, tried to locate relatives and friends whose whereabouts were still unknown, and I'm sure was able to offer psychological, if not physical, help to his parents. He was useful. I wasn't sure I could offer anything worthwhile except psychic support, but now and then I thought about those ghost schools.

My students were looking forward to more comforting holidays, wherever they'd find themselves. And till it was officially winter break, each hour of this and the following days would be an attempt to wrench them from daydreams back into the schoolroom.

We were working our way through an anthology of American writing, and we'd come to a sampler of Edwin Arlington Robinson's poems about the people of Tilbury Town. "Richard Cory" was always a favorite, a poem that worked even before holidays. It seldom failed to produce an emotional response and heated discussion once my overprivileged charges discovered that the wealthiest, most elegant and envied man in town commits suicide. While they search for explanations, I use the poem, which is all clues and no solution to the mystery, to encourage close reading. Of course, I never admit that we're doing that.

But suicide pulled my thoughts back to Phoebe, even though I no longer believed she'd taken her own life, and I was once again obsessed with trying to identify what I had to remember. No more missed pocketbooks!

For example, where was Dennis secretly staying? Where did—had—Toy lived? What was going on with them?

If Dennis wasn't at a hotel, he could be next to impossible to find. And he could be gone. We weren't going to know till he rang up some more credit card charges. I wondered if Mackenzie had checked for airline or train ticket charges within the last day.

Dennis as the killer was the only thing that made sense, or close to sense. Dennis, in debt and trying to end a relationship was the only person with a motive for both deaths, hateful as it was to think about his relationship with his mother in particular.

I tried my best to keep my eyes off Griffith, the closest thing this class had to Richard Cory. I was going to purge myself of my prejudices, and stop singling him out for scrutiny. I tried not to think about him, though it took entirely too much energy keeping a thought pushed back against the wall of the brain.

The discussion had roared along while I concentrated on my attempt to not think about Griffith. I tried to catch up. Stacy had just made the apt observation that nobody knew Richard Cory because—this showed she was reading the text closely—he was only described in terms of what he looked like and what he had. "Externally," she said with a proud smile. "Nobody spoke to him or knew him."

We were cruising around the question of how well anyone knows anyone else, when my attempts to not think about Griffith once again failed. But this time, I reconsidered him in the context of the poem. My assumptions about him made me a perfect example of the people of Tilbury Town. I'd watched him and judged him based on his externals—his wealth, his father's celebrity, his smirk, his silence in class, his mediocre grades, his popularity. I did not know the boy at all.

Thank you, Edwin Arlington Robinson.

But I still wished that Griffith didn't smirk. It would be so much easier to avoid prejudging him without that facial expression.

Of course, Griffith seldom spoke up in class, so waiting for him to explain himself would involve geologic increments of time. At the moment, he seemed unimpressed by the enthusiasm crackling around the room, and uninterested in joining the discussion. Instead, he slouched in his chair and watched his classmates impassively, almost as if he were enduring the session. There was nothing I could object to—not even a smirk now, and no open expression of boredom, or disagreement—and that in itself annoyed me.

"Maybe that's enough—maybe not having anybody know you—or realize that they don't know you—can drive a person to suicide," an always-earnest girl named Lili said.

I loved how this poem generated passionate observations that would be declared trite and embarrassing in a few years, but now were new and heartfelt. Ideas that boiled down to money being unable to buy happiness, or the pain of loneliness, or never judging a book by its cover.

The important thing was that they were thinking and talking and using the poem as their reference point, so they were actually practicing backing up their opinions and interpreting text. I didn't tell them that, either.

"We don't know what was in his past, on his mind," Jonesy Farmer said. "Maybe he had a secret driving him crazy."

Jonesy. I had to remember to find out about his father, Jesse, who'd also dated Phoebe. Not an "M," but maybe he'd know something more about her. Couldn't hurt, and maybe could help a lot. I added it to my mental checklist.

"What he said." Griffith had spoken. "That's right. You never really know what's going on with somebody. Even your good friends. Not really. He could be scared or something."

I was so enjoying the general level of enthusiasm and engagement that it took a minute to register that reticent Griffith was making history by participating. The Griff had spoken, backed Jonesy up. Jonesy looked happily dazed. I was also dazed. Those two sentences added up to more words than Griffith had spoken in class since the semester began. They were a strong testimonial to the bond between the two juniors, no matter what tensions or bullying I'd mistakenly thought I'd seen between them in the hallway.

Jonesy continued his argument. "He could have committed a crime. It could have been eating him up for a long time. Maybe he got his money illegally."

Griffith looked at his pal, frowned, then slouched even more dramatically and returned to impassivity. Even I could feel the temperature drop in the space between them. The joy and enthusiasm left Jonesy's face.

But Stacy shook her head and blurted her opinion out before I could call on her. "I don't think that's what the poem suggests *at all*! I think he's like a king—he's *born* to the money and the position! He's not a *criminal*!"

"But how would you know?" Jonesy asked. "If the point is that we don't know anybody, how would you know?"

"Because—because we're supposed to be looking at what Robinson said—"

"But he didn't say *why* he shot himself," a normally shy and silent boy added. He looked surprised by the fact that he'd spoken up.

"People who kill themselves are all crazy!" Dierdre said with passion. "And so was he. You have to be crazy to end your own life, and he had such a good life, anyway."

"That's the whole point!" somebody else said. "His life stunk. They just thought he had it all."

"So do I," Dierdre insisted. "He had looks and money and respect. What more can you want?"

"What isn't there, though?" I asked. "What makes for a happy life?"

Nothing like tossing out an impossible question debated for the past several thousand years, but as they didn't know enough to know that, they debated on.

I thought about happy and unhappy lives. I thought about my in-laws and all the hurricane victims, and knew their unhappiness was real, profound, perhaps permanent, but situational. It felt quantitatively different to be unhappy because unhappy things had happened to you versus being an inherently unhappy person, the way the imaginary but believable Richard Cory must have been, and Merilee was.

Even when life had been providing her with everything she wanted or needed, she always seemed vaguely discontented and ready to whine about whatever was still lacking or less than perfect, and that could range from a hangnail to a cataclysm. If a flood wiped out the entire Delaware Valley and swept most of its residents out to sea, Merilee would complain because it had spoiled a planned picnic.

I couldn't keep my mind in one place. It skittered from classroom to Phoebe, to the individuals she'd known, to the still-dangling threads, and back to the classroom, where the discussion was degenerating into a back-and-forth about whether rich people were happier than poor people. The group seemed to be moving toward the consensus that indeed it was easier to be happy with resources than without. "Then, why did Richard Cory put a bullet through his head?" I asked, and they looked startled. They'd forgotten the original question.

They went back to the imponderables, looked at the text again for a clue to a dark secret in his past, a crime darkening his soul—Jonesy again—to having those theories pooh-poohed, and back to loneliness. Acute, perpetual loneliness.

"Then, he should have *done* something about it," Stacy said in her usual emphatic style. As soon as she opened her mouth, exclamation points flashed in the air around her. "Nobody *has* to be lonely! He had all that money—why didn't he *do* something with it? *Help* other people, get involved in their lives. Then he wouldn't have been so *lonely!*"

I could almost see small lightbulbs flash over several heads in the class. Not Griffith's. He looked baffled by what Stacy had said. I turned my eyes and mind away from him and counted at least five juniors who gave every appearance of honestly considering the idea of helping others as a way of enriching one's own life. The little lightbulbs shimmered on. Thank you again, Edwin Arlington Robinson.

I hated to break the spell, but we didn't have much time left. "For tomorrow," I said, once I had them calmed down, "I'd like you to think about what you said and heard today, whether you agreed or disagreed, and write an essay—your opinion backed by whatever evidence you can or cannot find in the poem—as to why Richard Cory killed himself. There are no wrong answers. Simply defend your idea."

I braced myself for a replay of this morning's scene with the ninth graders. There were indeed groans and grumbles, but they were half-hearted. They were engaged with the idea, and as onerous as writing might be, they could see its point.

I hadn't eradicated misuse of the pronoun "it," but in a small way, for a few minutes at least, the poet, Stacy, and I, too, had done our bit for the future of humanity.

It sufficed.

Sixteen

Sasha's condo is *sui generis*. I am willing to bet there's no comparable place within the tristate area. Her father gave it to her during one of his divorces, and Sasha was wise enough never to probe the ethics or legality, or even to ask under what guise it had been economically advantageous—as surely it must have been—to get rid of the place that way and at that moment. If an opera were written about divorce court and accounting shenanigans, Sasha's father's life would provide the libretto.

He'd also left those furnishings he wasn't in the mood to move: mostly expensive, uncomfortably stark geometric shapes, plus a few more-beautiful Asian *tansus*. Scattered among them were Sasha's Goodwill "finds." She'd re-covered a tufted ebony wood–edged love seat in fake leopard skin and pillowed a

painfully carved wooden chair with red satin. But Sasha had also
had a brief engagement with an Englishman. The marriage never
happened, but the slipping apart was amicable, and when he
divested himself of a castle or country house and shipped a
container's load of furniture to his daughter in the States, he
earmarked some of it for Sasha. Hence chintz stuffed chairs
squatted among the angled tubes and solemn carved and padded
pieces. Add to that a few Spanish-influenced wooden chests and
a heavy-handed sprinkle of baroque accents—gilded mirrors
and picture frames—and you should have had a visual insult.
But Sasha melted the clashing edges and styles with a scarf
tossed here, a shawl there, and when necessary, by painting
solemn pieces in bright clean colors. Only her darkroom, seldom used in these digital days, its door generally closed, sym-
bolizing its separateness, was clinically efficient. Dark smooth
surfaces, shelves, and sink. In that room, all her style went into
her photographs. It stood, sealed beside the dining area like a
secret.

Elsewhere, she lived in the design equivalent of International
House where all were welcome. As if to demonstrate that, the
landscape painting she'd brought home from Phoebe's—a pallid,
dull scene to my taste—now hung on the dining area wall, and
despite a too-dark-too-much frame and washed-out canvas, it
now also felt a natural part of the eclectic décor.

I noticed another new piece relocated from Phoebe's, a gilded
Roman warrior about two feet tall. Why Sasha had wanted it, I
could not tell. The artist's sense of proportion was off, and the
warrior looked stringy and underweight, ineffectual.

"Phoebe loved that piece," Sasha said when she saw me eyeing it. *Chacun a son gout* indeed. I looked at it again. Even Sasha
had not yet been able to blend it into her mishmash décor. A
scarf covering the entire thing would be my plan.

"So what have you got about Phoebe?" she asked.

I told her the crumbs we'd gathered so far. They weren't
enough to interest an ant, let alone make a case. But she was in-

trigued by the news about Dennis and Toy. "And," I said, "Dennis did not go home to Chicago last week. He was using his credit card right here in Philly two, three days later."

"Where is he? Why would he lie that way?"

"Good questions. Could he have lied just to get away from us? He didn't want to be there, didn't want to be with people remembering his mother—fondly remembering her. So he lied. How's that for a theory?"

"Bad," she said. "Because he never worries about hurting people's feelings. He is not Mr. Sensitivity. He'd have just cut and run. Or said, 'I cannot stand you people. Adios.' Instead, he planned to have the lunch first so that he could catch that plane."

"He said."

"But he could as easily have let the lunch be afterwards and deserted us then." She shook her head. "His behavior has never made particular sense to me, but you could be right. It might have been about getting away from me. He tries to hide it, but it's absolutely true that he hates me."

"Why on earth? It's not like you stole his mommy's affections away from him."

She shrugged. "He's always begrudged my existence. I don't think he liked it that I got along with his mother. Not that he wanted to be with her, but I weakened his case that she was impossible to endure. I endured and enjoyed her."

We were both silent for a while.

"Do you think it was all about Toy?" I finally asked. "About getting rid of her?"

"That would be awful. He'd kill his mother as a setup for getting rid of a girlfriend?"

"Maybe not just that. But get rid of Mom and then make it a two-fer? Horrible but not impossible."

"I never thought of him as vicious," she said. "Annoying. Maybe even repugnant. Shady. Always on the fringe of what's not quite legal. Sneaky. But more likely to move away from his mother than have an open conflict. The only time I heard him bad-mouth her in her presence was last Sunday, and as you recall, she was dead, cremated, and in a martini shaker."

"He got awfully angry when you suggested that Phoebe might not have killed herself," I said mildly.

"That he did." She was quiet again, frowning slightly. "But even so . . ." She'd been holding Phoebe's pocketbook all along, and now she looked at it as if suddenly remembering that it was hanging from her shoulder. "I have to tell you, this isn't going to be nearly as interesting as the idea that Dennis has been secretly in town. Or that he and Toy . . ."

"Mackenzie's checking it out and I bet he finds out where he was and is. It just takes longer if he's been in a private home. However, that's all speculation and the pocketbook is real, so give it here."

"I looked in it." Her expression was suddenly that of a young child expecting to be chastised. "Before you called about it. Was that wrong? I mean tampering with something that might be evidence? Important? Messing up fingerprints and all?"

"No, no," I said. "Unless you got rid of its contents, which you did not."

"Then, that's the good news. But the bad news is that there is truly nothing interesting in it."

Of course I was sure my semi-trained eye would spot what she'd missed. My non-credentials had gone to my head.

"In fact," Sasha said, "I thought that was the only interesting thing about the bag—the fact that there wasn't anything interesting, meaning personal, in her pocketbook."

"You think somebody went through it before you? Took that mysterious something out—the interesting thing?"

Sasha shook her head and settled onto the leopard-print love seat. "That's what I thought at first, but then I really looked at the contents and changed my mind. I think she'd just experienced a getting-organized attack, and she died too soon after it for the normal flotsam to collect in there again. Everything was in separate see-through zip-up bags by categories, see?" She pulled one out now, a silvery mesh that held lipstick, comb, mirror, and face powder. "Cosmetics."

"Writing implements," Sasha said, "credit cards," pulling out two more bags, one orange, one green.

"Color coded, too," I murmured.

"This makes it easier to switch purses quickly, and she had this awesome collection." Sasha pulled out the little handheld version of the online calendar and address book. "I knew that anything on this would be on the computer, too, so that didn't seem significant, and that was pretty much that."

"No notebook or scraps of paper? What did she do with her random thoughts, shopping lists, memos to herself?"

"There's this, but look at it. It's got nothing interesting, either." She handed over a tiny soft-sided notebook. The used pages were gone, ripped out on the small perforated line. All that was still in it said, "dz. eggs, lib, b-dy crds, tpe." I tried to find subtle and meaningful coding there, but no matter how I looked at it, it seemed simply to be a list of chores. Phoebe had needed to buy eggs, birthday cards, and tape, and visit the library. Sasha was right. Hard to ascribe any significance to the list.

I shrugged. "Her money? A wallet?"

Sasha passed the entire pocketbook over to me. I understood why she'd appropriated it. It was a clever, crazy quilt of lizard skins dyed purple and topaz, immediately desirable, especially to the skinless shivering lizards left in its wake. I reached inside and was pulling out a slender wallet when the doorbell rang.

I looked at Sasha, who put her hands out, palms up. "I have no idea," she said. "It can't be my client. He's an impatient sort, but he gave me till tomorrow morning. If he . . ." She continued muttering to herself as she went to the door and looked through the peephole. "I don't believe it," she said, then turned and mouthed "Dennis."

"No."

She nodded vigorously.

Then there he was, walking—make that storming—through the door before Sasha had it fully opened.

"What the hell have you been telling people?" he demanded.

"Good afternoon to you, too, Dennis," she said. "Isn't this a surprise. I thought you were in Chicago."

"Obviously I'm not. And don't try to avoid the question."

"Why not? You're avoiding mine."

They stood in belligerent positions facing each other. "Why don't you both sit down?" I asked. I squashed Phoebe's purse down beside me. I was pretty sure Dennis wouldn't know this had been his mother's pocketbook, or notice that I had another bag, my own, at my feet.

He nodded brusquely, and he and Sasha found seats as far apart from each other as possible in the room. He was barely into a sitting position before he started up again. "The police asked me all kinds of questions. The Bordentown police!"

"In Chicago?" I asked softly.

He glared at me. "Here."

"Back so soon?" Sasha cooed.

He chose not to answer. He had questions of his own. "What did you tell them?" he demanded.

"Tell whom? About what?"

"The police! About me! You and your crazy ideas about my mother's—about Phoebe's death."

"They asked you about that?"

He shrugged. "They asked me lots of things. Why?"

Time to stop beating around the bush. "Was it maybe about Toy Rasmussen's violent death? You recall the name, right? The stager you hired? She was murdered," I said.

"Just because somebody recommended her and I hired her doesn't mean I'd—it doesn't make any sense, anyway. Use your brains—why would I?" He glared at Sasha. "Only somebody who hates me, who has been jealous of me and has undermined me forever every way she could think of—including now—only that one person would even think that."

The vanity of his paranoid and misplaced anger struck me. Sasha had been in his life—in fact, in his zip code—for only a few years. I hadn't heard her mention him, even in passing, in two decades, let alone bad-mouth him. He had not been on her mind at all.

But she'd been on his. He'd demonized her, carried her with him through all the intervening years, making her the villain behind his every ache and pain. I had a moment's panicked fear on her behalf, but he didn't seem about to inflict physical harm.

"I can't believe you told the police I *killed* her!"

"Which 'her' are you talking about?" Sasha asked quietly. "You're lumping everybody together."

"Toy," he said. "Her. Nobody killed my mother except my mother. But they asked me about her, too. About the circumstances surrounding her death."

"Well, that's good," Sasha said. "Finally."

"What the hell are you saying? You *did* turn them on me, didn't you? You told them I killed my mother? Is that what you said to them?" His skin had reached the color of a ripe eggplant, and I worried whether his head might explode while I watched.

"I only meant that they were finally considering the idea that somebody did her in. And I never said a word about you, Dennis, not because I think you wouldn't or couldn't, but because I never spoke with them about you or anybody else. Amanda and I found the . . . Toy. That's when we spoke with the police. They found you on their own. I, for one, thought you were in Chicago, the way you said you were."

"I had my reasons."

"If you're so innocent, even though you lied about where you'd be, why don't you drop the huffy act and just plain say what your reason for being here and saying you were there might be?" Sasha's color was darkening, too.

Dennis bit on his bottom lip as if to censor himself. "I had business, all right? Turns out, it was better trying to take care of certain things here, rather than in Chicago. I just—I didn't want to be hassled, is all. By you. By anybody."

Business. "What is it you do again?" I asked softly. "I thought you worked at Marshall Field's."

He waved that away with one hand. "Yeah, sure. You ever heard of the American Way? What's it to you if I'm looking to be more on my own?"

"I think the police talked with you because you were Toy's boyfriend." I kept my voice in a calm, soothe-the-savage-beast mode.

"*Were.* Was. As in past tense. It was over."

"Nothing quite like a ruptured romance to trigger other sorts of passions." I watched his face move around the color wheel again. We were approaching crimson when he finally took a deep breath that calmed him enough to speak.

"It wasn't like that. It was never a big thing, and then it was a friendly breakup. She moved here, what was supposed to happen? Look, I got her a job, didn't I? If I hated her or wanted her dead, why would I do that?"

We both stared at him. I don't think anybody blinked for much too long.

"Sweet mother of God!" he shouted. "Only you"—he scowled at Sasha again—"only you would even think of something that incredible! Like it was a setup? Something I planned? I can't believe you said that—thought that!" He grew silent for a moment. "No. I can believe it. It's just like you." He stood up.

My muscles tensed and I got ready to spring, but he simply stood there, looming.

"Good thing the police aren't as mentally disturbed as you are," he said. "They know I didn't do anything. Just make sure you don't go to them with any more of your crazy, vindictive theories."

"Or what?" Sasha stood up as well, looking at him eye-to-eye. There is much to be said in favor of being as tall as your enemies.

"I'm not wasting any more breath on you. Just stay away from me!"

"Stay away from you? You need help, Dennis. Look at me. I'm not in your city," she said. "I didn't burst into your apartment like a storm trooper. And I didn't lie about where I had to be or was."

"Where have you been, really?" I asked.

"None of your business," he snapped.

Sasha plowed on. "Stay away from you? I'd love to—if you'd stop stalking me!"

"Stalking! I—" He simply shook his head. Maybe the airflow he produced would cool him down. He looked like a stroke waiting to happen.

I know about sibling rivalry and sibling conflict, but this was a rarefied subset. They were former short-term stepsiblings still at war. I hoped that Sasha and Dennis were not typical. "Hey, you guys," I said. "Hey. This is a rough time. Simmer down."

"Don't involve me in anything else, do you hear?" he said. "That's all I have to say."

"What about the house?" Sasha asked. It was a valid question. It was not, however, a question Dennis wanted to answer. His color flared, he grimaced and fumed, but there it was between them: the house that was going to put money in his pockets.

"Sell it," he said.

"And you won't say I'm cheating you? I did something wrong or evil or malicious or—"

"Just sell it," he growled. "Not that anybody's going to rush to buy a place that had a murder in it."

"Two," Sasha said softly. "And I can reach you in which city?" she added.

He opened the door himself and slammed out. Sasha double-locked the door and turned to me with a long sigh.

"You were pushing it, dear friend," I said.

She shrugged. "So was he. But I'm glad the police talked to him, and I hope they keep tracking him."

"I thought you didn't think him capable of violence."

"Maybe I was wrong. Besides, Phoebe was killed in a cowardly way. That'd be like him. As for Toy—oh, I don't know. I hate him and I'd like him locked up even if he didn't do it."

Democracy is sometimes so unfair. Locking up whomever we didn't like is an enticing idea. But here we were, stuck with rule by law; and Dennis was gone, having managed to avoid explaining why he'd lied about his whereabouts after the memorial service. We had nothing more than we'd had before he barged in, and we couldn't lock him up.

Therefore, by all the rules of fair play (because of course, life does play fair, doesn't it? Doesn't it?), I would now get my reward for good behavior. I pulled Phoebe's purse out from under my thigh and opened it with a deep sigh of anticipation.

Phoebe's credit cards were in one of those cunning mesh bags, a purple one. The wallet I'd started to extract before Dennis arrived was a slender number holding only bills, coins, and—my anticipation went into happy high gear—receipts. *Now* I'd find something. Sasha probably hadn't even considered them.

I found lots of somethings, but unfortunately they were, without exception, extremely dull. Phoebe had bought stamps and gone to the supermarket—for those eggs on her list, I supposed. Also the ATM, where she'd withdrawn $200, not enough to believe anybody was threatening her or forcing her to make the withdrawal. She'd had lunch and left a 17 percent tip. She'd been to the dry cleaners and possibly still had clothing there. She'd bought something and pulled the tag off. It said it was a "Genuine Hoffer" and whatever that was, it said we should never settle for less. I sighed and tossed down the final contents, an appointment reminder for her dentist, a coupon for 20 percent off any purchase of towels at The Bubble, and a fabric-covered button.

Sasha watched me with a bemused expression. "Dull, right?"

I felt a completely irrational wave of indignation. How could Phoebe have exited this world without an incriminating letter in her pocketbook? Why not a slip showing a huge withdrawal from the bank—or even an out-of-line huge deposit? What about a telegram, or a matchbook from a seedy-sounding nightclub? Wasn't that supposed to happen? Why was nothing given me that I could cleverly analyze, that could provoke even a tiny "Aha!"?

Sasha was watching me, nodding. "You were warned," she said. "And so, my friend, if you have no further need of me, and you can't think of a way we can destroy Dennis without our going to prison, I will return to the editing job. I'd grumble about it, but they are paying me good money to work at breakneck speed."

I stood up. "And you're paying us good—"

"—not so good," she reminded me.

"—you're paying us pathetically small amounts of money to help you get to the bottom of this, and I'm afraid I haven't been much help at all. My apologies."

"Not your fault," she said. "It helped to know you believed me. And it helps to know that the cops asked Dennis about Phoebe, too. Maybe they are beginning to have doubts about her death. And I was thinking that if both women were killed by the same person, which seems logical, and if both times that person wanted the same thing, then if—when—the cops find out who killed Toy, we'll have our killer, too."

That should have been consolation, but it wasn't. I had no confidence in the murderer's being found. Toy's murder was too unscripted and messy, and Phoebe's too speculative, too theoretical.

"Thanks," I told Sasha.

"For what?"

"For being so foolishly optimistic. But keep your door locked," I said. "Don't let him back in, no matter what. Call the cops if he reappears. Don't let your client in until you double check that's who it is."

"Oh, Manda, Dennis is all talk when it comes to me, couldn't you tell? I mean he still wants me to make sure that house sells. How can I do that if he kills me first?"

"He'd cope with selling it himself. And he'd endure taking the entire profit."

She looked at me intently, then nodded. "I promise," she said.

"Good."

When all you've got going for you is an optimistic friend for whom you're grateful, you want, at the very least, to keep her alive.

Seventeen

Marc Wilkins lived with his replacement woman in the near northern suburbs. According to his schedule, he was teaching tonight, which was good since I couldn't come up with a reason why Ruby Osgood would need to see him again, let alone at home. I was reverting to being myself, and I didn't want to see Marc in any case.

Mackenzie was with me. We were multitasking. Sleuthing and dating. Kind of. Find out about Marc's whereabouts the night Phoebe died, then enjoy dessert somewhere in town afterwards. Our kind of a date. En route, I filled C.K. in with my various encounters, including the strange one with Dennis.

"He's here on business?" C.K. murmured. "Interestin'. Marshall Fields surely didn't send him here. So 'business' has to mean money. He's trying to dig up money in Philadelphia. Why here?" And then he was quiet for some time, working it through in his fashion until we pulled up to a garden-apartment complex that had seen better days. The grounds were sparsely planted, so that the winter landscape looked more bleak than it had to. The brick buildings' shutters and occasional planter box needed painting.

"Lacks curb appeal," I said. "I'm quoting the late Toy Rasmussen. Also doesn't look as if Marc Wilkins is in the money as he's reputed to be. Do you think Merilee's claim that he spent his inheritance on the business is true?"

"Could be, in which case I grant him his idiot credentials. Or it may simply be that he wants to appear hard up," Mackenzie said. "Easier on his wallet if he has less assets when he shows up in divorce court."

"Either way, better for our case. His conviction that Phoebe stole money, and might have had it on her is surely a reason to have gone to see her, to be 'M.' He could have been looking for cash or for whatever form she'd converted it into."

He laughed. "I hope you mean savings bonds, or a few shares of stock, not gold bullion or diamonds. How much money could she—if she had in fact taken any that didn't belong to her—how much could a person extract from a pet-accessory business? Maybe she converted it into those gold-foil-wrapped chocolate coins or paste jewelry." He lifted his hand to ring the bell. "Unless Marc's completely crazy, he'd know she couldn't have taken much."

"He keeps saying she did. Maybe there were hidden costs—remodeling the building—buying the building."

"That would have been still more insane. More likely his inheritance was small, and his lifestyle way over his head, and that's why he's living like this. Let's see what his woman knows." He rang the bell.

"What's our cover story? What did you say when you made the appointment?" I whispered, admittedly realizing it was a little late for this question.

"That—"

The door was opened by a sunny young woman who looked like she'd just stepped off the stage of the Grand Ole Opry. She had poufed blond hair, and wore red cowboy boots, black jeans and turtleneck, and a vest that had "Ashley" written in red sequins. The jeans looked stitched to her flesh. "Hi!" she said. "I've been expecting you, even though I don't know what I can tell you. I'm Ashley, Marky's fiancée. Please come in."

Marc's fiancée led us into the small living room with the panache of a baton twirler at the head of the band, and waved us onto the sofa. "I made cheese crisps," Ashley said. "Please, sit down and let me serve you. You must be thirsty. We have wine, sparkling water, beer, some of the hard stuff, coffee, tea, soda?"

This must have been her apartment. Marc had simply moved in. It had a young, temporary look, with posters tacked to the walls, board bookshelves balanced on concrete blocks, and carpeting that had been provided by a stingy landlord many years and tenants ago. I spotted the familiar girth and print of a "Fifteen-month Student Datebook" atop the bookshelves, along with a heavy text with "Abnormal Psychology" printed on its spine. I wondered where she was going to school.

I also wondered what on earth Ashley saw in Marc Wilkins. At this point, as her tenant, he couldn't seem her ticket to an easier life. He was a good-enough-looking man, especially if you liked a slightly dangerous darkness about the features, a withdrawn sullenness. But he was twice her age and a pompous letch, and even if her wardrobe could stand a redo, she was a great-looking, energy-filled young woman. Why him?

It took a while until our many assurances that we were comfortable and loved her cheese crisps and that sparkling water was precisely what we'd wanted satisfied her hostessing needs.

"How can I help you?" Ashley then said with open eagerness. I wondered if she'd been receptive to the appointment because we were much-needed entertainment. Maybe she was already a little bored with sulky Marc. Poor girl. That man was going to make all those bubbles in her personality go flat.

"We're investigators workin' on the Phoebe Ennis case," Mackenzie said. "We wanted to clarify a few things with you."

"Case?" Her eyes widened. "I thought—I heard she committed suicide. Why is that a case?"

"Just an expression," Mackenzie said. "Shorthand for case file. Did you know the deceased?"

"Not really." Ashley's cheeks reddened. "Not well. She—she came to see me once. She was upset about Marc and me." Ashley shrugged. "She said she wanted to talk sense with me about that, but really, she was just meddling. Marc said she really wanted him to loan them more money for the business. He'd had this inheritance. It wasn't that much, but it was nice enough, and he'd pretty much loaned the whole thing to those two women. I guess because Marc's wife was her partner, Phoebe was in a weird place, but still. She didn't have to come insult me, as if I were . . . She blamed me for Marc's decision to stop loaning them money, but I've never taken a cent from Marc. It wasn't my fault the business was failing. From everything I heard, it was her fault. All her fault."

"It must have upset the two of you, financially and emotionally, the way everything was tangled," I said. "Business and marriages and romances."

Mackenzie looked sideways at me, and I stopped. Maybe the kind of investigation we were pretending to do didn't touch on human emotions. "You understand that it wasn't a loan," he said. "Of course he anticipated sharing in the profits, but it wasn't ever a loan. Marc was the third partner. He put up the money to start the business."

"Marc did? It wasn't a loan?" Ashley looked at me, then at Mackenzie, her eyes slightly squinted. She looked as if she'd been left out of lots of loops and she was only now becoming aware of it.

"One question we have is whether you'll be making a legal claim against her estate," Mackenzie asked gently.

"Me? How would I? Marc would be the one to do that, I'd think."

"Will he be home soon?"

She checked her watch. "Not for several hours. You'll have to talk to him tomorrow. He's teaching tonight. The thing is, we aren't married, so I . . . I don't have any legal standing in this."

"You're his fiancée, correct?"

She shrugged. "Something like that."

"I asked because there is some confusion surrounding the disposition of her estate," Mackenzie said.

I have noticed that the two small words "her estate" calm and focus people. It did now, too.

"What kind of confusion?" Ashley asked. "And please, have more cheese crisps. I made way too many and they don't keep well, they get greasy, and Marc gets all angry if I've made things nobody eats. He's always saying, 'waste not, want not' and 'a penny saved,' blah, blah." She looked at us. "He checks what he calls my 'waste quotient' in the trash and garbage cans every night, can you believe it?"

All was not well in paradise, and Marc was the snake. I couldn't believe I felt pangs of sympathetic sisterhood for this child-bride-to-be, this husband-stealing young intruder. Nonetheless, I did.

Mackenzie took a deep breath. Something about the way he'd rearranged his facial muscles made me almost imagine him an insurance investigator, or whatever he was pretending to be. He had the look of one who'd had countless interviews with the mates of men who pawed through the garbage every night. "Things have gotten complicated because we've learned that Phoebe Ennis phoned a friend on the evening of her death to wish her bon voyage. This friend has come forth only now because she left that evening on a cruise, and she forgot about the specifics of the call until the unfortunate incident in the house this past week."

"That woman," Ashley said. "That woman who redoes your house when it's for sale. I read about her."

"Correct," Mackenzie said. "So did this woman, and it triggered the memory of her conversation with Mrs. Ennis. I must make it clear that we still don't know if it's relevant, but in any case, it appears that Mrs. Ennis spoke to this friend about a visitor she expected later that evening." He paused and looked at Ashley, giving her his premium blue-eyed beam. "It was Thursday evening, December first."

"Yes?" Ashley said politely when she realized she was expected to say something.

"Given what you've just said about the so-called loan, it might interest you to know that during that phone call, Mrs. Ennis mentioned the repayment of a debt."

"Phoebe Ennis said that? Kind of like a deathbed confession or something." Her voice was hushed. "Marc would be . . . he's pretty upset about losing all that money, and . . ." She shot a look toward the door when she said his name, as if she shouldn't have and she was worried about being caught at it.

As soon as this was all over, I was going to invite Ashley to lunch and make her reconsider this arrangement, if she hadn't reached the same conclusion on her own by then. She was studying abnormal psychology. She had to know her garbage-scanning boyfriend was not normal.

"Not quite a confession," Mackenzie said with a gentle chuckle. "But an interesting riddle, because she was talking about a debt owed to the visitor she expected that evening, and we don't know who that was, which complicates the disposition of her estate. The mystery man—or woman—who was to visit that evening is apparently owed that debt, which is, of course, not mentioned in her will."

"Maybe she paid it!" Ashley looked relieved. "The person

came to see her just the way she said, and she settled the issue. Nice, so she could die in peace. Not that it was nice that she did that to herself."

"That may be so," Mackenzie said slowly. Slowly enough to think a way around this, I suspected. "But we have no evidence of a payment. No cancelled check, no I.O.U., no large withdrawal from the bank." He shrugged. "Still, as you say, this may all be irrelevant, and perhaps not worth pursuing, but we do have to dot every 'i' and cross every 't,' as they say. If that was her wish—expressed to this friend, who has nothing at stake in this—her wish on the last day of her life, then we must try to support it."

While Mackenzie, the insurance investigator, trowelled it on, I watched poor Ashley's face. The mention of money produced a dreamy, wistful look, but she still didn't know where this was going. She wanted Marc to have been that mystery visitor, owed a great sum and repaid it.

"Only thing is, if he got the money, Marc should have told me, shouldn't he?"

We said nothing. As far as I was concerned, any wedge I could legitimately drive between these two was a good and honorable wedge.

"It should have made him happy. The inheritance was a kind of cushion, you know? The screenwriting hasn't been all that great lately, and teaching doesn't pay enough, given his marital situation. What night did you say it was again?"

Ashley's voice was like clear running water. Lovely. Maybe she really was a country singer. I had spotted a guitar propped against the far wall. "Marc might have phoned her, although I wouldn't know how to check. Can't you go over telephone records?"

"We can and will. We're just trying to narrow the field," Mackenzie said. "And the date was December first. A Thursday."

She stood up and took the fifteen-month planner off the shelf, shrugging, as if telling herself this was her datebook, and how was it going to answer any questions about Marc's where-abouts or phone calls?

"He teaches Thursday nights," she said as she flipped pages, "so I don't think . . ." Then she wrinkled her brow and shook her head. "Jeez," she said. "It would have been nice to have Marky be paid back, but it was somebody else. She must have owed lots of people money, then, and that's awful, but the fact is," she pointed at a page, "we were in Virginia, visiting my parents." She looked at Mackenzie. "It was Daddy's fiftieth birthday that Friday, so we drove down on Thursday evening to be there in time to help Mama set up the next day. Marc had to get somebody to cover his evening class so we could leave late afternoon." She looked at us. "It was something, that party. Lasted all weekend."

She suddenly laughed. "I just remembered. Poor Marky was grumpy part of the time because his cell phone fell into the toilet in a rest room while we were on the way south. Of course it was beyond ruined. Had to get a new one. So he couldn't have even made the call, unless he used Daddy and Mama's phone. But he wouldn't have been saying he was coming over that evening, that's for sure."

I knew this wasn't the relevant point, but I nonetheless wondered how Ashley's Daddy had felt about her beau, who was, I suspected, a few years older than he was.

Mackenzie closed his notebook. There wasn't anything more to find out. Marc Wilkins wasn't the mysterious visitor, much as I would have liked him to be, if only to spare Ashley some bumpy growing up.

"Should I have Marc call you?" Ashley asked.

Mackenzie looked as if he were filled with regret. "No need, ma'am," he said.

"I hope you find the right person," she whispered. She begged us to take home the rest of the cheese crisps, and I accepted a bag of them. Any man who is monitoring every morsel produced and digested in his household, making his beloved terrified of letting a few appetizers grow greasy, is a man to avoid. I wasn't all that much older than Ashley, perhaps five years, but I felt like her big sister—her negligent big sister if I didn't actively warn her off this man, as little good as that ever has done anyone.

"That was clever," I said when we were outside. "That mysterious phone call to the mysterious friend."

"All you've got to do is find a way to hint that money's involved, and it does it every time. Unfortunately."

We walked down the path to the car, and my feelings about the relationship spilled over. "What a waste," I said. "You'd think, studying psychology, she'd wonder about needing a daddy. She's going to wake up one morning and realize that he's nothing but . . ." Somewhere around then I realized that, speaking of relationships, the other half of mine hadn't been listening to a word. He had his cell phone out, and was getting ready to speed dial.

"Good thing it's earlier there," he said.

I didn't need to ask where, or who, or why.

"I'll be a minute before we get back on the road."

I sat in the car, listening to his soothing murmurs and suggestions from where he stood by the driver's-side door. His words seemed to come from quite a distance, and I could barely make them out, but they made it clear, once again, that as close and sympathetic as we might be, each of us still had a separate story, or at the very least, variations on a theme.

Mackenzie's evening, the way he'd tell it, was about finding out what he needed to know so as to get out in time to re-engage with the fracturing of his family and friends. And I, if I'd been asked to describe what had been going on, would have spun my tale around observation and worry about the future of the young woman in the apartment, and of my husband's smart and easy way of extracting information. Oh, and perhaps a moment's consideration of my own time crunch—papers waiting to be marked at home. But while we were inside the apartment I hadn't given a thought to the people who were living nonstop in his mind.

Maybe that should have made me sad, that renewed awareness of the spaces between people, and the unknowableness of others. But it didn't, because of the places that weren't unknown.

I got out of the car and went and stood close to him, and when he clicked the phone shut, I kissed him.

"What's that about?" he asked me.

"For starters, it's because you don't count the cheese crisps," I said.

Eighteen

The day bloomed clear and sparkling, as if winter had reconsidered and backed off a step. Days like this always feel like fresh starts, clean slates, and they promise to provide all the energy you'll need to get through them.

And it did feel that way. Opal greeted me with her usual sunny enthusiasm and said that it couldn't be a nicer day, could it now, and she wasn't one to rush south at the first chill of winter. She enjoyed the seasons, one by one, including this one in particular. "Call me cheimaphilic," she said.

"I don't think I can."

She chuckled. "Worse comes to worst, you get yourself a chittering-bite."

I stood there, waiting.

"Which one?" she asked.

"Both."

"Isn't it obvious? Call me fond of winter—"

"Okay," I said. "You are fond of winter."

She closed her eyes in mock annoyance. "And if it's too cold for you, I'd suggest a bit of bread in the mouth to keep your teeth from chattering."

"My ignorance is astounding," I said. "As must be evident on a daily basis."

She looked down and smiled, then told me that yesterday, once again, the hurricane collections had been remarkably generous. "Or maybe they always were," she said, and her wrinkles moved into a new, more dejected arrangement. "I thought about it last night, and those adorable children hinted at it, and I think now that we had—have—pirates and brigands in our hallways. Some collectors didn't make it to me with the full amount, I fear. Plus, the first week I was here I thought it safe enough if I put the money I received in the file cabinet. But sometimes, I have to leave the office for a second. I always close that gate there, but . . ." The webs of wrinkles on her face deepened until her features nearly disappeared. "If I ever find the wantwit who snatched that cash," she said, "I'm afraid I'll have a flagitious reaction."

"Wantwit," I repeated. "Perfect. That one shouldn't be lost."

"What's wrong with flagitious?"

"Its incomprehensibility?"

"Wicked or criminal," she said. "Shamefully so. Doesn't it sound that way? Why on earth should these gems become extinct?"

"We can't even blame it on global warming," I said.

"We're losing so many of them, all the time, it breaks my heart. I'm just doing my bit to try to push back doomsday," she said.

If I hadn't already been in an upbeat mood, Opal Codd's one-woman fight to save endangered vocabulary words certainly put me into one. The same crystal-clear, effervescent air seemed to fill the classroom as well, and I had a remarkably good home-room and morning.

By noon, I was able to take a necessary deep breath and eat lunch at my desk while I made a list of things I had to do about Phoebe. I wished we'd never promised Sasha that we'd look into it, but we had. When I'd finished my tuna salad sandwich, I still had time to make a phone call, and tick something off the list.

I thought it was fairly useless talking with Jesse Farmer. I didn't expect much. He wasn't on my "M" list, and even without having seen that initial in her book, I wouldn't think a man who'd murdered a woman he was dating would show up at her memorial with his son in tow. And since Sasha hadn't heard of Jesse Farmer, I didn't think it had been a very long-lived relationship. But still, maybe he'd have an idea, shine a light on an aspect of Phoebe that wasn't yet clear to me. I was indeed grasping at straws, but straws were all I had. I went to the office to check Jonesy's emergency contact numbers, and walked out into the hallway to phone his father. This wasn't school business, and I could count on being paid no attention by the students passing by.

Jesse Farmer's answering machine picked up and I listened to his message, said in the lulling voice of a jazz station DJ. He'd missed his calling, working as he did with antiques. I huddled over my phone, shielding it with my hand because students—loud students—were moving back and forth around me, en route in or out of the school. I identified myself after the beep. "But this isn't a school-related issue. No problem with Jonesy, so please don't worry on that account. I'm researching something and I be-lieve you could help me out. I'd love to talk with you if I could, at your convenience."

Let us hope his convenience dovetailed with my teaching hours. "Could you give me a call on my cell about what time would work? I'd be happy to come to your . . ." I realized I didn't know what he did with antiques. If he had a store, an auction house, if he was a restorer. "I'd be happy to come to you." I gave him my cell phone number. "I look forward to talking with you. Thanks in advance, Mr. Farmer."

I clicked the phone shut and looked up and saw Jonesy staring at me, gape-mouthed.

"I was walking by," he said. "Was that my father? That Mr. Farmer you were talking to?"

"I wasn't talking to him, only leaving a message."

"Yeah, but my father?"

I nodded.

"Why did you phone him?"

"It has nothing to do with you," I said. "Honestly. So don't worry."

"Nothing to do with me," he repeated. "Really. You phoned my father."

"I need information about something that has nothing to do with school and I think he can help me, and really, Jonesy, I think I've answered your question."

He kept shaking his head, watching me, then he mumbled, "Sorry," and hurried past me, outside.

Rushing off to polar poker, I supposed. Sitting in the park, fingers turning blue. Or, more logically, going to a nearby apartment. Student's parents out working, nobody home, and an hour to play. Griffith's apartment, I was sure—until I censored myself for always assigning anything I deemed negative to him.

I returned to my room and forgot about Jonesy till two periods later, when the juniors sauntered into my room, or at least some of them did. Others lagged at the door, eyeing one another, and changing the atmosphere with each step and gesture.

The second bell rang, and I realized that a sizeable proportion of the class was still outside the door, hovering in the hallway, and at its center, as I could have said without looking, was Griffith. I'd never seen him speak with any real heat or energy, never heard him tell anybody what to do or where to be, and yet he remained the core of whatever was going on.

This time, three boys were with him. One spoke, glancing at

Griffith while he did so, then he grew silent, as was his friend, while Jonesy gesticulated and turned away from the group.

I tried to think back to earlier in the semester, to see if I'd stored any memories of Jonesy as this constantly agitated young man. I couldn't, but perhaps that was because I'd been over-focused on Griffith and how much he annoyed me.

Griffith put a hand on Jonesy's shoulder. He didn't pull or tug, but the gesture was still a command, high school style, and Jonesy reacted with a glance at him, followed by floor-staring, looking chastised.

"Bell rang, gentlemen," I called out, and all three faces registered annoyed surprise. I was intruding on their lives.

Once everyone was settled, I collected their Richard Cory papers, and we looked at the two other poems by Robinson in our anthology: "Miniver Cheevy," who drank, oblivious to the life around him and "sighed for what was not," and "An Old Story."

> *Strange that I did not know him then.*
> *That friend of mine!*
> *I did not even show him then*
> *One friendly sign.*

I read that verse and couldn't help myself. I glanced at Griffith, hoping I wasn't reading something autobiographical. He was paying me no attention. His half-closed eyes were on the book in front of him, though I was sure he wasn't actually reading along.

He wasn't my friend. The poem wasn't about us.

When I got to the final lines:

> *I would have rid the earth of him*
> *Once, in my pride . . .*
> *I never knew the worth of him*
> *Until he died.*

Well, then. It had nothing to do with me, but the class was silent for a moment, thinking about its ideas.

"I want you to give this a try," I said, and their meditative expressions hardened and grew wary. "Robinson imagined an entire town and populated it with recognizable types. I know you aren't poets and you aren't expected to produce something eternal in a week, but I want you to observe and think, so that all of us, collectively, can create our imaginary town and its people. One poem about somebody. You can write it like this last one, the inner thoughts of somebody about somebody else, or paint a brief portrait as with 'Richard Cory' and 'Miniver Cheevy.' They're all very short stories, aren't they? Snapshots. If you're of a mind to do so, you can also illustrate your poem—show us what your Miniver or Richard looks like."

"Pepperville," somebody called out.

"What's that?"

"That's the town. Your town!"

Pepperville it was. I was delighted. No other class had come up with that, and more importantly, naming the town meant acceptance of the idea.

Of course, we had to thread through detailed questions about the assignment, specifics of length, deadline, format, and acceptable types. Extra credit for two poems? What would become of these? What if you had never noticed anybody, ever? Did you still have to write about a person? Couldn't it be a dog? Or trees?

They would all become Constitutional scholars some day, thanks to my class where they'd learned to examine any cluster of words with a microscope, in search of loopholes and possible exemptions.

While I answered their questions on automatic pilot, I stacked up the Richard Cory compositions they'd handed in, and flipped through them. Not that I could tell much by a two-second peek, but I could see that they'd at least mastered the required format and had used a computer so that I wouldn't have to un-scramble impossible handwriting. They all seemed adequate on that point—except one, which I pulled out of the pack.

By the time the bell rang, I thought they not only under-stood the weeks ahead, but accepted the idea. As they left the class, I tapped Jonesy on the shoulder, and as unobtrusively as I could, asked if he'd stay a minute.

"I've got—"

"I'll write you a note," I said, and I showed him his troubling composition. "What happened? Did you hand in an early draft by mistake?" I showed him what I'd received, half a page that ended midsentence with, "Perhaps he was in over his head with no way out. So he looked so, so what? Appearances can be "

He said nothing. I waited. Finally, he shook his head. "That's all I could write. I *tried*. That's all you can ask of anybody." He held his mouth tight with anger.

I waited a second, took a breath, and spoke softly. "You could have finished the sentence. Put a period in there. Or better still, you could have said why you felt unable to write the composi-tion."

He looked as if he might stay silent forever, as if everything he'd ever imagined having to say had dried up with that unfin-ished sentence.

"You've been a decent student up till now. You're interesting. I like your opinions, your ideas. Why stopper them now?"

"Because it's bull—it's stupid! It isn't real and it makes it all pretty. A poem! What good is that?"

"It was only a prompt. A way to get you thinking. A way to get you to express yourself, to think something through. It wasn't about Richard Cory, it was about you."

"Me? Why me? That man had everything and he offs him-self. There isn't one word about real problems or pressures, so what are you saying—I have it worse and if he killed himself—"

"Of course not! I didn't mean it that way. I meant the poem was about giving you a springboard so you could express yourself.

It's a famous poem, and the composition was a way for you to express your ideas about it, about whatever it prompted—even this anger you seem to be feeling about what he did, given his privilege. Writing an essay, practicing being able to express yourself—that's not a bad thing, it's a good thing. It's so you'll be heard, will know how to be heard. So you won't be unknown the way he was. Letting your ideas—your personality—be known."

"Why me? What do you mean it's about me?"

I took a deep breath. " 'You' meaning everybody. Mankind. Womankind. And you know that, Jonesy. Why are you twisting my words and intentions around?"

He stared at me without any emotion I could decipher.

"Am I not making sense?" I finally asked.

"If you mean do I understand what you're saying, I do. But you don't get it. I don't have anything to do with some stupid made-up person. He's not me! Besides, why do we have to keep talking about suicide and death? Why is that all you and the poets want to talk about?"

Phoebe. He'd been at Phoebe's memorial service, a memorial for a suicide. Had it upset him that much, derailed him this way? Maybe it was hard for him to express sorrow over the self-inflicted death of a woman he'd have considered ancient. "I'm sorry," I said. "I hadn't realized that Phoebe Ennis's suicide troubled you so much. I should have been more sensitive."

"Why bring her up? What are you trying to say? Just *say* it!"

I couldn't say anything. I was trying to listen through the static of his emotions to hear what he was actually saying. He was obviously going through a hard, defiant time, as witness the essay and his general touchiness. "Jonesy," I said softly as the bell rang for the next period. "I'm not pulling anything over on you. I don't have a secret agenda. If you'll think about all this, I'm sure you'll see that the poem is in the anthology, and the phone call was not about you, and—"

"I need that note," he said.

"What?"

"I'm late. The excuse note."

I wrote it out, intrigued that he worried about getting in trouble for entering class late, but seemed unconcerned about handing me the bare shadow of a composition in which he hadn't even bothered to complete a sentence.

I wanted to write this and the telephone episode off to adolescent hormones, but I wasn't sure. I'd told him that contacting his father had nothing to do with him, and it had been the truth. But now, given his reaction to that and to an innocuous poem and assignment, I really did want to ask his father about him.

Did that make me a liar?

Nineteen

Jesse Farmer returned my call within a half hour, but I was
teaching and had the phone off. I didn't get to check messages
till after school, by which time I had two messages, his and one
from Sasha, who wanted to be updated, perhaps over dinner
tonight.

His message suggested that he could either come to school
the next day, or we could talk on the phone, or meet at his
store—which he couldn't leave this particular day because staff
was out sick. He said he'd be there all day, and if that was my option, I should simply stop by.

I phoned Mackenzie and left a message about dinner on his
cell phone, asking him to leave a message on mine as to whether
it was a go. Pizza sounded good to me. Then I spent a moment

wondering how we all had functioned when we didn't have instant access to one another this way. Looking at the logistics of the day, and after checking the senior Farmer's address, I opted to visit him in his store. It was on my way home, on the edge of where the Colonial residential area of Society Hill eases into what was the Colonial commercial area of Old City where I live. It was also close to the pizzeria.

I realized that while I was now more interested in talking to Jesse Farmer about his son than about his own relationship with Phoebe, I still hoped for information—a name, a plan, a destination, an annoyance—that Phoebe had shared with him and that might lead somewhere. I wasn't counting on it, however.

The address he'd left on his message matched Jonesy's home address on the school files. He apparently lived above his store. I found it easily on Chestnut Street. It was within shouting distance of City Tavern, where having a mug of beer feels like a virtuous dip into history, knowing that the recipe was devised by George Washington and Thomas Jefferson. I thought briefly about inviting him to join me in a drink there, then remembered that we were meeting at the store because he couldn't leave it today.

Before I went in, I paused to admire the window display: an elegantly set table with small corner spotlights that made twisted silver candelabra gleam, heavily cut crystal goblets glint rainbow colors, silver settings glow, and the translucent porcelain radiate light. It was the sort of setting and ambience I doubt I will ever attain in my life. I wasn't sure I'd even want to, but the option would have been pleasant.

On a thick Oriental rug beneath the table, a life-sized china spaniel sat, looking upwards, and on a delicate gilded easel beside the table was a still life of roses such as I have never seen, looking as if they'd been flung onto a rumpled piece of pale yellow silk.

It was not instantly clear what category of objects was for sale. The name of his store, written in gold script, was *Extraordi-*

naire! Okay. A little pretentious, but descriptive. Anything that was special belonged here. The name seemed familiar, and I wondered how, or why, since I did not normally haunt "special" shops of this sort. Then I remembered: It had been on a card among Phoebe's refrigerator memorabilia.

The inside was as elegantly arranged as the window had been, and had none of the clutter I associate with consignment or antiques stores. Instead of a haphazard piling around, there were small mock-room arrangements, sofas and chairs gathered around coffee tables, the furniture accessorized with other extraordinary objects.

"Mr. Farmer?" I said to the man sitting behind a small desk.

He smiled and stood as I introduced myself, then pointed at a set of wing chairs that flanked a round table. "Might as well use them. They're comfortable and as nobody is exactly banging down the doors today, we should be able to talk in comfort. Is my son giving you trouble? I've been worrying about him. Mitch has been strained, I can tell, since I—we—since the divorce. Splitting time between us, shuttling back and forth, it's been a rough adjustment."

"It's difficult for everyone," I said. "But children do adjust."

"Guess you see a lot of it at that school."

I nodded. He was taking comfort from my platitudes, and I didn't know what else to say. His son wasn't giving me concern, precisely, though the unfinished essay and his non-explanation of it did concern me. But listening to his father protecting him, worrying about him, I was less and less inclined to present him as any sort of problem. The kid was going through a horrible time, and if his temper was frayed, it was understandable. Why make a few misunderstandings into something they were not, possibly escalate the tension and definitely increase his father's worries?

"Actually," I said after I'd settled into the leather-upholstered chair, "thanks for the heads up about what's going on at home. He does seem more tense than usual, but it's understandable, and not a problem. In fact, I didn't come here because of him. I wanted to talk with you about Phoebe Ennis."

"Really?" He blinked and frowned, and sat back, more deeply buried in his armchair. I could almost see him relocating me, pulling me from the predictable storage in his brain, and holding me, dangling, until he knew where to file me. "And why would that be?"

I had to refine my usual "investigating" riff, given that I was this man's son's teacher, so I explained about having a second job, and needing to follow up on some work we were doing for a legal firm.

"You're a part-time investigator?" He was a nice-looking man, his face deeply lined both with the frown I kept seeing between his eyes, and deep laugh lines. I had the sense he hadn't been using those laugh lines too often of late.

"I'm more of a clerical worker in an investigation firm. But it happens that in this case, I knew Phoebe Ennis years ago." I explained the connection. "I thought you, as someone who knew her socially, might be able to help us out."

"Socially? Where did you get that idea? You think I dated her?"

"You didn't?"

He shook his head. "Why would you think that?"

"Because you were there with Jonesy—sorry, I didn't mean to use his nickname."

He shook his head and smiled. "He's been called that since first grade. Farmer Jones. Nothing wrong with it, and don't worry. Go on."

"You were at her memorial service last Sunday, and you aren't in her address book, where I'd think she'd put an old friend, and . . . no matter. I'm embarrassed I leaped to conclusions and was obviously wrong. May I ask, then, what the connection was?"

He smiled, and stayed in the deep shadow of the chair. "Business."

"She was a customer?" Her house did not in any way resemble this store's elegant window, or the small and pleasant arrangements inside. But there had been that business card.

The slight frown again creased the skin between his eyes. "She was a client. She, ah, died before she consigned anything to the store—if, in fact, that's what she would have opted to do. We never got that far."

"I'm sorry. I'm not clear on the distinction between client and customer."

"She didn't buy things from me. She hired me to come out to her house in New Jersey and appraise a few things. I liked the woman, but not in a romantic manner. I liked her spirit and optimism. I'd been going through something less than an optimistic spell."

That seemed as much as he was willing to offer. "Was it just that one visit, then?" I asked.

"No. She wanted to talk more about options and certain issues pertaining to the appraisal, and we had dinner together—a business dinner. I phoned her after I'd done some research for her, and couldn't find her. I left a few messages, and then, reading the paper, I saw a small news article about her death being ruled a suicide. I was shocked, to put it mildly."

"Do I infer, then, that your dinner was close to the day she died?"

"From what I understand, it was the night before. I can't completely explain why I was so personally devastated by the news of her death, as I barely knew her. But when you're with someone twenty-four hours before they take their life, you have to think you missed some signal, some call for help or alert that might have saved her."

"But you didn't get any sense of depression or despair."

He shook his head. "I've replayed every word of the conversation many times, but it was all directed into the future. She wanted to get onto *Antiques Roadshow*, for heaven's sake. She thought I might know somebody who'd get her on it. She was wrong, but that isn't a suicidal-sounding woman, is it? There were other things we discussed as well, and they all involved the future. Why have all those questions about what to do next if you're going to erase any chance of it?"

I shook my head. "During the conversation, did she mention anybody else, or any annoyances, problems? Worries? Issues in the life of a widow?"

"Like I said, I couldn't find a single reason to think she was planning to kill herself. In fact, given that you're here, I'm wondering if she actually did."

I could feel how forced my close-lipped smile must look.

"You can't say, is that it?"

"I can say that nothing has been completely resolved."

He looked pensive, shaking his head, the worried frown in place again. "The implications are horrifying."

"Yes. There was a second death—definitely a murder—at the house this week, which was horrible itself, and casts further doubt on Phoebe's death."

He bit at his bottom lip and shook his head even more vigorously, negating it, refusing to allow such raw ugliness into this beautiful retreat.

"Obviously," I said, "it makes one think that there was something—or more than one something—in that house that somebody wanted." We had another brief quiet period. I finally decided that if he wasn't going to take the bait, I'd push it farther in front of him. "Phoebe always talked about her 'treasures,' but nobody thought she actually had any. They were precious to her, yes, but that's where it ended. Her house is so cluttered, and I'd think it was mostly kitsch."

Jesse Farmer sat, his lips closed, looking at me as if he were meditating with his eyes open and had no need, might never have a need, to speak.

"Did she have things of value?" I finally asked.

Now he leaned forward. "This may sound as if I'm being self-important, but I'm not going to answer that without some sort of police authority on your part. I realize I'm not a priest or psychiatrist, and that appraisals are not life-and-death issues, and you must know that this is particularly difficult saying to my son's English teacher, who I know is completely trustworthy. But you're sitting here wearing a different metaphorical hat, and so it's to that status, which is, you must admit, somewhat vague, that I have to say I do not divulge that information. I will not, except to those who come with warrants proving their purpose, and to legitimate heirs, and only then with proof. This has been my policy for years, since I opened the shop. It will come as no shock to hear that people use that kind of information for less than benign purposes. Look, you yourself hinted that two women might now have died because of something that seemed valuable to them. Something somebody else wanted.

"Nothing but trouble happens whether people think they have things of value that are actually worthless, or vice versa. So forgive me, but I can't give you the information you want."

He did not look about to bend, and I understood his reservation and thanked him for his time. "One last question," I said. "Did anybody, including Phoebe, know what the appraised value of the objects was?"

The frown reappeared, and he seemed to need to consider the question. Or perhaps he was simply tired of fending me off. Finally, he shook his head. "Only me. We never got to that third meeting. That's what I had been phoning her about the day I found out she was dead."

Brick wall time again. If nobody else knew, then it didn't matter what Phoebe actually had. I was thinking in circles, and creating my own maze. I had to find a way out to where the explanation of her death lay.

I thanked him again, and made my way through a lot of treasures in transition, from one proud owner to the next. A lot of stories were in this long peaceful room, and I wondered where Phoebe's fit into it.

* * *

Mackenzie was reading when I reached the pizzeria.

"Napoleon?" I said when I saw the writing on the spine.

"You're behaving like a teacher, upset I'm not doing my assigned homework." It was true, and it wasn't flattering, but he said it with a wink.

"I'm sorry. I only—"

"I know," he said. "Guilty as charged. I'm always complaining about not having time to do my regular reading for school, plus everything else. But you know you got me interested in the man, and now I'm close to the end—the poor guy's off in exile, and the party's over for him. I figured you might be delayed, and I'm kind of fascinated by this whole thing. People chop up their king and toss him out, screaming liberty, equality, fraternity—and wind up with an emperor. How does that happen? What in us leads to that criminal excess and then . . ." He smiled. "See? It is indeed related to my official course of study."

"You going to write your dissertation about the French Revolution?"

He made a *tsk*ing sound. "Don't think so. But who knows?"

"The same idea interested my ninth graders. The part where a good idea—the liberty, equality thing—goes over some cliff and becomes a new kind of oppression, as bad as the one they're throwing over ever was."

"Well," he said, "it's not a bad thing to become aware of. It didn't stop with the French Revolution."

Sasha bounced in at that point, red-faced and out of breath. "So hungry I practically ran here," she said as she sat down. "Let's order first, then tell me what you two Sherlocks have unearthed."

The pizzeria had perhaps not been the wisest choice of venue, as the noise was overpowering. People came to eat and shout, and with each beer downed, the group of young men near us grew louder and more raucous. Sasha, Mackenzie, and I huddled at our table near the window, talking in stage whispers, and after the sausage pizza arrived, we leaned over it so as to hear, thereby endangering our clothing.

"What's happening with the investigation? The one the cops are doing about Toy's murder?" Sasha asked. "I can't find anything out even though I check the Jersey papers every day."

Mackenzie shook his head. "Nothing, really."

"You've got a friend there, too?" I asked.

His shrug said, "But of course. Why ask?" "They've looked for anybody she knew, but she didn't know that many people well enough to have stirred up deliberate passions of that sort. Mostly knew clients, and all of them were apparently satisfied. Definitely not interested in killing her. She still had her wallet and money, so it doesn't sound like a junkie. She seemed legitimate, her business on the up and up. She did staging in Chicago, too, but apparently, an aunt in Philly promised her an interest in her real-estate business if she helped care for the woman. Hasn't happened yet, though. The old auntie is holding onto all her assets."

"One thing my friend told me," Mackenzie said, "was that they found evidence that the house had probably been broken into several times. A basement door had been messed with so that it didn't completely lock. But they can't tell if anybody was taking things."

"If you saw the house, you'd know why," I said. "But I'll bet they were, and that they were back again the day Toy interrupted them."

"Stealing the car wasn't their object, either," Mackenzie said. "Just convenient. They found her BMW abandoned on Delaware Avenue."

"Abandoned? In good shape?"

He nodded.

"When? How long before they found it?"

"That same day. Or night, really. Somebody was trying to steal it and the alarm went off, and for the first time in recent history, somebody noticed that a car alarm was signaling and called nine-one-one."

"The thief—the killer—locked it up and set the alarm before he abandoned it?"

"Guess so."

"Prints?"

"Nothing they can identify. Not even the would-be car thief's."

"It's winter. The driver wore gloves," I said. "Probably the guy trying to break in did, too."

Sasha gave a what's-to-be-done-about-it? lift of her shoulders. "What about Phoebe?" she said. "What's happening with that?"

"I'm about out of ideas," I confessed. "Marc was in Virginia that night, the blind-date guy was in California. Merilee? Who knows, but nothing to connect her with Phoebe that night, and it would be really hard for me to convince myself that the guy I talked with today had anything to do with her death."

"Who was he again?" she asked me.

"Jesse Farmer. He has a store called Extraordinaire! two blocks from here. Antiques and appraisals, and she apparently came to him for the latter." I eyed Sasha's crust. I happen to love crust, and would be so happy with an entire carb-loaded meal of pure crust alone that I'm astounded when people walk away from plates littered with it.

"Appraisal?" Sasha said with some wonder. "Of what?" Then she noticed my glance. "Take it," she said. "Please."

"Her treasures." We both smiled. I would have laughed, but it's hard and unaesthetic to eat and laugh at the same time.

"Did he actually say something was worthwhile?" Sasha asked.

"He wouldn't say anything. He never got to tell her whether it was or wasn't, but he saw her for a business dinner the night before she died, and he was emphatic about her not seeming depressed. She wanted to go on *Antiques Roadshow.*"

Sasha shook her head. "I loved her, but I can just imagine them looking at her refrigerator magnet collection, or the pottery puppies."

"There was that silver," I said. "That was good stuff, I think."

"But not exactly a treasure. The Berg family silver—or silver-plate for all I know—isn't going to wow them on *Antiques Road-show*. His royal highness Oscar Berg is not that well known."

"I feel I am being left out of a joke here, ladies," Mackenzie said. "That's impolite."

"I've told you about Phoebe's treasures," I insisted.

He shook his head. "You told me about the clutter in her house, her collections, but you're obviously laughing at something more."

"I never mentioned her, um, pretentiousness?"

"Meaning?"

"Oh, say, claims of royal ancestry?"

He raised one eyebrow. "I think I would have remembered that. Any special royal? Any special country's royalty? Where'd her family come from in Europe?"

Sasha sighed. "Her family, what she knew of it, has been here since Colonial times."

"Here, in a fledgling democracy, where royalty is generally not an easy commodity to find," he said. "Unless she meant it metaphorically. Theatrical royalty?"

Sasha shook her head.

"Okay, so she was delusional."

I put my hands out, palms up, then looked at the gesture that I had unconsciously made. A gesture of offering, but with empty palms. I put my hands on my lap. "She was illegitimate—does anybody even use that word anymore? She had a single mother who seems to also have lacked a resident and known father, and they were dirt poor, so these stories were spun around their origins. Something to help the girl hold her head up at school."

Sasha picked up the thread. "Nobody believed the stories except Phoebe. She took them to heart. Maybe because she had to. It was a survival mechanism and it got her through bad times. It was silly, but somehow endearing. Back when she was with my dad, she spent huge amounts of time on genealogical research—to no avail, as far as I know. And I think I'd know if she knew.

Everybody would have known. Honestly, when we looked at her computer, I thought we'd find all kinds of genealogical sites, but apparently not."

"She was researching live men, not dead ones," I said.

"You know, you went through that list of probably-didn't-do-it's and you left off Dennis! Are you forgetting Dennis?" Sasha asked. "Because you shouldn't. He's a given. If something under-handed's going on, Dennis is nearby. Trust me."

"Ah, yes," Mackenzie said. "Dennis. I thought you'd never ask."

Why had we needed to ask at all? The man was a little too into his Great Detective act, withholding information for maxi-mum dramatic effect. I wanted to remind him that it wouldn't have broken any international code of silence if he'd told us what-ever he knew about Dennis a half hour ago. But maybe this inno-cent game was his antidote to the other miseries he was coping with. If this provided a minor pressure valve, so be it.

Instead of saying anything, I looked at the pizza pan, which now held only one piece. I saw both Sasha and Mackenzie eye it and look away, politely.

"You guys split it," I said. "If I can have more of the crusts."

They gave me a decidedly David Copperfield look, and Sasha even tossed one of the crusts my way. "What about Den-nis?" I asked after happily munching through Sasha's leftovers. "Do we have to beg?"

"It appears my theory was correct," he said modestly. "Den-nis was tryin' to raise money by hustling out a mortgage on the house you both had inherited. The idea, of course, was to take out as much cash as they'd give him, and you wouldn't know about it, and ultimately, your half of the so-called profit, divided after the bank reclaimed its chunk, would be minuscule."

I sat in stunned silence. Sasha also took a while to regain the power of speech. "How could he do that? She left it to both of us. Isn't that illegal?"

"Well, of course, yes, if anybody catches you. But Dennis went in with his friend—"

"That lawyer!" Sasha said. "That smarmy lawyer buddy of his, I bet."

Mackenzie nodded. "Plus, a tiny blonde with big hair—her name, surprisingly, was Sasha Berg."

"Toy Rasmussen was pretending to be me? She was in on the scam with him?"

"They had the death certificate, and the papers on the house—which, by the way, has no mortgage on it. Apparently, Mr. Ennis had insurance that paid it off when he died. But you didn't know that, did you?"

Sasha shook her head. "I asked Dennis about equity in the house, and he said there wasn't much."

"Not so. Dennis was relying on bluster and smooth talk, and with his two friends and a lot of fast-talk and some documents, he was doing fine."

"He got it, then?" Every trace of the outdoor glow that had bustled in with Sasha was gone from her face, and her voice was only a whisper. I had to lip-read. "He took out all the money?" She closed her eyes and shook her head. "I don't care about the money, but I do care about his stealing it. And Toy!"

Mackenzie smiled. "It was a flawed plan. In fact, Toy's death derailed it. Once the house was a crime scene, appraisers couldn't get in, the mortgage company got more cautious about a house that might have a major stigma on it, somehow somebody found out that the victim and Sasha Berg were not one and the same, and the entire process ground to a halt. Otherwise, I'm not sure what would have happened."

"I am . . . I'm . . . I never trusted him, not even in junior high, but still. This is criminal, isn't it?"

Mackenzie nodded. "I think he'll face charges."

"Good!" Sasha said, her natural voice regained. "And good for you for finding out. You really are a great detective."

"Wait a minute," I said. "How could you have found out?"

He pulled back, an exaggerated expression of indignation on his face. "You're surprised?"

"Come on. How? It was a scam, and it was this week. How did you know where to look, what to ask? Who did you ask?"

"I told you. If he stayed in town—especially if he stayed and pretended to have gone—I was sure he was after money. Didn't you tell me his whole life had been shady schemes and grandiose failures? People don't change. He had money coming in the form of that house, so I tried to think of how he'd want to get still more. An' then I made a few calls to a few banks. Just checking whether a Mr. Dennis Allenby had been in to see the loan officer."

"And they told you?"

"I may have stretched the truth a little. I said I was trying to track him down. That I was handling some of the late Phoebe Ennis's estate, and we'd discovered a problem he needed to attend to, that he'd said he was heading to the bank to arrange a mortgage, and I was hoping I could catch him there. It took three banks before I found him."

"Why would they tell you that? Isn't it private?"

"I didn't ask for a single bit of information except whether he'd been there. Once I knew that he had been to one of them, once I knew there'd been an attempted crime, it wasn't that hard to call in a favor to get some of the law on my side—"

"Somebody on the force?" Sasha asked. "Somebody you used to work with?"

He nodded. "All we wanted was to know what he was trying. No big thing. Except, of course, to Dennis."

"And Toy. She was trying to rob me! I can't get over it—the two of them. And look where it got her!"

We were quiet for a moment. "Hey," I said. "Let's be really shallow and materialistic about this. There's no mortgage. That means a nice chunk of change for you someday."

"No thanks to him," she grumbled.

"Not much is thanks to him," I said. "But there's a further downside as far as I'm concerned. Toy's death hurt him. It didn't help anything."

"And to you, that means he had nothing to do with it," Mackenzie said as he collected Sasha's share of the dinner bill. We all stood and went over to the cashier.

"Doesn't it?" I asked.

He shrugged. "There are unintended consequences, and it's been my experience that criminals are seldom sharp enough to think them through. If they did any long-term planning, they wouldn't be criminals. She was conspiring with him. Truth was, he may have changed his mind, figured she'd signed the papers and he didn't need her anymore. Or afraid she'd somehow let slip what was going on."

"So Merilee and Dennis are still on the list," I said. "What do we do, flip a coin?"

"It would be nice to find a scrap of evidence first," Mackenzie murmured as he signed the credit card slip and opened the door to what had turned into an icy and blustery December night.

"My God but it's cold," Sasha said. "What happened to global *warming*?"

"Did you walk here?" I asked her, and when she said she had, I offered to drive her home. "I'm parked around the corner. Mackenzie's dropping me off, taking the car to go back to the office for a few hours, but he could drop you off first. Or second."

She stamped her feet and shook her head. "I'm on a health and fitness kick, and I'm sticking to it."

"I won't ask how pizza fits into that plan," I said, "but I will ask how long you've been on it."

She looked at her watch. "Since three minutes ago. I took a silent vow after eating that last piece of the pie. I need to burn off a few of those calories. No problem." She pulled the fake-zebra-skin collar of her black coat up.

"Start tomorrow," I said. "Maybe the windchill factor won't be as bad. Or try running in place. Inside your condo."

She smiled. "Do you feel horrible about corrupting me? I had such fine intentions. But I'll only agree if you'll come hang with me while Mackenzie works. What do you say? Have a cup of decaf. I have some stuff I want to talk with you about, anyway."

Stuff. Enough of crime, then. I knew what "stuff" was for Sasha. She'd met somebody. Again. And she didn't want to talk about him in front of Mackenzie, knowing he'd disapprove.

They'd long since ended their initial dislike of each other, but Sasha was aware of Mackenzie's incomprehension and mild irritation about her talent at finding the worst possible men as romantic partners. It stymied me, too, because she was otherwise close to sane. But each one was "different," and I braced myself for the particulars of her newest find.

I had no real urgency about going back to the empty loft. Macavity could wait. He had food and water, and it was Mackenzie for whom he yearned in any case.

Of course there were papers to mark, but there always were. "Deal," I said.

She nodded and we walked toward the car, where I got into the tiny back rather than force her six-foot-tall body into the necessary contortions. "If you're going to drag third parties into your car, and then be polite and accommodating, you should get yourself a four door and get rid of the Bug," she said.

"I'll tell you what. Once you're an heiress with all that house money, you can buy us a bigger car."

"I can see how it's going to be," she said. "People coming out of the woodwork to make claims. You know it isn't really going to be all that much, don't you? It's not exactly a palace."

And then, without anyone needing to say we needed a break from crime, we stopped talking about Phoebe, Toy, Dennis, and the house. Instead, we described our various days, weekend plans, how the people who'd been staying with Mackenzie's aunt and uncle were moving out of Louisiana altogether, and a dissertation idea rolling around in Mackenzie's head. "I'm intrigued by how high morals spin out of control into fanaticism and lawlessness," he said. "Maybe it all comes from reading that book about Napoleon."

We had to circle around because of one-way streets and to stop and start because of traffic, so the relatively short distance to Sasha's condo required a convoluted route and an inordinate amount of time.

"Could have walked it more quickly," I said.

"And burned off at least half a slice's worth of body fat," Sasha said. "Not that I'm sorry you thwarted me."

After Mackenzie had been quiet for several blocks, I leaned forward and tapped his shoulder. "Are you ready to tell us what it is?" I asked.

"Pardon?"

"What's on your mind? I saw that look you got at dinner, as if you mentally sidestepped into your own private space, and now, again. What's it about?"

He chuckled softly, and to my relief skipped the "Maybe we've been married too long because you're reading my mind" riff. "Okay," he said. "Where did you say Phoebe lived, Sasha?"

She squinted at him. "I know you too well to think you've forgotten, but here goes again: in New Jersey. Bordentown. She was born and bred in Jersey, though she did move around a little with all those marriages. Why?"

He took a deep breath. "Because there was, in fact, a king in Jersey. The king of Spain lived there."

"Gee, you'd think one of the requirements for that job would be living in Spain."

"The former king of Spain, then. Joseph Bonaparte. Napoleon's big brother."

"No," I said. "That's too—you're serious?"

He nodded. "Nappy got Elba, Joe got Bordentown. I didn't want to say it right out at dinner because I had to think about it for a while, because—"

"It changes everything."

He nodded again. "It's speculation, nothing more. Joseph

was going to be exiled, just like Napoleon, only he was going to be sent to Russia. He escaped to the States under a false name, carrying a suitcase full of jewels. But he also had around five million dollars worth of gold buried in Switzerland. Eventually, his manservant went back and retrieved it."

"Huh," Sasha said. "Five million dollars back then? That'd be—incredible now."

"So would five million," I said.

"Interesting how easily we can mention his stealing—it was stealing, right?—a fortune because it was long ago. And because he was a king in New Jersey."

"He often wintered in Philadelphia."

"Now you're being ridiculous—and when I buy you a bigger car, the most important thing will be a decent heating system. It's freezing in here." Sasha smacked the dashboard.

"My point being that it doesn't matter that much where Phoebe's family lived. Joseph's wife didn't accompany him, so there were also many liaisons."

I looked at him. "Then Phoebe could, indeed, be—"

"Dear God," Sasha said softly. "Remember how she'd be drawing those charts when we were in junior high? Always looking for the illustrious ancestor? Poor Phoebe. She'd have been so thrilled to know."

"Nothing to know," our chauffeur reminded us. "Family legend could have created that story. You tell it enough generations, it becomes history. No way to prove anything. But there's something else. The legislature passed a bill that allowed him—a non-citizen—to buy land. He had about a thousand acres, and a mansion, Point Breeze, filled with the treasures of Europe—"

"Point Breeze!" I said. "Phoebe's maiden name was Breeze. DeBreeze. From Breeze?"

"Maybe. Doesn't have to be. Somebody in her family could have decided to adopt the name. In any case, there was a huge fire—supposedly set by an angry Russian woman."

"All those treasures lost," I said. "Pity." We were by now sitting, idling in what would have been a great parking spot, down the street from Sasha's place. Mackenzie finished his tale.

"That's the interesting part. The story is that the good people of Bordentown came to the rescue. They carried the paintings and statues and whatnots to safety. And then, according to the story, they returned everything."

"Really?" Sasha and I asked in unison.

"You're cynics," Mackenzie said with a shrug. "But I agree. I find the official story a little hard to believe. I mean we've got a man living like the king he was, with money he stole and smuggled out, money basically taken from the common people of Italy and Spain. He's a nice guy, but still, he represents the opposite of the democracy these people are building. His mansion is surrounded by ordinary, hard-working people. Small farmers, laborers. And suddenly, the treasure house—treasures gotten by nothing this man did, but through his brother's conquests that more or less stand for everything we weren't supposed to stand for—is up for grabs."

"So you're saying—people grabbed."

"Most people obviously didn't. Their inventory seemed pretty complete when it was over. I'd think that nearly everybody returned whatever they took. But *everybody*? I don't think human nature changes, no matter how prettily the history books word it."

"So even if Phoebe wasn't his descendant, she still might have had something that failed to be returned after the fire. Is that a polite way of putting it? One—or more—of her treasures might truly be just that. Ill-gotten or given to the pretty woman with whom he slept," Sasha said.

"But who would know this story?" I asked. "Who on our list is a student of history and would know this?"

"There's the rub," Mackenzie said. "Go figure that out, you two. Once you do, we're home free."

Twenty

"What do you think it could be, that treasure?" I asked as we opened the outer door to Sasha's building. "And shouldn't that door be locked?"

"Could be treasures," she said, then she looked at me quizzically. "It never is, till after nine P.M."

"I know, but shouldn't it be, all the time?"

A car pulled away from the curb, and startled me.

"You're getting twitchy and weird." She closed the door behind her.

She was right, but that didn't mean I could un-twitch. My mind felt clogged with potential dangers, as if Mackenzie's information about Bonaparte had loosened items otherwise safely bolted down. Who now was a threat? Who knew enough to kill Phoebe and Toy?

"Why do you look like a deer in the headlights?" Sasha asked. "Come on. I'll make you decaf or tea. Or are you afraid Dennis is going to come back and rant again?"

"It's not that." Maybe it was. Too many questions about Dennis. But too many questions now about too many people.

Jesse Farmer. Not an "M," but who knew what Phoebe might have meant by that letter? He'd been doing research for her. He'd know about the kind of valuables a Bonaparte might have owned. Maybe he was planning to rip Phoebe off.

"Not to worry," Sasha said. "Dennis would be too scared to, now that his little scam has been foiled. But if he does show up, I am going to personally kill him for what he was trying to do to me. Come on. A flight of stairs never hurt anybody, and it'll burn off one half a bite of sausage." We started up.

Sasha's condo was once part of a grand house, now sliced into three units, one on each floor. It makes for the kind of high-ceilinged spaciousness that is rare in newer buildings, but if you're in a twitchy kind of mood, it's also obvious that it was never designed to be a fortress, the way so many city apartment buildings are. There wasn't any real lobby, only a narrow entry sliced off the original house's more gracious one, with a staircase straight ahead, mail cubbies that were once open, but after some pilfering, were now covered with locked doors, and an elevator that hadn't worked within recent memory.

"Phoebe always said her 'treasures,' plural," Sasha said. "Maybe there are lots of them. Then again, she would do things like pick up one of her pink crystal pyramids, or the plate with Charles and Diana painted on it when she said that, and I'm pretty sure those things never belonged to the Bonapartes."

We went into Sasha's condo, which, unlike the building it-self, had a spacious entryway leading down a short hall to the living room.

I closed the door but stopped mid-motion.

"What?" Sasha asked.

"Listen."

She appeared to, then she shook her head. "What?"

"That horn. Did you hear it? Two honks, then a stop, then two honks."

She pulled back in an exaggerated and stagy reaction. "Dear friend," she said, "you are in deep trouble. Is it living with a crime-obsessed man that's doing it? Was it seeing Toy dead? Or are you paranoid?"

"Didn't you hear it?"

Before she spoke, she looked at me with an expression you never want to see on anybody's face whose opinion you value. "If I heard a horn, so what?" she finally said quietly. "People honk night and day. It's a rude city."

"Didn't it sound like a signal?"

"People who hear or see patterns in random events are in big trouble, pal. But even if it was a signal—why think it's a bad one? Maybe it's Romeo saying, 'Juliet, I've got wheels, so come on down.' "

Her worried expression made me realize I was tuned up tightly in a way that wasn't helpful and didn't make particular sense. "Thanks," I said. "I guess I needed that. It's just that this week—"

Now she spoke much more warmly. "I know. Me, too. And I don't know how anybody's supposed to pull away and regain balance, but you have to, don't you? You especially. You have to keep telling yourself that Toy—con artist that we now know her to be—was nonetheless just in the wrong place—or the right one, where the supposed treasures lay. Or, what it sounds like, the place somebody had been robbing with great regularity since Phoebe died." She walked ahead of me into the living room, then turned and, head tilted slightly, watched me as if waiting for something she'd expected.

I remembered. "Tell me about him," I said. "What's wonderful and unique about him?"

"I thought you'd never ask." She unbuttoned her coat and tossed it and her long black scarf onto an ottoman. "Coffee? Tea? Something stronger?"

"I'm going to need to work when I get home, but tea would be great." I needed warming up, and I left my coat on for a moment longer. Sasha might be economizing, given the current cost of gas, so I said nothing about how chilly it was in here.

Jesse Farmer, I thought again. But Toy? Why, then, go after Toy?

"Make yourself at home." She went into the kitchen, talking nonstop as she did. "He is really different," she said.

As was every other man, every other time, I didn't have to listen that attentively because I'd heard all this before. Why didn't the two murders, the two deaths, fit into one piece?

"Honestly," Sasha said. "I think I've found him."

"Where?"

Dennis was the one who needed money, who had motives for both murders, sordid as those motives might be.

"Met him on a blind date my aunt arranged!" Sasha burst out laughing. "Surprised you, didn't I? No bar, no online service— my aunt Cassie!" It sounded as if she clanged the spoon against the cup on purpose, as if we'd hit some prize on a quiz show. I was shocked into attention by her answer. Religious great-aunts' matchmaking was not high on Sasha's list of favorites.

"Don't tell me," I said. "Based on the little I've heard about great-aunt Cassie, he's a man of the cloth, right?"

"Not quite," she said. "Unless cloth means he's well dressed. He's actually a scientist, an oceanographer, who . . . "

She continued to talk, but I no longer really heard her because the din of everything else—people, need for money, knowing about Bonaparte—was now fighting for space against a third factor, and this one was here, nearby. Something was wrong, but what?

I listened. No more horn. No noise outside at all. Was that all it was? The shock of silence?

No. The horn had stopped its two at a time message a while back. This had just happened.

I looked around, but the room was, as always, a mélange of styles that combined to suggest another era, one you should recall and be able to identify, but couldn't. I saw the same unknowable time and place. Nothing moved, nothing had a new, unnatural protrusion, silhouette, or dent.

From the kitchen, Sasha described the scientist's hair and smile, muffling whatever other sounds I might have otherwise heard. But even so, something had shifted. Was there now a shadow where there hadn't been one? Sasha had turned on only one floor lamp in her passage through the room, and its circle of light did not reach into the corners.

I barely breathed, I was straining so hard to hear and see. It— whatever it was—wasn't here in the living area, but beyond; in the shadows of the dining area, under the long satiny cloth covering the table, behind the brocade drapery. I stood up slowly, trying to avoid any floor squeaks, any shift in furniture.

And then I saw it, the slightest bulge in the brocade drapes, the shift of darker shadow on dark cloth. I grabbed the first solid and moveable object near me and slowly advanced toward the drapes, my hand gripping what I suddenly realized was the ugly statue—the scrawny centurian in his sculpted tunic. Skinny Caesar. He was made of metal, so I didn't care that his muscles were weak-looking. I gripped it tightly, as if it were enchanted and had the power of that metallic legionnaire. As if his short knife would protect me.

I advanced, my eyes on the drapery. I thought I saw it move again, the slightest sucking inward, pulling back in on itself.

The teapot screamed, and I nearly did, too. But that high, ungodly warning meant only that the water had boiled. The scream died off as Sasha removed the pot from the burner.

I reached the drapery, stood there, trying to breathe, then with my right arm brandishing Caesar, I put my left hand on the edge of the drape.

The scream was Sasha's this time. "For God's sake, what are you—"

I half turned, and moved my head to make her come closer. She was carrying a pot of boiling water, an even better weapon than the Roman statue.

"Amanda, really—you'll kill somebody!"

My eyes wide—how many ways could I silently signal somebody to be quiet? In any case, I'd failed to get the message across, but seeing is believing, so while she shouted at me, I whipped the drapery back.

And revealed nothing. No one.

"What in God's name were you—"

"I saw movement—"

"The window's open! Air currents do that." She was giving me that look again, and I could understand how, from her point of view, I deserved it. But she was wrong.

"Sit down," she said, brandishing the teapot until I was afraid she'd use it on me. "And put that down. It isn't a—"

"Somebody's here," I whispered, nonetheless sitting on a dining-table chair. I kept hold of the soldier, needing all the help I could get. From where I sat, I could see into Sasha's bedroom, which looked still and unoccupied. Her window curtains were pulled back with ties. Nobody could hide behind them, and nobody could hide under her bed, where, she'd once proudly shown me, she had drawers for extra clothing storage. It was a spacious flat, but it did not have an infinite number of rooms. There was the bathroom, off of Sasha's bedroom, and—

"Dennis? You think Dennis is in my house?"

"Listen, Sasha—"

"You're out of your—"

"Shhh!" I said.

"I'm worried about you," she whispered.

I felt as if we were closed in a box charged with extra ions, electrical waves—something. As if everything had been drenched in colors so intense they hurt the eyeballs. And every sound, however tiny, buzzed and roared into my brain. I heard a squeak, an old floorboard's complaint, and my back muscles tightened and my heart beat still faster.

Somebody was in this apartment. I had heard something, I knew it. Something I couldn't account for, even if I couldn't remember what it had been. I refused to believe it was pure coincidence that tonight, for the first time ever, some random thief would break into Sasha's condo in order to rob her. Coincidences happened, but not that many. Not now. Whoever was here had to do with Phoebe and Toy, and that house, and probably with Joseph Bonaparte.

Phoebe must have known. She'd somehow finally put the family legends together, read Bordentown history, found a site online—I didn't know how, but I was sure she knew.

My mind kaleidoscoped. The spinning elements swirled: Phoebe, Toy, the king of Spain in New Jersey, the appraisals, the idling car outside tonight, the honks. The joyride in the BMW. "Sorry," said once too often.

I felt sick.

The colors around me swirled and ran together, and I was afraid I might faint. "Call nine-one-one," I said.

"Are you crazy? Why?"

I stood up again despite Sasha's soft protest and the hand with which she grabbed me. I shrugged off her hand and pointed to the closed darkroom door across from us and moved closer to it. It was the only space we couldn't see.

She shook her head. "It's always closed," she whispered. "It doesn't mean anybody's hiding—"

I shook my head. It was the only thing that made sense. The person behind it had heard the signal, the warning beeps, had not had time to get out before we entered, had hidden behind the only closed door.

Sasha frowned and shook her head again.

I ignored her, then turned and whispered, "Bring the kettle, the teapot."

"No!" she whispered back. "That's horrible! You could—"

"Two people were murdered," I snapped, my voice wobbling out of control. "It isn't going to turn into four!"

"Nobody's here! You're imagining all this and scaring me! Put that thing down and get yourself—"

This time we both heard it, though I couldn't have said what the wheezed, full-of-air noise was. A small scream? Someone inhaling mightily in order to have the strength for an attack? "You're right," I said. "Put the kettle back."

"But I heard it," Sasha whispered. "OhmyGod. Dennis?" Her voice got louder. "I'll kill him! How dare he—how dare he!"

"No," I whispered. "Not Dennis." I felt my eyes well up. "Please—just call!

"Why are you—"

"Call!"

"Okay, but don't *do* anything until I—"

Wrong. I wasn't going to give the person behind the door the advantage of flinging it open and springing on me.

Besides, I knew who was behind there.

Armed with Little Caesar, I took a deep breath and whipped the door open, my arm held high as Sasha screamed, "NO! Don't do that!"

"Call!" I shouted, trying to see into the dark of the room. The dim, faraway living-room floor lamp gave the windowless space the merest outline and blurry glint of bottles, countertops, the stainless faucet.

I blinked, then blinked again, and for a third time, heard the noise.

A sob.

And then, loudly, a voice screaming, "Don't shoot me! Don't kill me!"

I knew that voice. I'd been right.

I could not remember ever so acutely wanting to have been wrong.

Twenty-one

Jonesy Farmer sat on Sasha's sofa between the two of us. I still held the skinny centurion that Jonesy, hearing Sasha's protests, had thought was a gun.

"What are you doing in my home?" Sasha demanded.

It was an unnecessary question. He'd been sitting in the far corner of the darkroom, clutching the rosewood case that held the ornate silver.

"Why were you in my darkroom?" It was her sanctum, hers alone. Of all this young man's crimes, right now, Sasha was most horrified by that one.

"I couldn't get out the window in time. You came upstairs fast, and I had the box and . . ." He shook his head. "I was scared," he mumbled. "I thought I'd be able to stay in there till you went to bed, and I could leave then." His eyes were still half filled with liquid, and he blinked furiously, ashamed, even at this most ridiculous moment, of crying.

"I've warned you about that fire escape," I said to Sasha. "And open windows with no grates on them."

"I had no idea I had to protect myself against Philly Prep kids," she said, her hands in fists. She tapped the rosewood box of silver. "How did you know about this?"

He looked at her, still fighting for control. I wasn't sure if he was more horrified at what he'd done or at having been found crying. "I saw you take it."

"You were watching me?"

"The house, not you."

"And you knew what was valuable, didn't you?" I asked rhetorically, because it hadn't been Jesse Farmer, although he'd known the worth of Phoebe's treasures. "You saw the report your father was going to deliver to Phoebe." I wanted him to deny it, to explain why he hadn't done any of the things I knew he had.

"It was on the computer," he said. "He was going to print it out and mail it to her."

"Were you along for that business dinner? Is that how you knew to look? To be interested?"

"It was my week with him. My Dad. We—he—lives upstairs from the store and he's weird about leaving me alone on his weeks. It's like I'm a kid to him. Besides, he thought it would be interesting for me to learn more about what he did. Get a head for business, is what he always says."

Some lesson learned. Along with everyone else who'd been hurt along the way, I felt terrible for Jesse Farmer, who had so innocently played a role in all this.

"I don't get it," Sasha said. "I just don't. You killed my friend, a really nice person. You poisoned her. Why? Why on earth?"

"I didn't mean to! I swear it. I wanted her to fall asleep so I could take stuff and she'd never know—she had so much! She'd told my dad she had problems sleeping, I knew she'd have had to have her doctor give her stuff, so I put two pills in her drink, to be sure she'd sleep. It was only one drink. How was I supposed to know she'd been drinking before I got there? I got so . . . I just left."

We were guarding him, but we didn't really have to. He was defeated in more ways than I could count. "I still don't get it, kid," Sasha said. "What do you want with engraved sterling, or whatever else you took?"

He looked down at his hands and shook his head. "I didn't take anything that time."

But the thoughts of money had answered that for me already. "You were in debt, weren't you?" I said. "That perpetual poker game. Big debt, it must have been. That's what those conferences with Griffith were about. Did he charge interest, too? And then, you thought Phoebe's treasures would solve everything, but poor Phoebe died."

He swallowed hard.

"So you siphoned funds from the hurricane money. How? Strong-arming kids in the hall? I don't care how. I can think of a dozen ways. And you still went back to that house in Jersey when you could. It was kind of like your ATM machine, wasn't it?"

"My father would have killed me. He doesn't like Griffith. He warned me, said he'd pull me out of that school if I got too mixed up with the rich kids."

"What exactly does Griffith have to do with this?"

"He loaned me money to play. I kept losing until I owed him so much with interest and all. I . . . I'm not rich like he is, and I shouldn't have played, but they make fun of you if you don't. You're out, you're nothing. You're one of the losers. I know I shouldn't care, but I did."

We were silent for a moment. "You don't have a car, do you?" I asked. He shook his head, as if ashamed. "So when you went back to Jersey to see what else was there, you needed a lift?"

He nodded.

Griffith, I thought. He had an SUV.

"But the day you—the day the woman was in the house and you were surprised—Griffith left you there. That's why you took her BMW. To get home." I felt a moment's shameful, but nonetheless powerful, gladness that Griffith was involved; that Griffith would be in trouble himself.

"How did you know?" Jonesy asked. "But not Griffith—Casey. Griffith loaned him the car."

So much for that. Griffith, I was sure, was one of those people who'd skim through life creating situations for which his cohorts paid, while he himself did not. He had an invisible shield that made him impervious. I could only hope it had an expiration date on its warranty.

"I didn't mean to hurt anybody," Jonesy said, his voice catching again. "I thought somebody was going to hurt me! She came around a corner and screamed and punched me! I grabbed something near me—a cane, I think it was, just to protect myself, not to hurt anybody, but then—she was so little, I guess that's why . . ."

I could only shake my head. There was no point saying the obvious. He could have called for help. He could have stayed.

He could have said no to stealing funds meant for innocent people in distress they hadn't caused.

He could have understood that Griffith was a pernicious influence, and that he, not Griffith, would be the one to pay for whatever their relationship produced.

He could have admitted his debt and culpability to his father before anything more serious than being punished was the result.

Jonesy's eyes widened at the sound of the approaching siren. "One more thing," I said. "Why did you go see Phoebe that night? Why did she think you were there?"

"For stamps."

"Pardon me?"

"At dinner the night before, she asked me if I collected anything, and my dad said stamps. I really haven't for a while, but she said her son had a collection he didn't care about. She said I could see it—maybe have it if I liked it."

She'd offered an act of kindness. Set out cookies for Mitch, her "M," because his father didn't use the nickname "Jonesy." There hadn't ever been a second glass of wine. Her visitor was underage. She was protecting him, taking care of him. Putting out cookies.

The sirens grew deafening, then shut off.

We waited in silence. There was nothing left to say.

Twenty-two

Mackenzie arrived shortly after the police escorted Jonesy out of the condo. I was still sitting on the sofa. Sasha and I had barely spoken a word for the first ten minutes, after which she'd put her hand on my arm and said, "You call me when you're ready," and she kindly found busywork tidying up her darkroom. I wasn't ready to talk about the thoughts swirling in my mind. Not even my mind was ready. It was too tired.

Mackenzie looked as he did most of the time lately, as if he'd barely emerged as the winner in a battle with his own demons and divided loyalties.

I knew, then. Knew what I thought, what I wanted to say. I

took a deep breath and patted the seat next to me. When he was beside me, I said, "This isn't the adventure I want to be having right now."

He nodded slowly and put his arm around me. "Me, neither," he said.

Twenty-three

"Happy New Year!" Mackenzie's kiss was followed by a click of our champagne glasses.

"I think it will be," I said. "But it does feel odd to not be freezing on New Year's Eve. Actually—all of this feels odd."

"But right?"

"But right." We sat on beach chairs on a friend-of-a-friend's rooftop garden, the party's laughter and tooting party-horns fading into a chorus of "Auld Lang Syne" rising up from open windows below. I felt dizzy, and not from the champagne. Life had never spun as quickly as it had these past weeks. In the movie reel of my mind, I'd said a magical sentence there on Sasha's sofa. Because if neither of us was having the adventure we wanted at the moment, then—poof!—pick another adventure.

So we did.

Of course, it was there—here—waiting for us to realize it. And for all that I felt tied to and part of my teaching life, it was the end of a semester and a relatively easy time to disengage. I tried handling the loose edges as much as I could. After we talked about it, Rachel Leary, the school counselor, promised to work on a program that would discuss the issues of gambling and peer pressure. As usual, she was willing to buck huge cultural pressures, which is why she's one of my heroes.

My headmaster cloaked his relief in getting rid of me by spouting convoluted hymns of praise to my "Mission of Mercy." Of course I'd miss the students—or most of them, but I was hoping to help a city in which every school had been damaged to some extent, a city with students and staff spread around the country in exile, a city rebuilding its system in every sense.

Sad to leave Pepperville, as the students had dubbed it, but some of them had promised to write. And of those, a handful would. And I had promised to return to testify, sign statements, do whatever I could to mitigate what happened to Jonesy. I wanted him to have a chance to grow back into the good person he was intended to be.

I'd be back for happier occasions, too, for the prom and graduation, if so invited.

As always, the students would move on. This time, so would I.

As Opal Codd said sweetly my last day, her apopemptic word for me was "agathism."

Once again, I could do no more than smile and ask her to translate. "My dear," she said, "apopemptic! Pertaining to farewell, of course."

"Of course. But 'agathism'? A belief in Agatha Christie?"

"That's nice, too, dear, but it actually is the concept that all is for the better."

I'd had fits of giggles and anxiety trying to hold on to agathism while we turned our lives in a new direction with dizzying speed. Things weren't supposed to happen that fast. That same click of the fingers and our loft was rented and Mackenzie's advisor at Penn agreed that New Orleans, with its less than stellar crime-fighting past and post-catastrophic rebuilding, was a gigantic Petri dish for criminologists. The only trouble he might have in writing a dissertation here was narrowing down the appallingly numerous possibilities.

But sometimes it felt as if we were moving so fast, we'd broken the sound barrier. "I don't even know what I'll actually do there," I lamented during one such fit.

"That's why it's an adventure," Mackenzie reminded me. "For both of us. But while you're finding what you'll do next, why not think about where you've been? The adventures you've already had. You've always said you wanted to write."

I had, but . . . "What adventures?" I thought of storm-ravaged cities, plunges into the unknown, lions and tigers and Hemingway. Bodily combat. I drew a blank.

"At school," he said. "These past few years. Even these past few weeks. You've certainly got stories."

I certainly did. It was, indeed, an idea.

The only household member who was less than gleeful about the prospect of new adventures was the cat. Macavity is by feline nature a conservative who likes everything to remain as it is. Furniture is not to be moved, let alone his own self. However, Macavity is by feline nature pragmatic, and by the second day after we'd all relocated into the tiny studio apartment a friend of a friend had found for us, he'd come out from under the bed and was exploring his new quarters and food location and declaring it acceptable. And Louisiana has fine winged insects to entertain him every time we open a window.

And so we moved at warp speed, finding a tenant for our loft, storing possessions that wouldn't fit in the new quarters, changing all manner of addresses, becoming overly familiar with Bubble Wrap, newspaper and cartons, and a great round of good-bye-for-nows. Good-bye to Philly Prep, to Penn, to Ozzie Bright Investigations.

And to the irreplaceables: my sister, her family, and our friends. But we'd talk, we'd e-mail, we'd visit, and we'd be back when it was time for yet another adventure.

My parents in Florida, of course, would simply be at a different angle to us than they currently were. My mother at first thought my leaving Philly Prep meant I was having a baby, but she reconciled herself to reality and was intrigued by the move more than anything. She knew that her cell phone could dial a new area code as easily as it had been hitting 215. She'd be able to remind me of my biological clock wherever I might be.

In the meantime, during the whirl of good-byes and the multitude of arrangements, Sasha and her oceanographer—who did, indeed, look as if he might be her next husband, and a wonderful one at that—threw us a "pack-em-up" party ("Not that we want them to go, but—" the invitation said). I hadn't known we knew that many people, or that there was that much Bubble Wrap available in North America.

My brother-in-law Sam was among the many partygoing packers. Sam is a quiet man, so when I heard him say, "My God! What's this? What's this doing here?" I felt a rush of panic.

When I saw what he was looking at, I felt a rush of horror.

The less-than-thrilling painting Sasha had given me was still on the floor, propped against the wall, close to the entry. I simply had had too much on my mind, and that painting was never a part of it, so it stayed down there on the floor, migrating closer and closer to the door, as if preparing to leave on its own.

I worked at convincing myself that the open door all but covered it, and my dear friend, for all her comings and goings at the loft these past weeks, had never noticed as she whisked past.

I still didn't like it. It was too dark, and it was too still a life, if that is an acceptable opinion. But I had never wanted Sasha to know.

Too bad for me that Sam had fixated on it. Sasha possessed a radar that felt Sam's interest even though she'd been at the opposite end of the loft, packing books. She walked over in time to see Sam lift the painting from its place on the floor, and hold it up, turning so as to get more light on it.

She looked at him, then at me. "You know," she said, "I have no particular bond to that painting."

"Oh, don't misinterpret the fact that—I've been trying to decide where to hang—"

"—or if you even keep it. I only wanted you to have a Phoebe-souvenir. We could find something else, like the skinny Caesar man. You seemed quite attached to it at my place that night."

"No, I—"

"When did you get this?" Sam asked. "Where?"

"I gave it to her," Sasha said. "It had belonged to a friend of mine. It had sentimental value."

"It has more than that," he said. "Who was your friend?"

"A housewife in Jersey who collected anything and everything. Matchbooks, refrigerator magnets, homely statues, paintings . . ."

"And this," Sam said in a reverent tone. "Of course I could be wrong, and this could be a brilliant reproduction or copy, but it certainly looks like Willem Kalf's work. I'd bet it was, except housewives in New Jersey do not have Kalf on their walls."

"Who was he?" I asked.

"Dutch, seventeenth century. Studied in Paris. Known for *pronkstilleven*—ostentatious still lifes—because of the expensive objects he'd make a part of the painting." The amazement on our faces must have been obvious, because he laughed. "I was an art history major, remember?"

I didn't. I quite unfairly tended to think of lawyer Sam as having been born in a three-piece suit.

"I loved the Dutch masters most of all," he said.

"One Jersey housewife did indeed own a Kalf," Sasha said

with a big smile. "And, to be honest, some other doozies as well, like the still life I now have at home."

"That—Phoebe? How do you know?"

"Jesse Farmer's appraisal. I rehired him. He had a list of eight objects he'd seen at the house: the silver I took, the landscape, another small painting, an Italian bowl, a Chinese bowl, a ring, and believe it or not, one of those damnable porcelain doo-dads. Luckily, none of the real treasures would be easy for a kid to pawn, that's why Jonesy must have left them. Until he came for the silver. So now, I have seven goodies and you've got the eighth. And Dennis? He's probably going to jail for attempted bank fraud, so he gets zilch."

"This painting is valuable?"

"Incredibly so," Sam said, his voice near a whisper, yet audible all over the room, apparently. Packing ceased, Bubble Wrap no longer popped, and I felt as if I were in a surrealistic dream.

I shook myself back to reality. "Then I couldn't—"

"Sam, you've ruined my surprise," Sasha said. Then she grinned at me. "I was planning a big ta-DAH! kind of announcement later in the evening. But so be it. Bottom line is: You will keep it," she said. "And you should sell it."

"Oh, no! I love—"

"No you don't. I know you think I haven't noticed it sitting there, looking horribly out of place. Wrong. I don't like it either—it was only a souvenir, remember? I'll give you one of the commemorative plates she collected, how's that? I'll give you all of them!"

"You take it," I said. "She left it to you. Dennis said you could have everything in the house."

"I know, and I'm giving you this, and suggesting that you put it up for auction. Fund your new life. Don't worry about money for a while."

"A long while," Sam said.

"Use it for good—or go crazy and blow it. Consider it your fee—a gift of thanks—for finding out what happened to Phoebe."

I shook my head. "I barely did. I really can't!"

"You have to! Giving it to you makes me feel like Queen Isabella, sending you off on your great adventure. Find the new world, you two. Go!"

And so we did. The auction is next month and the painting is being treated as if it were royalty. As if, in fact, it were a king's treasure, which, apparently, it was.

Phoebe would be so proud.

"Happy New Year," Mackenzie said again.

It was a pretty sure thing.

GILLIAN ROBERTS won the Anthony Award for Best First Mystery for *Caught Dead in Philadelphia.* She is also the author of *Philly Stakes, I'd Rather Be in Philadelphia, With Friends Like These . . . , How I Spent My Summer Vacation, In the Dead of Summer, The Mummers' Curse, The Bluest Blood, Adam and Evil, Helen Hath No Fury, Claire and Present Danger,* and *Till the End of Tom.* Formerly an English teacher in Philadelphia, Gillian Roberts now lives in California. Her website address is www.GillianRoberts.com—and she enjoys receiving fan e-mail at Judygilly@aol.com.

About the Type

This book was set in Garamond, a typeface originally designed by the Parisian typecutter Claude Garamond (1480–1561). Garamond's distinguished romans and italics first appeared in *Opera Ciceronis* in 1543–44. The Garamond types are clear, open, and elegant.